House
Fires

The

Iowa

Short

Fiction

Award

University of

Iowa Press

Iowa City

*Nancy
Reisman*

*House
Fires*

*For Nancy —
With much admiration & love —
Always, I wish you happiness & fulfillment
& all good things — Nancy

11/99 Buffalo*

University of Iowa Press, Iowa City 52242

Copyright © 1999 by Nancy Reisman

Printed in the United States of America

http://www.uiowa.edu/~uipress

Printed on acid-free paper

Library of Congress Cataloging-in-Publication Data

Reisman, Nancy, 1961–

House fires / Nancy Reisman.

p.   cm.—(The Iowa short fiction award)

ISBN 0-87745-692-5

1. United States—Social life and customs—20th century—

Fiction.   I. Title.   II. Series.

PS3568.E5135H68   1999

813'.54—dc21   99-29218

99   00   01   02   03   P   5   4   3   2   1

For my family

For Sadie

Contents

ACKNOWLEDGMENTS

I am grateful for the support of the Institute
for Creative Writing at the University of
Wisconsin, the Heekin Group Foundation,
the Rhode Island State Council on the
Arts, and the Fine Arts Work Center in
Provincetown.

Many thanks to the Providence Area Writers,
the Creative Writing faculty at the
University of Wisconsin, my colleagues at
the Rhode Island School of Design, and my
Madison writing group. I am indebted to
several kind and tireless readers: Jon Loomis,
Jesse Lee Kercheval, Ron Wallace, Linda
Reisman, Ronna Johnson, Ann Harleman,
Hester Kaplan, Judith McClain, F. M. Dowell,
and Jean Marie Lutes.

For their invaluable encouragement and
support, I thank these readers and many
other friends, mentors, and loved ones,
among them the Reisman and Estry families,
Laury Rappaport, Howard Norman, Jane
Shore, Robert McClure Smith, Karen
Donovan, Walker Rumble, Jennifer and Doug
Boone, Margaret Lewis, Jill Polk, Pamela
Perry, Melissa Zieve, and William Waltz.

Several of the stories in this collection have
previously appeared in journals and
anthologies. "House Fires," "The Good Life,"
and "Sharks" appeared in *Glimmer Train*.
"Edie in Winter" and "Strays" appeared,
respectively, as prize-winning stories in the
eighth and ninth editions of *American
Fiction*. "Dreaming of the Snail Life"
appeared in the *Kenyon Review*. "Girl

on a Couch" appeared in *Press*. "Heart of Hearts" appeared in *Lilith*. "Confessions," which won the 1996 Raymond Carver Award, appeared in *Toyon*. "Common Light" appeared in the *Sonora Review*.

House
Fires

House Fires

When Randi died, my family went haywire: one by one we shorted out. My father, a dignified cardiologist, took to drinking and belligerence. My mother's mannered calm gave way to hysteria. I became pale and inept and forgot how to hold conversations.

My sister was killed at night by fire; afterward, the indigo black sky seemed intolerable. Ordinary flames left us stricken and obsessed. Her last minutes seemed a vast unlit space I could neither penetrate nor ignore. In my attempts to comprehend them, I went as far as lowering my fingers over lit matches and holding my breath. I ended up writing Randi secret notes, which I left crumpled in the kitchen trash. *Wake up and jump out a window.*

Do this scene over again, some way I can see it: a rescue, a sprained ankle, momentary coughing, an embrace on the street, in the light of fire engines. Here, steady yourself. Let me wrap your ankle. I will bring you blankets. Within weeks I took to dressing in Randi's old clothes, castoff sweaters, worn jeans, dresses from her past: some of them held traces of her crushed-lilac scent. I'd wear them until my mother made me take them off, or until there was nothing of Randi left in them.

The house Randi lived in was a two-family in New Haven I saw only once, after the fire; the surviving structure was roofless, open along the western side, char and ash and air where Randi's room had been. Left over were objects from storage: books she didn't use, an olive raincoat, camping equipment, all smoke damaged. The fire was caused by faulty wiring and fanned by high winds, the sort of thing you'd never anticipate. Imagine, for example, your life is rising, the proof is everywhere, at your Ivy League law review, in your lovemaking, in the mirror. Certainty crests, crests again. You work impossibly hard and sleep heavily, sleep through the first scent of smoke. When do you realize you are trapped in sheets of flame?

Her voice burned. Her intellect burned. I don't know what to say about her soul. Randi's body reminded me of certain sea pebbles: white, smooth, perfectly separate. That night she was sleeping, a woman wrapped in quilts, a woman turned inward, a self on a bed. No one reported hearing her—no cries, no calls. Did she, at the end, remain asleep? Did she wake to the knowledge of fire and nothing else, not even herself?

That winter I became unsure of my skin: it seemed too thin and insubstantial to contain me. At night I felt a sudden panic and imagined spilling out into the dark air, slipping beneath the sound of stray sirens, dissipating. Near my parents' house a local diner burned, and I stayed at the window biting my nails and watching the sky grow chalky. I couldn't ignore the ways fire annihilates: the objects that steady us—landmarks, banisters, familiar walls—disappear or char down to remnants. An address no longer counts; a phone number drops away. Proof of the past vanishes and the infrastructure of our days collapses into chaos. It is pure loss, and yet, coming upon someone else's fire, we pull over to the side of the road, stand in the street, stare from the top of the hill at the gorgeous and terrible flames. In some living room the family photos are seared off the wall; outside the house we *stand back, stand back* but can't leave.

On the worst nights I crept downstairs to my parents' dark family room and turned on late movies: *Stella Dallas, Splendor in the Grass, Shampoo*. I would watch anything. At first I fell into film because of the story lines, but it also seemed a world impervious to fire. Even celluloid, which can so easily shrivel from heat—a sudden melting on screen, burns blooming over a city street or hotel lobby or a woman's bewildered face—seemed salvageable. The image curls away into brown arcs and blank space; the film breaks; the projectionist snaps off the machine. But wait, and the film begins again, skipping a few lines of dialogue, losing a gesture. The damaged reel will be replaced by a new, flawless print. Finally, somewhere, there was recourse.

Eventually, I studied film; now on my insomniac nights I read theory. I return to Bazin, who wrote in the aftermath of World War II and, nevertheless, insisted on unity. He thought that film's promise and purpose was to elucidate the real, to reveal the patterns already before us, and he believed that unity of space and time were paramount. So he relied on long shots: if a scene includes a man and a woman in a room, the camera should give us a clear view of both the characters and the space, all within a frame. No jump cuts, no breaks in time. When the scene is whole, we witness the simultaneous body language, the woman stirring her coffee as the man stares into his lap, the man leaning forward as the woman says his name, the thickness of the oak table dividing them, the strange juxtaposition of their tensed bodies and troubled faces against extravagant floral wallpaper. How small they appear stumbling down a hill in the snow; how terribly close in the hospital elevator they must take together. Each shot re-veals the shifts in power. I like this idea; I am drawn to Bazin's faith. But is wholeness itself illusory? So often I see things in pieces.

Picture, for example, my mother the months after Randi died, a forty-eight-year-old woman weeping into her coffee, weeping into the houseplants, slamming doors when contradicted, then weeping behind one or another slammed door. Every evening after six, she'd prepare an impressive dinner none of us could eat. You could film her for minutes at a distance, a woman alone in an immaculate kitchen, snapping green beans and fishing Kleenex from her pocket, then calling, "Dinner everyone," as if there were ten of us. Or you could abandon Bazin's principle and film her face in close-up, film the lined hands, the manicured nails, elaborate rings and traces of arthritis, fingers breaking and break-ing the beans, and then cut to a shot of my father pretending to work but actually drawing squares on a notepad. Watch my fa-ther refill his Glenlivet, see in close-up the heavy lines beneath the eyes, a single twitch at the corner of his mouth, and hear my mother's voice, "Dinner everyone." Or you could view the plush empty rooms of the house, one after another, then cut to my fa-ther's face, his sip of scotch. Cut to me, disheveled, on the floor of the living room, thumbing the classifieds without looking at them, headphones over my ears. Hear the sound of those snap-ping beans. Cut to my mother's face, then to the wintry lawn, "Dinner everyone."

I hear my father's voice swim out of the dark. Beyond the win-dow blue snow accumulates over the college lawns. It is Vermont. It is December. His voice seems to emanate from the band of falling snow rather than the phone line; we are nearly mutes. He almost chokes on my name but then repeats it, breathlessly, "Amy," over the miles of cable between Boston and Bennington, across the 5 A.M. blue dark. He says that Randi was in a fire. What do you mean? I say.

She was in it. She didn't get out.

My mouth tastes of metal and the night flattens into slabs of light and dark, the snow into two-dimensional flecks. I brush my hair. I dial the busline, write a schedule on a drugstore receipt, dress myself in a sweater and leggings, find matching shoes. In dawn light I board a bus that travels past fields of snow and stripped silver trees, stopping in tiny towns along the Connecticut River valley. Two seats away from me, a woman hums songs from West Side Story, and once the driver stops to tell a man in the back to put out his cigarette. The air becomes increasingly white as we drive and the daylight thickens. All the way down the highway snow falls, small frenzied flakes that seem never to end.

In New Haven we held hands. My parents seemed crushed and ancient, and our gaits dropped off to a shuffle. On the grounds of Yale the three of us walked in a row, hand-in-hand: sometimes I was on the outside to the left and sometimes I was in the middle. At a restaurant table my father touched my hand, then clasped my mother's, then knotted his own together while a waiter brought us coffee and plates of eggs we ignored. At the funeral in Newton, my parents held hands at the graveside, and when I stepped back, away from the rest of the mourners, they appeared to be at the very edge of the grave, heads bowed; a gust of wind could have knocked them in. They were gripping each other's hands and didn't sway or lean or turn, becoming in that moment a still shot of snow-flecked hair, shoulders in overcoats, almost trembling, a small bridge of hands. Aunt Natalie shepherded me from the funeral parlor to the graveside to my parents' house and into a chair; she held my hand, and later other relatives and friends would take one hand or the other and hold it, sometimes purposefully, sometimes almost absently, as they sat with plates in their laps and spooned up mild foods, offering me pieces of bagel or sliced cucumbers. The Orthodox women on my father's side of the family wore dark velvet hats with delicate brims; their warm, soap-scented hands stroked my stubby, nail-bitten fingers. It was as if in all this handholding we would find the missing hands or reconstruct them somehow.

My thirteen-year-old cousin, Ellen, held my hand to tug me away from the living room, to tell me that Randi had explained sex to her. "She was the best," Ellen said. "She knew everything. I wish she weren't dead." All at once, Ellen burst into tears and clung onto me, crying into my navy dress. We swayed in the kitchen for several minutes, Ellen's soft animal sounds rising, my silence wrapping and wrapping them. I kissed Ellen on the forehead and watched the weather arrive in the backyard. Then Aunt Natalie found us and helped me upstairs to nap.

After a week of visits from relatives and friends, gifts of coffeecakes and casseroles and pots of soup, everyone disappeared. There were the three of us. For a few weeks I kept an eye on my mother, who sometimes needed help getting dressed. The kingsized bed dwarfed her; she would lie on the right side, the quilt gathered around her, propping her head just enough to see me pull blouses and pants out of her closet and wave them in the air before her. She would shake her head at one outfit, shake her head at another, eventually shrug at something. I'd turn on the shower for her and get the temperature right. I'd wait until she was done and hand her a towel. By then she was ready to be on her own. "Okay, doll," she'd say, and then I would falter. I did have projects to work on: I had taken incompletes in all my fall classes but could hardly think about the sociology of militarism or the French subjunctive. In truth, I could hardly think. I watched my late movies, got up in time for *Good Morning America*, and napped during the day. To occupy myself, I often folded laundry.

My father went back to work almost immediately. I thought it was because in his office there were people he could save. Or because he didn't know what else to do. He claimed that, since he'd cosigned all of Randi's law school loans, he couldn't afford a longer leave. No one believed him. One of my father's partners, Barry Levitz, suggested that my parents leave the country. "Take a real vacation," Barry said. "Go to the Azores. Go to France." This was something my mother wanted and my father resisted. A week before my spring semester was to begin in Vermont, she pulled me aside and asked me to go with them to Paris. It seemed an unsavory idea. And shouldn't I try school? "I can't go now," I said. "I don't have a passport."

"We can't go without you," my mother said. "We couldn't leave you here alone."

"You should go," I said. "Eat pastry. Go to the Louvre. I'll be okay."

My mother pursed her lips and gave me a once-over: I'd been wearing a bathrobe for two days.

"I'll call you in Paris," I said. "Anyway, I have to go back to school."

"We'll talk later," she said.

But no one went anywhere.

If I were to film that first month, I would want to focus on small gestures, small sounds, a sort of bewildered scratching against the largeness of the space around us, the largeness of each day. But for how long would that work on the screen? There ought to be narrative development, but of what sort, and how should it be filmed?

The following months in Newton, we all had a propensity for breaking things. Bright drinks fell to the floor. Lamps sat too close to the edges of tables. The patio door slammed too hard, breaking a spring. "Nuts," my mother would say. Picture, then, a shot of a hand knocking backwards into a juice glass, the glass shattering, bright orange spilling over the white linoleum floor.

"Shut up," my father says. "Just shut up." This at dinner, while my mother and I grasp at conversation about the unexpected pigeons at the birdfeeder or the recipe for stuffed cabbage or what is at the Newton Cinema. A faint pinkness creeps up through his cheeks and forehead, over his balding scalp. He is not drunk. He is a man I've never met before. My mother bites the inside of her cheek: she holds firmly to the belief that dinner conversation is both a right and an obligation. Silence at the table is uncivilized. She stares at the roast potatoes and julienned carrots on her plate and says, as if he were a child, "Abe, you don't have to eat with us tonight."

One night, he grunts and stays. One night, he takes his plate off to the study. My mother is utterly white and gray, her skin more drawn, the pale blue of her eyes washed out, her jawline rigid. Her conversation with me becomes even more tenuous, bits of chaff thrown into the air. *I bought apples today. The gas man will be here Thursday morning. Buddy Stern is getting married again.* The scene repeats itself until my mother just shakes her head, tears up, and drops whatever line of conversation she's started. I stay catatonic through dessert.

Would it be more cinematic to hear the voice, the low shout, "shut up," and cut to me alone, an hour later, striking a match, my index finger racing through the flame? What does it mean to pair my father's voice with that action? To follow it with shots of my mother's sudden entrance into my room, her hard slap across my face, the gash made with the edge of her ring, my right cheek slowly welling blood?

We are both stunned, my mother and I. Her mouth shapes a perfect, cerise-lipsticked O. My face stings as she pulls me into the bathroom and jams my burned fingertip under the cold water. Red bruises form on my wrist where she grips it. "Don't you ever," she says. In the mirror I see her glance at the cut on my cheek. Neither one of us touches it.

Later the shock wears off. One day I try on Randi's blue satin prom dress, pour myself some Glenlivet, and lounge in Randi's room, reading my mother's back issues of *National Geographic* and sifting through photographs of Randi's old boyfriends and high school triumphs: Randi at a diving meet arrowing into a pool; Randi and Alex Goldman waving from a ski lift; Randi in a black strapless dress, drinking a Bud. I find Randi at eighteen in an emerald green sweatshirt, thick amber hair cut to shoulder length, head tipped onto Bob D'Amato's shoulder. She is the cat with the canary, and sexy, brainy Bob D'Amato wraps both arms around her, his teeth astonishingly white. My mother walks into the room, colors at the sight of me, and slaps me on both cheeks. Neither one of us is surprised. I say nothing. I take off the dress in front of her, rehang it in Randi's closet, and slip on my jeans and sweatshirt.

A week later, when I mistakenly set the table for four, my mother slaps me again and I mechanically clear the fourth place. My father lifts his head from the stack of mail he is sorting. "Marian." He shakes his head ever so slightly. Then they are both stock still, staring at each other. They don't notice my exit from the room.

How would an audience's view change if I cut back and forth between the slaps and the wailing I hear late at night from my parents' room, or between the slaps and the latest instances of my mother's social decline—her skittishness in supermarkets and clothing stores, her new awkwardness with friends? Would it be more accurate? Or too overt, too manipulative? Montage can be tricky and coercive, which is why advertisers and other propagandists embrace it. But the wailing is important.

Most mornings, even then, my mother kissed me and smoothed my hair.

My father, on the other hand, could not easily greet me. He rose in the morning for work, he left the house, he called my mother once in the afternoon, he returned at six and secluded himself. Perhaps that is when he wept. He shouted when his brooding was interrupted. *Get out of here.* I crumbled; Randi was the one who could shout back. And yelling was not part of our relationship: when I was small, one stern look would keep me in line. So I began to move stealthily when he was home, slipping past him into empty rooms, avoiding him in the hallway, though this could backfire. *What's the matter with you, are you a mouse?*

Appease, I thought, appease. I left ridiculous notes in his briefcase—*Have a good day!*—along with packages of Fig Newtons or oatmeal bars or peanut butter cups. During a break in the cold weather I washed his car. He acknowledged nothing. In previous years I would have found a thank-you note on my dresser; he might have taken me to lunch. It's true that his solicitude had always coexisted with a controlled bluster, an arrogance I'd witnessed from the sidelines of medical meetings and in unsatisfactory restaurants. But he'd always responded to appeasement, to the phrase "I see your point," to the free drink sent by the manager. And always he was protective of my mother, of Randi, of me. We were beautiful, he said, we were smart, we were angels. Especially Randi.

It's vacation. We are in Maine. I am picking blueberries with my mother, and my father and Randi are on the dock, fishing. Randi must be about nine. I am seven. I watch my father tug at her ponytail; she grins up at him, then reels in a sunfish big enough to keep. My father holds the hooked fish in the air, where it flops about. He and Randi grin and grin. She is slick as an eel in her green one-piece. I stuff my mouth with blueberries.

"Hey," my mother says. "Save those."

I open my hand and offer her several half-crushed berries. She relents and eats a few, but moves the bucket out of my reach and hands me a Styrofoam cup to use for picking. When I look out toward the dock again, Randi is holding up the now-dead fish and waving it in the direction of my mother. My mother stands up and waves back. "Great," she yells. "Marvelous."

Fantasy 1: I happen to be in New Haven and arrive at the scene of the fire in time to pull Randi out alive. Everyone is stunned by my courage and skill, even the fire squad. Randi and I hug each other and cry. Before I can berate her for being in that house, on that night, for being asleep too long, for exposing me to endless wrath and sorrow, she apologizes. She also apologizes for ever calling me an airhead.

Fantasy 2: Randi's house goes up in flames, but she escapes unscathed. This moment of threat and escape—the sirens, the flames, the coldness of the night—shakes Randi enough that she sheds a layer of arrogance. She begins calling me long distance and sending gifts through the mail. She tells me how lucky she feels to be my sister.

Fantasy 3: I am the one who escapes the fire. Randi rescues me, takes me to a good hotel, and stays up until I fall asleep. The next day, everything is fine. She gives me her favorite sweater and we order room service.

Fantasy 4: I am the one who escapes the fire. I do it without Randi's help. She is amazed at my bravery and luck. She admits to her friends that she underestimated me. "She was always sweet," Randi says, "but I thought she was hapless. Was I ever wrong." After that she wants us to take vacations together. "Let's go where you want," she says.

Fantasy 5: There is no fire.

I thought about the fish in Maine. I thought I was dying. In the bathroom I would read the label on my father's package of razor blades and assess the blueness of the veins in my wrists. Then I would sit on the white tile floor, weep, and wait for the weeping to recede into a distanced calm. It was then I felt Randi's absence in its cleanest form: an endless, zero-gravity drifting, a world of lonely air.

Contemplating the razor blade left me oddly belligerent. I'd leave matchbooks around the house for my mother to scoop up and hide. The day I dropped an heirloom teacup and she slapped me, I began to sing "Oklahoma!" as I swept up the shards of china roses. I cleared my father's drinks before he was finished with them, and one night at dinner when he spouted about wanting silence, I surprised all of us by telling him to find a monastery. But these moments were rare and left my parents increasingly convinced that I had no sense of judgment: all common sense had perished with Randi.

After four months in Newton, I looked as if I'd been living underground. I was pale as a nightcrawler, and thin: I'd lost ten pounds and my clothes hung about me. I became disoriented in traffic and my old shyness surfaced with strangers. But I began small forays into the neighborhood, alone. Evenings at the cinema by myself. I favored independent films with offbeat characters who traveled a lot, or films where someone escaped from one country into another, took trains, or rode bicycles long distances. I would buy my ticket and hang about the lobby, reading the posted movie reviews and jumping if anyone bumped into me or asked me the time. After a few weeks, the man at the concession started giving me medium-sized popcorn when I ordered small. He said nothing about it, just took my money and smiled and went on to the next customer.

That April, I turned twenty-one. It was a mild, muddy day, and in the afternoon I took the train into the city and bought myself a spring dress, a print of blue roses, which I wore out of the store. Aunt Natalie called from New York and sent red tulips. My father left me a pair of silver earrings on the breakfast table, and before dinner he took out the Polaroid. Although we had always taken photographs on our birthdays, no one had touched the camera since Thanksgiving; there was relief and pleasure in my father's retrieval of it. He was almost jovial, loading my arms with tulips, photographing me alone, photographing me with my mother, orchestrating shots for my mother to take of me with him, and, finally, setting the self-timer and rushing over for a photo of the three of us. We laid the photos out on the table, watched ourselves emerge through the murky green and yellow stages of each print: my mother's smile a bit taut, my father's face a bit flushed, my lips together in small smiles, all of us surprised.

"Look at the two of you," my father said. "Beautiful." He kissed my mother's cheek. "Beautiful," he said. He kissed me on the forehead.

"Such a pretty dress," my mother said.

We sat down to salmon and asparagus. My father uncorked a bottle of Sauvignon Blanc and poured glasses for the three of us. He asked me about my day in Boston. He asked me whether I was getting bored in Newton.

"Maybe it's time to go to school again," he said.

I pictured Vermont, mountains, unbridled green.

"Take a look at Brandeis," he said. "Take a look at Harvard." Both schools were within ten miles of the house.

"I hadn't thought of them," I said.

"What would you want to study?" my mother said. "Anthropology? Wasn't that it?"

"Maybe," I said, "that could be interesting," even though I only wanted to watch films. My father tapped his fork against the table and then speared a piece of salmon. "Hmm," he said, waving the fork in figure eights. "Nothing wrong with anthropology, but you'd have to be serious about a field like that. You'd have to want graduate school."

"Oh."

"I didn't go to graduate school," my mother said.

"It's a different era," my father said.

"I'll give it some thought," I said.

"Abe, she can't know if she wants graduate school before she's taken any courses."

"I'm just saying," my father said. "Be practical. What's so bad about being practical? Amy, what about biology?"

I shrugged.

"Or computers," my father said.

"Maybe," I said.

"Abe," my mother said, "if she wants to study anthropology, let her study anthropology."

"Anthropology's fine. Amy, go ahead, study anthropology. Marian, don't misinterpret me."

"I think I heard you correctly," my mother said, "Anyway, Amy, we're happy to get you a car. The Green Line is a pain in the neck."

"Thank you," I said.

"We can start looking this week," my father said. "I have a patient in the business."

No one mentioned Bennington, a place I had liked, a place not so very far from Newton. I didn't say that I missed the mountains. I didn't say I'd forgotten how to be on my own but wanted to remember, if I could. Why spoil my own birthday, the shimmer of those tulips, the most peace we'd had since Randi's death? So I changed the subject. I asked my mother about her gardening plans.

Later my mother brought out the cake, angel food studded with strawberries. She sliced it and handed out the slices and sang to me. My father cheerfully mumbled along. At the end of the singing there was nothing for me to do but eat: she had brought no candles.

The lack was so striking that I found myself staring at the cake and not lifting a fork. I glanced up at each of my parents and back down at the cake. I shrugged. I blew air across the top of the slice. "For luck," I said. I stuck my fork into airy whiteness.

"Was that necessary?" my mother said.

"Was what necessary? There weren't candles," I said.

"And you know why," my mother said.

I looked down at the rose-print dress, my thin white arms. Suddenly, I felt ridiculous, a bony, flawed girl trying to pass for pretty, trying to pass for whole. I almost nodded assent. But it was my birthday. I was twenty-one. I should have been in a bar drinking champagne with college buddies. I should have been kissing a man. "Birthday cakes usually have candles," I said.

"If you don't want the cake, don't eat it," my mother said.

"What's the matter with the cake?" my father said.

"I just wanted something to wish on."

My mother bit her lip.

"Can't you appreciate that your mother baked you a cake?" my father said.

I tried to keep my tone even, but the words came out clipped. "Thanks for the cake," I said to my mother.

"What's that snottiness?" my father said.

"You think I'm going to give you lit candles?" my mother said. "After what you did?"

"What did she do?" my father said.

"Two fingers," I said. "Two fingers and there aren't even scars."

"Don't talk to me about scars," my mother said.

"Scars," I said, "show up after injuries. Some people have appendix scars. There's a movie called *Scarface* I don't think you'd like."

"Amy, be quiet," my father said.

"It's stupid, Mom," I said. "Not even one birthday candle. I would have blown it out. I would have made a wish and blown it out."

"Shut up," my father said.

"I don't want to shut up." I rose and began to clear the table. "I'll go talk somewhere else."

"You sit down," my father said. "You eat that cake."

"I'm not hungry," I said.

My father grabbed me by the arm and pushed me down into the chair. He picked up a forkful of cake and shoved it at my mouth. He held it there, gripping my forearm, until I bit into the piece. When he moved his hand away, I spit it back at him.

"That's it," he said.

I tried to make a dash for the door, but before I could sidestep him, my father grabbed me by the shoulders and shoved me back against the wall. "What's *wrong* with you?" he shouted. He was shaking me, his face fierce and red, his breath heavy with liquor and fish. "Answer me," he shouted. Twice my head banged back against the wall. I closed my eyes. "Answer me," he repeated. I began humming a two-note phrase, the first note slightly higher than the second—*see saw see saw*. I didn't move.

"*Abe*," I heard my mother say. "Abe."

His hands released, and I sensed him backing away from me. When I opened my eyes, he was beside his chair, incredulous, gazing at his palms. He sagged and looked up at me. "Amy," he said. His voice caught, and he regained it only long enough to say my mother's name. "Marian," he was begging, "Marian," and weeping. He fell back into his chair, and my mother went to him then, held him, rocked him, my father leaning his head against her belly, sobbing. Like a sleepwalker, I left the house.

Most of this took place within three or four minutes, for part of which I was sightless. Should I stick with my stream of perception, including darkness, or should I reconstruct what I did not see and film mise-en-scène from a medium shot? Should my mother be in the frame at all times?

Afterward, neither of my parents mentioned that night. The cake vanished. The photographs vanished. For a few days my father whistled comfortless, unidentifiable tunes. My mother remained watchful. I became a different Amy: sly, calculating, untouchable. I did not eat meals with my parents. Or talk. I quietly sold off the one piece of stock I owned and converted the proceeds into traveler's checks. I emptied my bank account. I scouted the house for cash.

A week after my birthday, when my mother was at the supermarket, I left a note on the counter and left Newton. I took with me no photos or mementos. My departure from the house seemed as ordinary as any other: I locked the side door, picked my way across the rain-puddled walk. I counted my change for the Green Line train, switched to the Red Line, crossed the traffic-filled blocks between South Station and the Trailways terminal. Somewhere in Ohio, I called my father's office and left a message for Barry Levitz. The buses I rode wove on across the country, through flat expanses of prairie, into mountains, stopping at Burger Kings and Pizza Huts and twenty-four-hour truckstops. I washed and brushed my teeth in the restaurant bathrooms and lived on grilled cheese and french fries. Within a few days I reached California.

For a couple of nights I stayed at the Hilton near Union Square in San Francisco, walked the city, and invented possible aliases for myself, mixing in the names of streets: Melissa Grant, Joan Vallejo, Margaret Montgomery. I renamed myself Amy Montgomery and moved to Berkeley with that name, to a shared house near Rockridge. For the first six months I contacted my parents only through Barry, calling the office from pay phones.

It's me. Tell them I'm fine.

Where are you?

I'll call you in a couple of weeks.

I never said where I was and never stayed on the line more than two minutes. Was this cruel? I feared my parents would fly to San Francisco and comb the streets for me. I don't think I was wrong.

Those first months, I kept to myself. I smoked clove cigarettes and sat in cheap Chinese restaurants eating soup and reading about silent movie greats. I went to matinees alone. After a year of working in cafes, I landed a staff assistant job at KQED and enrolled in film classes. I began to live in a social world.

I have lived in Berkeley for six years: sometimes I think I stay here simply because the pomegranate trees surprise me, because of the shock of green in February, because I still find the bay beautiful. I have befriended several women. Sometimes I have boyfriends, interesting men inclined toward social justice or film, who can speak fluent Spanish or know how to backpack. I have not fallen in love.

I could say, yes, time heals. I wouldn't be wrong, but there are scars we can't always name. I cannot help but think we were disfigured to begin with, and the fire illuminated the twists to our hearts and limbs. I have visited my parents in Newton a few times. The first time, I insisted on staying at the Marriott. They came to meet me there for dinner and I wept to see them. My mother sat close beside me, stroking my hand. My father was pale and lost. "Would you come back to Boston?" he said. "My Amy, won't you come back?"

"I can't," I said. "This is all I can do."

Some nights I wake up and the air smells of eucalyptus and gardenias; my skin is warm. For an instant I could be a young girl named Amy, my sister sleeping, my father listening to Mozart, eyes closed, my mother reading in the bath. I know why theorists now write about seduction and desire. And I know why they want us to wake up, to see the seams in films, to remember that images and sounds are pasted together. How else can we keep from tumbling, blindly, into fantasy? How will we know if we have, in the larger scheme of things, been pushed against a wall?

And yet for me there is still the dream of making internal life visible. Of finding characters I can believe in. The hope that, this time, my trust will not be betrayed. There is the dream of wholeness. The dream of reconciliation. And there is my desire for a simple plot, for the unity that never quite arrives in daily life, for true closure. These days, I look for the sort of closure that is not false and is not death. Is there such a thing?

I know this: fire blooms, blooms again, marking us, dismantling what we believed inviolable. At times we can do nothing but record its stunning recklessness. Later, we sift through the ashes by hand.

I. Buffalo Series

Edie in Winter

1948

Edie Cole is fourth in line at Mendelsohn's bakery when her heart falls to her feet. No one remarks on the flutter that crosses her face, her sudden loss of breath: Buffalo is frozen, and the cold has knocked the wind out of most customers walking in from the street. It's nearly Shabbas, and Mendelsohn's has stayed open longer than usual—everyone's in a hurry. The December sky has already turned pink, shafts of light coloring the bakery air and Edie's coat and boots. "Arthur Blum," Gary Mendelsohn says. "That handsome Arthur," Gloria Mendelsohn says, wistfully. All the married women nod. Ruth Brodsky sighs. Edie swallows hard and feels her throat turn to dust.

Nora Lang swivels her head in Edie's direction. "Wasn't he sweet on you?"

Edie's face reddens, and she turns to study the nearly empty dessert case.

"*Nora*," Gloria says.

"I don't mean anything by it," Nora says. She pats Edie on the shoulder, and Edie offers up a queasy smile. Then she flails in the net of women's voices.

"He was at Normandy. A hero."

"They gave him all the decorations."

"Still not married—Edie, did you know that?"

"Still pining over Judy Shumaker, is he?"

"Oh no, too long ago. I heard he fell for a Catholic girl in New York."

"Really, Nora, you shouldn't."

"That's what I heard."

"Well, I heard he wanted to marry a French girl, Jewish, out of the camps, but she wouldn't leave Europe."

"After the camps she wouldn't leave?"

"He's been living in New York."

"He must be thirty by now."

"Minnie Abrams is in New York."

"Minnie's married. In Brooklyn."

"He lives in Manhattan?"

"He's staying at his cousin Rita's, off Hertel."

"I heard he was staying at the Statler Hotel."

"You're kidding."

"You know he's a lawyer now."

"What can I get for you, Edie?"

Edie looks up suddenly and drops her package of smoked fish, her first graders' papers, her gloves. Her glasses slide down her nose and her woolen scarf drags as she bends down to retrieve them. "My challah," Edie says. Her voice seems clogged and small. She clears her throat. "And that last honeycake."

By the time Edie reaches her block, the neighborhood is turning blue. She hugs her packages and almost runs out of breath. She has to find Manny: if he's not home, she'll call him at the bookstore. She pictures him shuffling between the cluttered stacks and the tilting shelves, sorting boxes from the Martinson estate. How mulish and sad-eyed and shy he is, even with the customers he likes. How calming they find the store's easy quiet. But if Arthur pushes the door open, that calm will scramble, the dust itself will vanish, and Manny's face will revert to the face of a boy. A face Edie hasn't seen for years.

And if, instead, Manny sees Arthur from a distance, on the street? No matter that it's Shabbas, that the houses have hushed, that Manny is due home for dinner. *Arthur, Arthur*, he'll call, and Arthur will turn to find Manny doused in twilight. They'll disappear downtown before she can catch either one of them.

Edie pushes the front door open and hurries down the hall to the kitchen. Wet snow slides off her boots and puddles on the floor. The table is set for supper. In the corner, Manny polishes his shoes. He nods hello and returns to buffing the brown leather.

In candlelight Manny is luminous. Even now, after years of their routines, Edie has not stopped noticing the grace of his shoulders, the narrow torso, slim legs, the knob of bone in his wrist. How tentatively he moves. A distant yearning curdles in her belly. He's her brother. But some nights longing rises in her, and she is back at the lake, it's summer, a stinging heat, the shock of the water at Crystal Beach. They are diving, floating, while their sisters read novels onshore and braid each other's hair: white fabric in the distance. *Edie! Manny!* Someone is calling. Edie ignores it, but Manny takes a step toward shore, turns his head toward the sound. If she tells him to stop and wait, if she says "two more minutes," he'll stay, patiently, but he will be leaning toward the others. He has always been like that, coming when called.

Manny mumbles the Shabbas prayers and passes her a slice of challah. They chew in silence until he coughs and says, "Edie, did you hear? Arthur's back." His eyes flutter. "Can you believe it?"

She takes a hard sip of sweet wine. "Really? I heard a rumor."

"I saw him," Manny says. He forks up his potatoes, but he is elsewhere, in a private, unreachable country.

Wasn't he sweet on you?

The last time she saw Arthur, he stood in the parlor of the old house on Butler Avenue, biting his lip. Dark, unruly curls fell across his forehead; his eyelashes seemed unusually thick. In the years of Manny's friendship with Arthur, the dozens of Sundays they'd taken her to the pictures, she'd never seen Arthur silenced; that day, his chatter evaporated. Edie's mother, still alive, still walking, pressed a tin of mandelbrot into his hands and pinched his cheek and told him to take good care of himself overseas; she retreated to the kitchen, blowing her nose and calling Edie's sisters to come with her. When the others were gone, Arthur stood close to Manny, his hands on Manny's shoulders. Manny wept openly. "Manny?" their mother called. Edie stood a few feet away. She was twenty-two then, wearing a dress of her sister Sylvia's, blue sprinkled with fine white dots, her hair brushed out in long waves. "Pretty Edie," Sylvia had called her. In the shadowy parlor Arthur glanced at her and pressed his lips against Manny's forehead. Then he stepped back, his hands sliding down Manny's arms, his fingers twining around Manny's.

"Manny, honey, give Edie her time with Arthur," their mother called.

"I'll write every week," Manny said, and backed away, disappearing into the dining room. Her sisters voices floated from the kitchen. *Manny, you need a handkerchief?* They murmured about the war, about Manny's bad knee, about being a man. *There's plenty you can do here.*

Arthur's hands trembled. He turned to Edie, giving her a look she couldn't fully comprehend, a begging-for-mercy sort of look. He hugged her hard, wept into her waved hair. No man had ever held her like this, pulled her so close she might lose her breath; she could feel his muscle and bones and skin beneath the layers of clothes. Her body seemed too light, too fragile for the yearning rushing through it. Arthur whispered to her, "Look out for Manny, okay?" Then he pulled back and kissed her on the cheek, the way she kissed her mother, and left her bewildered.

For a few days Edie's left hand was an object of discussion in the neighborhood; had Arthur transformed it, or was it as ordinary as ever? "Maybe he's saving up," Nora said. "Maybe he's afraid something will happen to him," Ruth Brodsky said. *Absence makes the heart grow fonder*, her older sisters repeated. In the months that followed, Edie and Manny wrote letters to Arthur and clenched their jaws during news broadcasts. For a time Manny barely spoke, and, when he did, it was privately, to Edie. "Do you think he'll come back?" That year, Manny fell into the first of his bad spells, weeks when he couldn't get out of bed. It was then that Edie grasped what looking out for Manny might mean.

Now it's as if the moment of the blue-and-white dress never occurred. Manny's spells have become routine. Edie's grown plump, and she still doesn't know how to date. The awkward ones ask her out, or the older, fat ones she can never bring herself to kiss. No one she would press close against the way she did saying good-bye to Arthur. A few times a year, she puts on her good maroon dress, clips on gold earrings, applies matching lipstick, and sits in a dim kosher restaurant, dabbing her lips with her napkin and listening to someone's bachelor cousin or someone's friend's brother chew lake whitefish. Her body is rigid; there's no feeling in her legs. She's receded to a knot of muscle in her ribcage. Later, he takes her for a walk in the neighborhood. He holds her limp hand. In front of her building he kisses her on the cheek. Hope pours out of his lips. Her skin crawls. She smiles. *Thanks for the lovely evening.*

Manny falls asleep early, on the couch, to the sounds of jazz combos aired over the radio. Dating seems utterly beyond him: each year he becomes more reclusive. When she returns from these evenings and finds him, sprawled out like a beautiful animal, waves of tenderness leave her in tears.

On Saturday afternoon when the doorbell rings, Edie is aproned and dowdy. Out the window she spots Arthur, the same strong jaw, the same broad lips, the same chocolate-drop eyes. His hair is cropped closely, tiny darts of gray creeping in. *That handsome Arthur.* Edie rushes to her bedroom, throws her apron on the floor, and fumbles through her handbag for a lipstick. She snaps on her gold earrings and reddens her lips while the bell rings again and Manny calls from the bathroom, "Edie, would you get that?"

When she opens the front door, the reality of Arthur surprises her: the smoothness of his face, his slightly chipped tooth, the lush weave of his camel coat, the tang of his skin when he rushes in to kiss her.

"*Edie.* How wonderful you look." For several seconds she's wrapped in his bear hug; she closes her eyes and feels her muscles loosen, as if she had slipped into a bath. "I've brought you something," he says. Beyond him light snow has begun to fall. He tucks her fingers around a box of chocolate-covered cherries.

"So nice of you," she says.

In the foyer he squeezes her hands and a warm flush races through her. "It's been much too long," he says, but before she has time to take his coat, Manny is there, cutting past her, embracing Arthur.

"Told you I'd be here," Arthur whispers.

Edie furrows her brow and tugs at Manny's sleeve. "Let Arthur take his coat off."

"Of course," Manny says, and awkwardly backs away.

She waves the box of chocolates like a shield. "Look what he brought."

"Open them," Arthur says. "They're lovely."

When she offers the box to Manny, Arthur kisses her hand.

She sets out the English teacups, slices the honeycake, arranges and rearranges the tray. When she enters the parlor, Manny and Arthur are side by side on the sofa—Manny leaning slightly forward, glancing at the floor as she nears, Arthur's arms spread across the sofa back. With a face like that, Arthur could be in Hollywood, she thinks, he could be a leading man. She pours the tea and serves the cake and pulls up the heavy rocking chair. "How long are you in town?" she says.

Arthur shifts his body forward and shrugs. "I don't know yet." He sips tea and samples the honeycake. "A beautiful tea set." He leans far enough in her direction to touch her hand. "Tell me about you, Edie." Manny rolls a spoon back and forth across his palms.

"Did Manny tell you I'm a teacher now?" She stumbles over the details. "Reading, yes. And math. And oh, we do projects, we decorate the room."

Arthur picks up the conversation and carries her with it. "First graders? I bet you're great with children. Have you been to Manhattan? Really, Edie, you should visit. And how are your sisters?"

Edie answers and blushes and smiles at him. She starts to regain her composure. There are things she wants to know: why he stopped writing and what went on in England and France, why he stayed away from Buffalo for so long. He seems untouched by the war, more self-possessed than ever. "What happened?" she asks, but his attention has begun to stray.

Let's not talk about the war. Let's talk about Manny. Manny, have a chocolate. Really, you'll love them. Edie? No? Manny savor it — wonderful, yes? What about this bookstore of yours? You're not giving everything away, are you? Is he, Edie? Manny, you have to charge enough to make a profit, you know. You have to pay the rent. How like you, Manny. What do you make of Henry Wallace, Manny? He's more than a spoiler, I think. More chocolate, Manny? Manny. Manny.

Manny's face is soft, he looks almost tipsy, but Edie forces her smile and finally excuses herself, walks down the hall to the bathroom. It smells of shaving tonic, a spill in the sink. Flat shaving lather films over the shelf top; Manny's unrinsed razor and brush lie between the taps. He never leaves things this way. She stays in the bathroom an extra five minutes to clean up the mess, refold the towels, redo her lipstick.

When she returns to the parlor, the sofa is empty and the men are pulling on their coats and hats.

"We're going to Arthur's cousin Rita's," Manny says. He fingers the buttons on his coat; when he glances at Edie, his voice weakens. "Tonight Arthur's taking me out to dinner."

"We should go to Oliver's," Arthur says. "We should have prime rib." He brushes off his hat and beams at Edie. "*Thank you*," he says, as if she's offered him a Chevrolet.

She gives him a tight smile and takes a step back. "Nice to see you, Arthur."

Manny's already at the door. "Oh *Edie*," Arthur says, his voice intimate. He strides toward her and runs his palm along her cheek. His scent rushes over her again.

She bites her lip, then nods. "Have a good time," she finally says.

Edie skips dinner and eats tinned olives while she plans lessons for the week. At school she's been reading fairy tales. Rapunzel. The Frog King. Briar Rose. All of them have saviors, all undergo transformations. Evil lurks in certain women and certain animals. The stories are like warnings—she isn't sure of what—but enchantment still draws her. She plans through Wednesday and gives up, paces the flat, finishes the olives without tasting them. In the bathroom she spreads cold cream over her face and becomes a mask, big eyes peeping out from a layer of white stucco, eyebrows thick above them. The pink of her lips and tongue jumps out against the whiteness. Below the stiff suits of weekdays and the frumpy dresses of home, the rest of her is also white and pink, but she fears the pink will seep out of her; she can feel herself fading into potato paleness. She's nearly thirty and everyone in the neighborhood knows it. When Edie rinses off the cold cream, her face in the mirror seems nondescript, almost absent, and the small hope, *Pretty Edie*, eludes her. She undresses, pulls on a prim flannel nightgown, and returns her reflection; her broad shoulders and heavy breasts make the nightgown float down like a tent. She buttons the collar to keep the ruffle along the neckline from swelling too much.

Manny returns late at night. In the morning, there's a new fedora on the hatrack, Manny's name sewn in gold thread on the inner lining. Expensive. She whisks eggs and milk, drops the broken shells into the garbage pail, and pours the mixture into a hot skillet. Manny takes his time washing and dressing, but from the kitchen Edie can hear him whistling. *Whistling.* It sounds vaguely like Benny Goodman. And, when he comes into the kitchen, he is smiling. From a few feet away she can smell his best aftershave.

"Nice hat," Edie says.

"Uh huh. A beauty. Arthur got it."

She peppers the eggs and keeps her eyes on the skillet.

His voice wavers slightly. "A late birthday present."

Only after the waver does Edie smile. "That's nice." She gestures at the counter. "Jam on your toast?"

Her class is full of round-faced Polish children and dark-eyed Italians, the girls wearing thick braids and gold crosses, the boys practicing curse words in the coat room. All day they pinch and push and clamor. Miss Cole, they say, tell one about a king. Miss Cole, tell about a princess.

"First, tell me again what we read Friday." Edie says, "Why did Briar Rose fall asleep?"

"She's under a spell," Teresa says.

"She was *cursed*," Joey Csznowski says.

"By the wise woman," Angela says, "the one who didn't get invited to the party."

"The one who lost her shoe," Paul says.

"No," Mary says.

"That's another one," Anthony says.

"What will save her?" Edie says.

"The soldiers," Joey Santora says.

"The prince," Lucille says.

"How?" Edie says.

The boys elbow each other and snicker. A few of the girls cover their mouths.

"What happens next?" Edie says.

"They live contented to the end of their days," Angela says.

"Yes," Teresa sighs, "that's how it ends."

All week, Manny skips supper and stays out late. Edie doesn't sleep until she hears him come in—eleven, midnight, later. He's abandoned his early morning walks, his seven o'clock coffee and newspaper. She leaves for school without seeing him. Late Thursday afternoon, she stops by the bookstore. The sign on the door is handwritten in someone else's script. *Closed for the day.*

Edie visits her sisters: she reads to Sylvia's little ones, diapers Dora's baby, drinks tea in their kitchens, and says nothing about Manny or Arthur. She spends Shabbas at Marilyn's but otherwise eats alone, leaving plates in the icebox for Manny. Some nights she falls into a heavy blank sleep; some nights she's awake until she hears the key in the lock, Manny's footsteps in the hall. One night she waits until Manny's movements have stopped; at two o'clock she stands in his doorway, gauging the depth of his breathing. Then she enters his room. He's asleep in his clothes— his best trousers, an unfamiliar shirt. The room smells faintly of whiskey and aftershave and something sharper than either. It's almost intoxicating, that smell. She wants to lie down on the bed next to him, to wake him up and remind him who she is. But he'd be shocked to find her there, he'd push her away, and the shame of simply watching him overwhelms her. She does not cover him with a blanket; she closes the door and in the kitchen makes herself a cup of tea. She sweeps and mops the floor and dusts the living room furniture until 3:30.

"Where did you get that shirt?"
"What shirt?"
"The one on top of the laundry basket. It's linen."
"It's Arthur's."
"Why doesn't he wash his own?"
"He lent it to me."
"You wear linen shirts to the bookstore?"
"I'll wash it myself." Manny picks up the newspaper and fortresses himself in the reading chair.

Edie tucks the shirt more deeply into the laundry basket. Later, when she loads the wash, she sniffs at it. Manny's scent, riddled with smoke.

The day of the snowstorm, school closes early and there is bedlam in the coat room. The boys push each other and trample stray mittens, Mary's forgotten to use the bathroom before pulling on her woolens, Joey Csznowski keeps pulling Lucille's hat off, and Matthew repeatedly shouts, "snowball war, snowball war." How enormous and slow Edie is in this swarm of small, restless bodies. Why should this make her tear up? She buttons them into their coats and watches them depart in noisy clumps, led away by harried mothers. In her boots and coat and hat, Edie returns to the classroom and erases the board.

The streetcar is slow to arrive and already the snow falls heavily. An inch or more an hour, the driver says. Cars skid as they turn onto residential streets, and the sidewalks are already emptying. No one is bothering to shovel; cleared paths will vanish in minutes. Edie wraps an extra scarf around her head before she gets off at her stop, so only her glasses peek out. Snowflakes on their surface melt in small patches.

Manny isn't home yet, and she telephones the store: no answer. She fills pitchers with water and lays out candles and matches in case the power goes out. She puts on a pot of soup, boils noodles, and layers them with egg and raisins and apples for kugel, waits. Through the window the city air seems pearly and opaque, even though it's only two o'clock. She turns on the radio news, crochets, watches the minute hand on the living room clock. Finally, she dials Arthur's cousin.

"Rita? It's Edie Cole."

"Edie, how are you? Such a storm."

"Terrible. I wondered if Manny was there."

"Manny? No. He's not out in this, is he?"

"He must be checking the store. You know he worries about floods."

"All those books."

"Can I speak to Arthur?"

"*Arthur.* If he'd just listen to me. I told him, I said I heard about a storm. He drove to Toronto for the day and now he's stuck. He called from a hotel, thank God."

"Toronto?"

"Oh Edie, you know Arthur. Friends everywhere, and he always has to say hello."

"Sure," Edie says, "I know how he is."

Manny is not at Marilyn's or Dora's. When Edie dials Sylvia's house, she hears the click that means Marta Block has picked up on the party line they share: she'll have to watch what she says.

"Sylvia, are you all home safe?"

"We're fine. Eli got in a couple of hours ago."

"And the children? Did Manny help you get them home?"

"Oh, I didn't ask. He's got his hands full with that store. Emily Eisenberg helped me out."

"All right then."

"By the way, Edie, have you seen Arthur Blum?"

"He visited." Edie hesitates. "And brought chocolates. He sends his best."

When the kugel is out of the oven, she layers on her woolens, pulls on her overcoat and fake fur hat. The snow is stinging, blinding, already drifting to midcalf. She doesn't know where she's going, and she can barely see across the street. Parked cars have metamorphosed into mounds of snow. When she reaches the intersection a few blocks over, the red glow of the traffic signal seems to hover by itself. One plow drives by. Edie tries to wipe her glasses, but the snow smears and freezes on the outside, while the inside fogs from her breath. She pictures them, Manny and Arthur, laughing in the lounge of Buffalo's Statler Hotel, the only hotel she knows: they are beyond the snow, far beyond Edie. For a mile she lumbers through drifts, her fingers and toes numbing, her legs heavy and unsteady.

"Manne–e–e Manne–e–e." A few blocks from the store, she starts calling, but the wind swallows up her voice. The store is dark, locked: she takes off her gloves and rummages in her coat pocket for keys. Inside the bookstore, the deafening gusts are muted to a soft whoosh. *Mannee?* She walks the perimeter of the store, takes the flashlight from the desk, checks the basement. It's dry but cold, musty, and empty of Manny.

Stacks of Latin and Greek textbooks form a barricade on the far side of Manny's desk; the front shelf displays *The Settlement Cookbook*, *Visiting Scotland*, and *The Great American West*. From Manny's phone she dials the flat, tightens a fist around the receiver, and counts a dozen rings. Finally, she hangs up.

The brother she knows would never go off to Toronto without telling. Edie's Manny always leaves notes: he calls her, he leaves messages in the school office. She paces up and down the wood floor, a wet trail melting from her coat and boots, water rolling down her ankles, seeping into her socks. If she calls her sisters back, she'll have to tell about Arthur.

The cash register is locked, but the desk drawers are open. Receipts. Letters from other used-book dealers. Queries from professors. A pint bottle of Scotch whisky, a chocolate bar, stamps. A cigarbox of other letters, some from Arthur. Recent postmarks. She can't help but touch them, open them. *My dear Manny*, the letters all begin, and mostly tell where Arthur is living, where he is working, name his Army friends and Manhattan friends. She skims along the lines. *Thank you for the wonderful books. . . . When did you start reading plays? . . . I am finally myself again, no longer sad. . . . The very idea of Buffalo wears me out, a coffin of a city. But you are there, Manny, and I'll try.* The latest, from September, says, *I mean it, come to New York.*

Come to New York? I mean it. He sounded like he meant it when he told Edie, *Really, you should visit.* That's what people say. And of course they've stayed in touch, they are best friends, why shouldn't they? For an instant Edie's lips quiver, and then she staunches the impulse, stills, feeling her spine become rigid, her face stiff. She replaces the letters in the cigarbox, wraps herself up again, reenters the storm. The visibility is only a few feet.

Not long after Edie arrives home, the electricity goes out. She spends the night upright on the couch, watching the ghostly streets, crocheting socks for Dora's baby, lighting candle after candle.

By morning Edie is red-eyed and frayed, and it isn't until noon that the storm settles into light snow and the city begins to dig out. Early in the afternoon, Manny calls on a line steeped in static.

"Terrible storm," he says.

Edie bursts into tears. "Why didn't you call me?"

"I tried. You didn't answer. Then there was a problem with the phone."

"The electricity, not the phone. Where are you?"

"Rita's."

"You didn't call here."

"I did, Edie, I swear, Marta picked up to dial."

"Manny—"

"Marta, are you listening? Tell Edie."

"I was here."

"Maybe you were in the bathroom."

"I would have heard the phone ring."

"Not if you were running water, Edie. Maybe you were running water."

At the beginning of February Edie redecorates the classroom, hanging red hearts edged with paper doilies. The children make cards for their mothers, writing, *I love you* or *My Valentine*, and writing their names, the letters blocky and awkward.

Manny is home when she gets there; for three days he stays home, lying in bed, the lights out. The first night, he comes to the table for supper, then returns to his room. After that Edie takes him trays. She brings the radio to his room, and she sits in the parlor, reading, until ten o'clock; these nights, her sleep is deep and uninterrupted.

On Thursday evening Arthur rings the bell.

"He's not feeling well," Edie says.

"I know. I'm here to see him."

"Leave him alone."

"Edie," Arthur says. He takes her hands. He squeezes her fingers and rubs his thumb across her skin. "Let me see him."

She relents. She busies herself in the kitchen and lets Arthur go to Manny's bedroom. But she creeps back toward the hallway as she hears their voices rise. Only a few clear words: *the only way . . . I can't . . . stubborn . . . you don't know.*

Then Manny bursts out the door and heads for the bathroom. She can tell by the flush on his skin, his pursed lips, and drooping neck that he's crying. Arthur follows to the bathroom, but Manny's already shut the door. Edie hurries down the hall and pulls Arthur away, out into the parlor.

"Why is he crying?"

"Edie—"

"I want to know why he's crying."

"We had a disagreement, that's all."

"He hasn't cried for months. He was fine before."

"I don't want him to cry."

"Well, stop it. You started it, you stop it."

"That's what I'm trying to do here, Edie."

They stand in the parlor, glaring and silent, until Manny opens the door and shuffles down the hallway, holding his head. "I've got a headache," he says. "I've got a real headache." When he reaches the parlor, he gazes at the two of them. "Edie, stay out of it."

"Why are you so upset?"

"It isn't your business."

"What do you mean?"

"Just leave me alone. You never leave me alone."

Edie's eyes narrow and her voice goes cold. "I see." She starts toward the kitchen and calls back, "Arthur, you can show yourself out."

Then she is burning, clanging skillets against saucepans. He'll leave again, and what will she have? Manny, broken, months of his headaches and sleeping and crying, months of leaning on her, months of resenting her for being there to lean on. No one to shore her up, to kiss her on the lips, no bed of tenderness.

She hears the door close, the lock click as they walk out of the flat. From the window she can see their bodies melt into the dark, first Arthur, then Manny. Once again, Manny resumes his late-night routine, while Edie's silence extends like lake ice.

Edie knows that it's only a matter of time before Arthur returns to New York; he's seen too much, he doesn't belong in Buffalo. *A coffin of a city.* She watches for signs, and in a week they become clear to her. Manny has begun to drip humility again, he's jittery, solicitous: the way he acts when he's afraid.

"What are you teaching now, Edie? I brought you some books, for the kids, this one has trains . . . Edie? Do we need anything at the market? . . . Edie I can get those shoes repaired for you, you want them repaired?"

Finally, he tells her. It's Sunday afternoon. He shuffles and stares at his feet. "Arthur's going back to New York."

"Oh?"

They sit down at the kitchen table, the pause between them like a live thing.

"He asked me to go with him," Manny mumbles.

"I see."

With effort, he looks her in the face. "I need . . ."

"What?"

"You're the only one who knows."

"What?" Edie says.

"You *know*."

"I don't know anything."

"Edie, don't do this."

"I'm not doing anything."

"*Please*," Manny begs.

He's waiting for her to fill the gap she always fills, to say it will be fine, to say, *You'll love Manhattan, I'll visit you there.* To tell him he can always come back. "What is it, Manny?" Edie says.

"Help me," he says.

"I help you all the time."

Without Edie, Manny takes the suitcases from the storage closet, launders his boxers, undershirts, socks, picks out towels and linens. Without her, he makes arrangements for the store. Without her, he counts his money and visits Sylvia, Marilyn, and Dora. Edie pretends to ignore every act, every gesture: she teaches her classes, shops on her regular shopping days, cooks the usual suppers.

On the morning of the departure, Manny paces the flat and sweats through his shirt. His suitcases stand in neat rows at the door. His store files are in the bedroom for Sylvia's Eli to pick up. Edie rocks in their mother's rocker, making no attempt at conversation. Blue yarn spills over her lap and her knitting needles click; she concentrates on the baby blanket as if it were the child.

When the yellow taxicab honks in front of the house, Edie rises and kisses Manny on the cheek and hands him a packed lunch for the train. Then she returns to the rocking chair and takes up her needles. Manny hesitates, nervous, at the door, as if waiting for something else.

"Take care of yourself, Edie," he says.

"I will." She steals a glance at the window; she can see Arthur emerge from the cab and approach the front door. He knocks but does not come in.

"Just a minute," Manny says. He hands one suitcase out to Arthur and turns back to Edie again. "Well," he says, "good-bye then."

Edie doesn't drop a stitch. "Good-bye, Manny." She peers at the blanket.

It isn't until the door closes that Edie looks up, then moves to the window. The neighborhood seems grayer than ever against the brightness of the taxi. The driver and Arthur lift the suitcases into the trunk, while Manny takes quick glances back at the house. He has always had a graceful silhouette. For the briefest instant, Edie moves into the lamplight near the window, so Manny can see her looking out. There is too much of her and not enough beauty, she thinks, and she quickly retreats. In the parlor's shadows the radiator hisses, the clock ticks. The slam of car doors echoes over the ice outside, and Edie drops back into the rocker, crosses her arms over her chest, and rocks.

Heart of Hearts

Ben Abrams was not a bad man; he was a practical man confused by grief, which swept through him to my family. I want to say he visited sorrow upon us, as drowning people will, but that is disingenuous. Ben simply mirrored our own blinding currents. Mine.

Ben started out a poor boy in Buffalo and met his great love, Edith Rosenberg, just after the war. At a Rochester wedding reception he saw her slipping into the shadows and sneaking an extra glass of wine behind her father's back—a willowy beauty, properly shy with men. She blushed when she realized she'd been seen, but kept her composure as her cousin introduced Ben; she smiled, accepted one dance, dismissed him. *Edith*, he repeated to himself, *Edith*. From their first awkward conversation, he believed she'd hung the moon, and her presence in this world shook him loose from our neighborhood in Buffalo, emptied his savings account, pulled him to Rochester where he worked like an animal and prayed he would be worthy, and where, eventually, he met with her father behind closed doors. He agreed to stay in Rochester. He agreed to take a house on the Rosenberg's street. On his knees he proposed.

Ben loved Edith with a mute ferocity punctuated by grand gestures: buckets of roses, pearls from Gamler's. At the breakfast table she'd find gold bracelets, diamond studs, a ring of tiny sapphires. Edith accepted his devotion with apparent serenity: who knows whether she was happy. She saw her mother every day, learned to cook French, and, later, spent most of her waking hours with her children. In summer they stayed in a cottage at Crystal Beach. In winter she taught the children to skate. On Saturday nights Ben took her out for dinner and she wore the diamond studs. She was otherwise careless about the jewelry: her girls wore the pearls for dress-up. The oldest was five, the second daughter four, and the boy about two when Edith died, her blood rife with cancer. It was 1953 and the doctors were all but helpless. Ben's strength stayed with him through her illness, those long nights at her bedside; he prayed with the fervor of a Hasid, a blind optimism gracing him until the end. When she died, he became unmoored. He wandered his furniture store at night, touching the chairs and sofas as if they were her body. His mother-in-law cooked supper for the children and got them to bed. The little girls and his young son were invisible to him; it was as if they existed only in relation to his beautiful Edith.

That June, before the lilacs browned, Ben appeared on our front porch. He stood downwind of the bush, not touching the blossoms, numb to the impulse to crush his face against them. He wore a deep brown suit, a dark tie, removed his hat when Sam walked out onto the porch: a man paying his respects. They had been ushers at each other's weddings. Sam, in his weekend workshirt and trousers, took Ben's face in his hands, hugged him, patted him on the back, led him to the rocker on the sunny corner of the porch. Ben moved with the stiff-jointed swaying of a marionette, an uninhabited man. He spoke little. They sat together in the mild breeze, Sam asking questions with definite, easy answers and telling news of the neighborhood he otherwise wouldn't repeat: *What do you recommend in sofas, Ben? Thursday's thunderstorm hit Rochester? I hear your cousin Frieda's off to college.* After twenty minutes Ben rose, fingered the brim of his hat, and stepped out onto the front walk, refusing Sam's invitations to stay and offers to escort him elsewhere.

Edith had only been gone a month then, but Ben began to spend whole weekends in Buffalo, leaving his children with his in-laws, automatically driving west, following back roads lined by cornfields and orchards, emerging into our close and crowded neighborhood. He wandered from the house of one friend or relative to another. Door after door opened to him, and as he walked down one street and up another, aunts and cousins would line the sidewalk, watching, as if their gazes would safeguard his arrival somewhere else.

I don't remember the first time he stayed for a meal: what I remember is his flat, fish-eyed gaze as he ate a bowl of soup. One afternoon I handed him a teacup and discovered his skin tone had become more olive and pink. There was a flicker of a smile when my daughter Sarah smeared her face with pudding. When his eyes regained expression, I noticed how large, how round they were—the color of woods, fur, sleep. He gazed at my belly as I moved about the room: I was pregnant again, just showing. There was, by August, the sort of intensity to his look I had heard women talk of when he was younger and a single man. I turned away to tend to Sarah and the back of my blouse burned.

Those nights, after Ben had left for Rochester and Sarah had fallen asleep, I would hold Sam to me as I had at no other time. Our marriage was a passionate one, and our intimate pleasures had been curtailed only in the months after Sarah's birth. But those nights of Ben's first visits we crushed ourselves against each other, swayed and moaned with the fierceness of prayer, as if we had seen how the world might end and in our coupling would stave it off.

In late summer Ben came alive. He began to arrive with gifts: tomatoes, sweet corn, baskets of peaches. His voice regained its resonance and surety, a more natural timbre. He told old stories. *When Sam and I were ten*, he'd say. *When Mrs. Moscowitz caught Sam behind the ball park . . . When Arnie Stein was drunk at shul. . . .* In the afternoons he walked the neighborhood with Sam and Sarah. Twice I heard him laugh; each time, a craving rose up in me.

Soon the gifts began to change. One week Ben brought a bud vase, one week perfumed writing paper. One week he gave me a velvet-lined box; inside, an extravagant gold hair clip.

I knew I should not keep it.

"It's lovely," I said, "but Ben."

"Try it on," he said.

Sam's mouth opened and closed on air.

"Perhaps later," I said.

"No, no, wear it today," Ben said.

"Something to save for your girls," I said.

His face folded in on itself. "You don't like it?"

"I told you, it's lovely."

"Then try it. What can it hurt?"

I looked to Sam, who was sliding behind his newspaper.

"Go ahead," Ben said.

I relented, pulled my hair out of the loose bun I wore, brushed it back, twisted it, and set the clip in place.

"That's beautiful, your hair like that."

"Sam?" I said.

A few seconds passed. "Don't you think? Sam?" Ben said.

Sam dropped the paper for an instant. "Nice."

When it came time for Sam and Sarah to leave for their walk, Ben insisted I join them, promising to help me clean the dishes. We all drove over to Delaware Park, and he slipped his arm through mine as we crossed the green lawns, while Sarah ran circles around the maples, Sam behind her, threatening to catch up. Sam was lifting Sarah in the air, spinning her around, when Ben leaned over and kissed me on the forehead. We were standing very close. I blushed. Stray red leaves curled across the grass. "It's getting to be autumn," I said. I called to Sarah. "Look at the leaves." My voice instantly brought her back to me, as I knew it would, Sam following along.

That day, before he returned to Rochester, Ben kissed my hand. We were standing in the doorway, in clear view of the entire neighborhood. He held my wrist for several seconds, a man in a trance, his mouth pressing against my knuckles.

"He's lonely, Sam," I said that night. "He's lonely and grateful." I put the hair clip on the top closet shelf and climbed into bed. Sam nodded at me, his curls falling thick over his forehead. He wrapped his hands in my hair and, slowly, wrapped his body around mine.

But for weeks after we did not sleep entwined. At night Sam would offer up a solemn kiss and turn to the far side of the bed, his movements heavy and doltish. He did not touch me. My skin became the shell of a more solitary creature, thick with loneliness. I thought of Ben, the pressure of his mouth against my wrist, and then I became more human, my breathing quickened, my thighs dampened and warmed. I imagined Ben's fingers circling over my breasts. Sam would shift in bed or slip into light snoring, and I'd freeze, an animal caught in light. Once or twice I reached over to him, hoping to bring him back and blot Ben from my mind. But Sam pulled further away, curled into himself at the edge of the bed.

On the loneliest night yet, when the dream of Ben was so strong I felt him in the room, I tried to break away by stroking Sam's shoulders and back, slipping my hands beneath his nightclothes, pressing against his chest. He pulled away. "Marilyn, get some sleep." It was as if he smelled Ben on my skin. I left our bed and checked on Sarah. She slept soundly, curled on her side the way Sam did. In her room there was peace, and I stayed in the rocker by her crib, dozing, waking, watching her roll, fling an arm over her head, find her thumb. Nothing compared to her small mouth, the wild dark curls that she'd inherited from Sam, the texture of her face, her light breathing. Hers was the room in which my visions of Ben vanished. At 5 A.M. I rose, scrubbed myself with hot water and soap, and brewed the morning coffee.

The last Sunday Ben and I were alone together, he brought me late roses. Sam said nothing. He left the house to check on his mother. He did not take Sarah, though he had promised her the afternoon. She wailed as he hurried away from the house. I told Ben I hadn't much time, there was bread to bake. Instead of leaving, he hovered near me in the kitchen, watching the clouds of flour float above my hands, rolling a pinch of dough between his thumb and his forefinger, staring at my face. Sarah would not play by herself and clung to my legs until I lifted her up and gave her a piece of dough to knead. I finished the dough and began to clean the table. The kitchen seemed to narrow—Ben filling more and more of it—and I flushed under his gaze. My hands trembled and I barely spoke: the dreams were coming loose. Ben seemed unperturbed by my silence. Finally, I stuttered that Sarah and I were also expected at Sam's mother's house.

He reached over and took my floury hand, rubbed his fingers over my skin, then leaned across the table and kissed me on the cheek, hesitating after the kiss, breathing against the side of my face. A warm, familiar flush ran through to my legs.

He waited for my response. For a moment I was paralyzed, feeling his breath against me. I touched my fingers to my lips, thinking only *kiss*, forgetting everything but *kiss*. Then a small piece of dough slapped the floor. Sarah began to fuss, and suddenly I was three steps away from Ben, holding her. She buried her face in my dress.

"What is it honey? Are you ready to go to Nana's?"

Ben stepped back, licked his lips, dropped his gaze to the floor, glanced up at the clock. "I'll be back in town next week," he said.

I spoke without thinking. "Good. We'll all see you then."

The next week, I invited my mother-in-law and Sam's cousin Irv to the house, and regularly began to fill our house with Sunday guests: my sister Sylvia and her husband, Eli, Sam's uncles, friends from the neighborhood. This left no time for Ben to be alone with me. He barely disguised his impatience. He sulked and sent me imploring looks, but kept returning. I pretended to notice nothing. I did not explain to Sam my decision to invite other guests, nor did he ask. But finally the coldness that had come upon our marriage began to thaw.

Were it not for my sister Edie, we would have gone on with our Sunday afternoons and forgotten those strange, confused weeks, perhaps forgotten even the desire that colored them. Ben would have drifted back to Rochester, married one of the spinster Rosenberg women or devoted himself to his children. But Edie. She was always an undeniable force in our world—awkward, provincial, headstrong. I can say now that she is the sister I loved the least, the one I found it hardest to protect. She alternately bullied the rest of us and crumbled into shyness so painful we rushed to her deliverance. Twice a week I visited her with Sarah; I'd solicit news of her first graders, her knowledge of child development. Around children Edie softened into a loving woman. Then I could tolerate her oddness and manipulations, and in this way we could live as sisters. But she behaved poorly with Sam, fawning over him, sneering about his insurance job. At parties she remained mum or made unpredictable gaffes; holidays were marred by her sudden outbursts. I did not invite her to visit with Ben.

It was late October. Company filled the parlor—Ben, Sylvia, Eli, Sam's mother, Sylvia's two boys—when Edie walked in, opening the door without knocking, hauling a bushel of apples, Cortlands she'd bought at the farmer's market. The boys raced up and down the hallway, Sarah tagging after them. Ben smoked a cigarette and pretended to listen to Sam's mother, who was gossiping in Yiddish. "Oh Edie," I said, "hello." Ben's head swiveled like a weathervane in wild wind: forgetting, he scanned the room for the face of his own Edith. My sister waited, plump and pale, her glasses obscuring her wide hazel eyes. She set down the apples, scooped up Sarah, and held her like a shield.

"You remember Ben Abrams?" I said.

Edie nodded and stared at the air to the right of Ben's face. "I'm sorry about your loss," she said. Her eyes darted to the left and then back to the smoke rising from his cigarette.

"Edie, doll, beautiful apples," Sam's mother said.

"Have one," Edie said. "Let me pick one out for you."

"Be sure to bake it. These teeth are too old."

"Oh."

Sarah pulled at Edie's glasses, the thick frames angling down

Edie's face, and Edie pried her fingers off the lenses. "Not the glasses, Sarah. I have sweets for you."

Sam's mother resumed her Yiddish stories. The boys began to shoot marbles in the hallway. Eli held apples up to the light and praised them.

I left for the kitchen, but I could hear Sylvia making conversation, telling Ben that Edie was a teacher, asking what kind of apples the market offered. The sweet rolls on the stove had cooled enough to be served. I told myself that the apples were a kind gesture. But Edie knew better than to arrive unannounced, to enter my house without knocking. Sylvia would tell me to be grateful Edie hadn't done worse: as a young girl she'd thrown tantrums only our brother, Manny, could calm. Soft-hearted Manny. At turns Edie lorded over him and coddled him. Well into adulthood she kept house for him as if he were her husband: outsiders mistook them for a married couple. Then Manny up and moved to Manhattan. Edie's small eccentricities mushroomed. She loitered in front of Manny's old bookstore. She wandered the streets at five A.M. Scrappy pink curlers hung in her hair as she went about her marketing. Rag dolls, baby dolls, and stuffed animals began to fill her flat. I pretended they were for Sarah's benefit.

I stacked the sweet rolls on a platter and returned to the parlor. Chocolate stuck to Sarah's fingers and lips. I took her from Edie; her small chubby arms curved tightly around my neck. Edie was already inching toward the door, Ben's gaze on her at full intensity. She did not say a word but glanced at Ben and awkwardly curtsied; it was a girl's gesture, one that didn't fit Edie anymore, one I hoped she would not repeat. From the window I watched her hurry down the block to her flat, an index finger in her mouth.

One evening a few weeks later, Edie arrived at our door carrying dresses: the maroon wool she wore at holidays, a plain navy shirtwaist, a beige suit a size too small. She wanted advice on what to wear to dinner with Ben. The back of my neck prickled.

"Maybe you should get something new," I said.

She frowned. "There isn't time. You don't like these, do you?"

I leaned against the parlor door. "These are fine. But why not treat yourself?"

"What should I do?" Agitation screwed up her face: her forehead pinched, her nose swelled, her lips flattened and slanted downward.

"Let me look at these," I said. "Would you check on Sarah?"

Her face reassembled itself, and she hurried down the hall to the nursery. I rifled through my bedroom closet. Most often Edie wore a size or two larger than mine, but with the pregnancies I'd acquired a range. Sam looked up from the insurance papers he had spread out over our bed. "What are you doing?"

"Finding a dress for Edie."

"Special occasion?"

I hesitated. "Maybe," I said. "I think she wants to try some new styles."

He shrugged. Edie had spurned two of his cousins, good if ordinary men, and he'd long since given up on her. "Couldn't hurt."

I lingered over an unattractive brown-and-white striped dress my mother-in-law had given me. Then I picked a green-and-white print that would bring out Edie's eyes, white beads, earrings. From outside the nursery I could hear Edie singing "Dedicated to You" to Sarah. Her beautiful, rich alto seemed to emanate from another body. I walked in the room and she let a verse drop. "Look who's here," she said to Sarah.

"Hi pumpkin." I kissed Sarah's chubby face. "Having a good time with Aunt Edie?" I held up the dress for Edie to examine. "I thought green might be a good color for you. Something to try."

She pressed it against herself, stroked the fabric. "You think so?"

"See if you like it. If not, wear the navy one and dress it up a bit, some beads or a scarf. You can borrow some of mine."

"Okay," Edie said, nodding too much. "Okay."

When she left I lay down on the sofa and closed my eyes, drifting until I could almost feel Ben's hands.

There was a second date. After a month Edie stopped asking my advice and became more secretive about her meetings with Ben. I don't know when their romance began in earnest. He shortened his visits to our flat, then abandoned them. Edie stopped walking the neighborhood in curlers and put away her dolls. She bought a salmon lipstick. The talk began, at first lighthearted, not unkind. Ben and Edie had been seen walking together, nice for them. *She knows about loneliness, your sister*, women at the market told me. *She has some wisdom for this man.*

Then my sister Dora called to say she'd run into Edie and Ben at the pictures on a Saturday night. She mentioned the new lipstick.

"What about him?"

"Ben? Hair slicked back, a new suit. Not at all a widower. Sylvia says I should mind my own business, but it's shameful, *scandalous*, his wife six months in the grave and the two of them running around like that."

I imagined Ben's body beneath the new suit, the tailored shirts and bleached underclothes slipping away, revealing pale skin, thick muscle, tangled patches of dark hair, heat. A sharp salt on my tongue. I bit a slice of lemon and waxed the parlor floor. Shame. Scandal. Trouble honed itself on ordinary life, the line dividing them as fine as Sarah's hair. Everyone knew of Edie's loneliness. No one knew that Ben had kissed my face, or that he'd flown toward me in dreams and I had not run. No one but Sam had recognized the peculiar tone of Ben's visits to our flat, and Sam had come back to me. We were again a physical couple. Every night, Sam held me, Sarah called to me, the child inside me rolled and kicked; there was simply no room for Ben. But in my private moments, he appeared.

Edie was wrong for him, of course. And I knew she was un-accustomed to the attentions of men. I didn't caution her. He kissed her hand at dinner, the way he'd kissed mine, the way he'd kissed Edith Rosenberg, those warm lips pressing, lingering. She responded with gratitude, perhaps with lust: I couldn't bring myself to discuss him with her. For her part, Edie was too skittish to bring him up.

When I found Edith Rosenberg's pearls on Edie's bureau, I knew Ben was serious. There was no mistaking those drop ear-rings, that eighteen-inch strand—both too luminous to be false. They lay in the open on her mirrored dresser tray, pearls and reflections of pearls adding up to opulence.

I touched them. Tentatively at first, tracing them with my fingertips. I pulled the strung pearls across the back of my hand, held them against my cheek and lips, lifted them into the light. My sister lumbered through the door. "Edie," I said.

We stood there for a moment, pearls shimmering between us. Then Edie tugged them from my hands and carefully laid them in a velvet case, her face expressionless.

This is my last image of Ben: He stands on the sidewalk, dapper, hands in his pockets, as if deciding whether or not to ring our front bell. Lake winds have kicked up, and our street appears gray and abandoned. I set our empty milk bottles on the porch and call to him.

"Ben? Are you looking for Edie? Ben?"

"What?"

"Are you seeing Edie this weekend?"

Doffing his hat then, embarrassed. "How are you? Yes."

They did not wait until the anniversary of Edith Abrams's death, although Sylvia told Edie they should. This meant sacrifice. Edie had always weakened at the thought of white lace and rose-filled bouquets: over the years she'd built up a dowry with enough money for a satin gown and a large reception. But Ben arranged a quiet ceremony in Rochester, performed by the rabbi who had married him to Edith Rosenberg. I doubt my Edie argued. No one else intervened on her behalf. My sister Dora traveled to Rochester, but I was well into my eight month by the wedding date, confined to bed. Sylvia's youngest was ill. When Dora returned, she said little: the flowers were lovely. Ben's children did not attend.

During the last weeks of my pregnancy I napped in the afternoons, Sarah beside me, kicking in her sleep. I would wake imagining Ben's bed, where Edie slept. She had never felt a man's touch over the whole of her body. I pictured Ben, patient, amorous. He would kiss her face, her shoulders, her hands. Slowly, quietly, he'd trace the contours of her body. He'd embrace her. For the first time since girlhood, she would feel desirable. Her intense shyness would give way to the fierce, blind coupling that would irrevocably bind her to him.

I grimaced; I could not sustain such generosity. Other visions rose up in me. I knew that Edie desperately needed Ben's tenderness and would be crushed by his indifference, but that knowledge did not move me. For a time I decided the fault would lie with her: Edie would remain trapped by her own shyness. Ben might beseech her, but she was too fearful to let him touch her. Their marriage would be chaste from the start.

Or perhaps Edie would let him touch her but would not relax enough to take pleasure in their intimacy. Ben, seeing this, would close his eyes and try to imagine a more responsive woman. As time went on, his imaginings would take the place of the flesh-and-blood Edie.

I chastised myself for these thoughts. Then I would grant her the children, the two girls and the little boy, who, having lost their mother, must have been lost themselves. But I pictured crumpled, faceless girls howling when they heard Ben say the name Edie, his pet name for their mother. I pictured the two year old wailing. More likely, the girls screamed at nothing, said nothing, complied with Edie's every request. Edie would fear for them. The boy would have clung to Edie, not allowing her out of his sight. And Edie would equal the attachment. This seemed acceptable to me: Edie would spend all her time with the children; Ben, with his furniture.

In less selfish moods, I realized that the fact of this marriage, less than a year after Edith Rosenberg's death, must have been scandal to everyone in Rochester. I imagined the neighbors appalled at Ben, who seemed to be replacing one Edie with another, the Rosenbergs mortified and unkind. And after our Edie was seen wearing the drop pearls? The family would stop speaking to him. Here my thoughts of Edie would soften. What friends would she have? Her marriage, begun with tenderness and hope, would quickly deteriorate. A tragedy.

And the final tragic moment would arrive quietly, after supper, Edie alone, rinsing plates and finally realizing what everyone else had seen and Ben had not: that he was still desperately in love with Edith Rosenberg and that his heart had no room for any other kind of Edith.

I knew I was tainted by envy: my mind would not allow Edie happiness. I never spoke of this. I did not interfere.

When my labor began, Edie bought a train ticket and reappeared in Buffalo. She wore a plain woolen dress, no lipstick. Through a long, difficult labor, Edie stayed beside me, holding my hand, speaking to me the way she spoke to Sarah, to the children in her classes, in the most secure and soothing of voices. Jacob was born red and wrinkled and fierce, and Edie, in the days of my exhaustion, walked him through the flat and sang to him, sprawled on the floor with Sarah and drew castles while he slept, cooked our meals, and watched over all of us while Sam was off at work.

After a week she told me she was not returning to Rochester.

"What?"

"I'll stay in Buffalo now."

"He's your *husband*," I said.

I realized then that she was not wearing her ring. She shook her head. "I'll teach again in September. I'll find another flat."

"What happened?"

"Your Jacob, he needs a little sun. See the yellow on him?"

"Edie, what are you telling me?"

A momentary dullness fell over her face. "I'll start the wash now."

I tried once more and got a low, imperious, "I'm staying put." She said nothing more. She smiled and stroked Jacob's head. It was then that the weight of my visions pulled me to earth, and I felt my blood and bones crush inward. I slipped to the floor, dizzy with my curses on her marriage. Edie observed me, distant, curious. "Think about what you want for supper," she said. She placed Jacob in my arms and left the room. He was not crying.

I buried my questions alongside my wayward desires. Some evenings, I prayed. Edie and I returned to our habits, our weekday teas, our talk of children and infants, our guarded pleasantries. In winter Sam shoveled her walkway. In spring she helped plant our garden. Our middle years spread before us, and we entered each one as if Ben had never walked through our lives, as if there had been no other Edith, as if nothing but love lay in our heart of hearts.

Confessions

___

            The day before I left for Fort Benning, I promised Manny I wouldn't marry. We were in love: it was an easy promise to make. A mild breeze swept through my neighborhood, carrying the scent of grass, roses, water. A fat blue Chevy rolled down Hertel Avenue; a Checker cab parked up the block. Long strips of sunlight split through cumulus clouds, variegating the street, and we walked aimlessly, simply to walk. It was as if we'd found the heart of leisure. The war seemed a distant, forgettable obligation, and I was conscious only of Manny— slim, sinew and bone, his hatbrim a bit askew, slight limp to his left, barely perceptible. The lines of his face converged in polished angles, like sculpted wood, olive, his eyes mahogany. All giving off heat. All on the verge, I felt, of melting into me, nearly liquid, transforming us in the way only sex transforms. That week, we had twice made love, and there on Hertel Avenue, in the lull of a Buffalo afternoon, more than anything I wanted to kiss him. Impossible. I shifted my gait to the left and bumped into him as we walked.

Manny stroked his cheek, once, twice, as if wiping off an idea. "Arthur, don't get yourself killed," he said.

My stomach fluttered. "I won't, of course." I smiled with all my teeth. "We'll win and I'll be back."

"I know that," he said. "I know."

I brushed up against his shoulder. Sirens passed in the distance; in their wake the streets seemed unnaturally empty. Our steps fell a half-beat apart, like an echo, a muted argument. Block after block we said nothing. The pattern of silence broke when a DeSoto pulled up to the curb and a bald-headed man asked for directions to Delaware Avenue. The car drove on and Manny cleared his throat. "What if you meet a woman? A Garbo type. A looker."

I rolled my eyes. "Manny, I'm coming back."

He licked his lips and frowned.

"Shouldn't *I* be worried?" I tugged his hat. "What if you fall for Ruth Brodsky while I'm gone?"

Manny snorted a laugh. "I'll never marry. I'm not marrying anyone." He gazed at me directly, his eyes both shadow and light. "You know that."

"Me neither," I said. "Not anyone."

Some weeks, everyone in Buffalo expected me to marry Rhoda Feinstein; some weeks, Becky Strauss; some weeks, Manny's sister Edie. The idea was that we would marry, settle in Buffalo or maybe Kenmore, I would finish law school and pick up in business where my father left off. This was what my father would have wanted, strongly favoring Becky, a German Jew whose family belonged to Beth Zion: Edie and Rhoda were daughters of Russian immigrants, working people. My mother would have no part in matchmaking and refused my father's requests to fix me up with this or that daughter of friends. From the start she knew I loved Manny. She accepted this without comment; we never spoke of it directly. After my father died, Manny practically moved in with us, delivering groceries to the house, brewing pots of tea, asking guests to leave when my mother seemed tired. He brought her bouquets of daisies, bakery shortbread, picture books. She reciprocated by regularly setting a place for Manny at dinner, and, later, pointedly leaving the house for hours of errands. "Your friend Manny," she would tell me, "you can trust him."

My father's death did not leave my mother utterly bereft: as always she was a social woman, running committees at the temple, planning Hadassah events, volunteering at the hospital. Within her circle of friends she was well loved. But her own family lived in Manhattan. My older brother, Simon, a brutish, uncharitable man, had married his equal and settled in Miami. And my mother was not close with my father's relatives, well-meaning, narrow-thinking brothers- and sisters-in-law who swarmed around her after my father's heart attack. My departure rattled her into silence. The morning I left, she was red-eyed and heartsick but insisted she had the flu. I wrote to her constantly, sending short notes with amateurish thumbnail sketches of landscapes and English cottages. When the landscapes became grim, I sketched Buffalo from memory.

I received a few love letters in Manny's hand, signed with the name Ruth, no return address. Otherwise, our letters were light, never daring passion. I wrote to him as often as I could, chatty descriptions of incidentals: English weather, Bing Crosby, impressions of men in my company. I did not write of sex or death; I skirted fear. *Garbo is not here. I miss you.* My French was improving. I'd read a bit of Shaw. But after Normandy I read nothing. My letters became sporadic and brief. At first the villages I traveled through were intact, nearly whole, the surrounding farms deceptively peaceful. I thought I might, somehow, skirt the violence. Then one morning as we crossed east through an open pasture, the air thickened with flies, a stench swept toward us, and we came upon the bodies of animals, cows dismembered by artillery. Cow parts littered the pasture—a hind quarter, bits of hide stuck to a fence, the partially scavenged head of a calf. Our company fell silent, a few men leaning against fenceposts to retch. That night, I did not eat. I lighted cigarette after cigarette and waited for the rumbling of distant air raids. I dozed in raw, half-hour bits, waking to the black air and sickly quiet, calmed back to sleep only by the rhythms of other men's breathing.

Of course, the animals were simply a prelude. Ahead lay roads and fields sodden with death. Men like cows, in parts. Shy, skinny Mike Jessup, shot in the abdomen and thigh. A German boy, bleeding from the mouth, running toward me and collapsing. Joey Santora, handsome and lewd, eaten by a grenade. After I'd seen several dead men, I learned a temporary numbness: in the presence of the bodies I'd react only to smaller things—a boot heel's moon of uneven wear, a bloody wristwatch in the grass. I did not speak of these things, although at night, awake, I would watch them rise in the dark. In my letters home there were no unburied bodies, burned cities, rumors of camps. No stink, no despair, no terror. No tremors, no dizzy spells. Of Germany I wrote about a single courtyard of apple trees, verdant in a pocked and cratered neighborhood. *I prefer the orchards of Lockport,* I wrote. *Look in on my mother, would you? Regards to your family.* In short, I did not mention the war. Nor did I allude to the encounters that kept me sane, the back rooms of certain pubs or a private named O'Neill who made love to me ten miles from the front, rescuing me at the brink of nervous collapse.

I miss you, I repeated. *I miss you.* I held my breath and watched the Arthur I was—a boy on a lark—dissolve. In spite of my secrecy with Manny, I'd never felt real paranoia: in Europe all surety unraveled. Long before the German surrender, I was an insomniac. Afterward, I fell asleep imagining I too would wake in separate pieces, a leg in a bright green field, an arm among the ruins of a music hall. The early mornings were rank with nausea; I often woke crying and sick. More than once, O'Neill was beside me, patting me on the back. "At least I slept," I'd tell him.

"Me too," he'd say. Then he'd light cigarettes for both of us and comment on the weather.

I smoked until my hands did not tremble, lighting a second cigarette after the first.

Not long before the end of my tour, I transferred to the DP camp in Landsberg. I knew some Yiddish—Manny had taught me—and translators were scarce. Most of the Landsberg DPs had survived Dachau; when I got there, the camp had 6,000 DPs, 5,000 of them Jews desperate for news of family and for transport to Palestine. The camp seemed an island of filth: no working sanitation, no fuel for heat. Everyone had scabies. I feared my mind would give way altogether, yet the DPs were resilient, already schooling their children. For days at a time, I'd hear tales of atrocity and manage a veneer of calm. Then, as a young father described the Polish farmhouse where he'd left his infant son, or a woman recounted the night she'd last seen her mother, the day would break apart in front of me, a kaleidoscope of sky and barracks and grim, exhausted faces. Spoken language fragmented into noise. I'd pause, hold up my hands, leave the man or woman midsentence, pace beyond the barracks, smoke a cigarette. Time would pass. Then the pieces of the afternoon would reassemble themselves, I would apologize in two or three languages, and ask the man, the woman to please continue the story.

A few weeks before my discharge, I met Anna. Her brown cotton dress fell almost to her feet, exaggerating her already frightening scrawniness. She was half-Polish and half-French, the daughter of a philosophy professor, and she'd been at university at the start of the war. I spoke to her in French. She wanted to find her cousin, she told me, a Parisian named Justine. Everyone else was dead.

A routine interview, but later, alone, I pictured Anna's face. She had an odd, plantlike delicacy: a small frame, an elegant neck, an oval face, eyes large and dark, fringed by even darker lashes. Her manner was reserved, her gaze disarmingly frank.

Daily, I looked for her. I gave her my cigarettes to smoke or barter: she accepted them with a measured nod and slipped them in the pocket of her dress. I gave her the chocolate I'd saved. I gave her books Manny sent to me, novels and poems in English, a language she spoke with some effort. Sometimes we strolled through the camp together. Sometimes we sat together and read.

At night I felt an urgency to record what I'd heard and seen, but I'd stopped keeping a diary, and when I began my letters to Manny, I wrote:

Dear Manny,
It's all true about the camps. I am using the Yiddish you taught me.

Dear Manny,
A rainstorm today. Thanks for helping Mother pack up the house.

Dear Manny,
The sky is so clear I've found eight constellations.
The Jews here have set up a school.
Mother adores Manhattan.

Dear Manny,
I can taste the end. Meet me in New York?

My mother had left Buffalo for good and had taken a large apartment on the Upper East Side. Plenty of room to spare, she wrote. I knew then that I would settle in New York; Buffalo's provincialism could only cause me harm. Somehow I'd convince Manny to move.

As I readied to return to the States, I met Anna as often as I could. Some of the DPs assumed I was courting her. My commander spoke of proper conduct; perhaps he recognized my impulsive nature, assumed that I would take sexual advantage. But in fact my impulsiveness peaked as Anna and I were reading Shakespeare's sonnets—Anna one line, I the next—outside the brick barracks. Around us the air bubbled with Yiddish and Polish, Czech, Hungarian, bits of Russian, broken English. *"That time of year thou mayst*—mayst?—*in me behold,"* she read.

"Mayst—it's old, c'est un mot vieux, it means may, can, pouvoir. *When yellow leaves, or none, or few do hang . . ."*

"Upon those . . . boughs . . . What is this, boughs?"

I held my arms out. "Like a tree. The branch, the arm. Le bras d'un arbre."

"Un arbre," she whispered.

Upon those boughs which shake against the cold . . .

She scanned the lines silently, intent, her lips shaping the words, and then she read words aloud—quick glances at me to confirm pronunciation, a hint of a smile.

I wanted to touch her face, press my face against her hair. I read my lines with decreasing comprehension. After two sonnets I said, "I want to tell you something."

She marked the page with her thumb.

"I fall in love with men. You understand?"

She shrugged. "I had a cousin like that. A boy, a man, who desired men."

"Did that trouble you?"

"It troubled my parents."

"And you?"

"He was my favorite cousin. Polish. From Warsaw." Anna touched my hand, a gesture both soothing and electric. "He would have liked you very much."

Clouds passed beneath other clouds. Two men argued in Yiddish about kitchen sanitation. In the distance, several women—bobbing brown and gray figures—sorted through a shipment of clothes. I told her I'd be leaving for New York. It was then that the barracks around us took on a pointillist quality, the light seeming to fall in separate particles. I breathed into the bottom of my lungs and asked whether she thought we should marry.

"What?"

"We would stay in New York," I said. "That's where my mother lives now. New York."

"There is no man?"

"Yes. There is a man. Manny."

"A man named Manny." She laughed and covered her mouth with her hand.

"His nickname. His pet name."

"You love him."

"Yes."

"But you ask me to marry you."

"Yes."

She fingered the binding of the book, tilted her head, scraped a shoe in the dirt. "You will make the arrangements?" she said.

I held her then. I lifted her against me, and we swayed in the open air amidst the swarm of DPs and army personnel, the odors of cooking and sweat and sewage, the light filtered through layers of clouds, indirect, as if all light were interior.

When I walked into the New York apartment with Anna, my mother kissed us and cried. Anna blushed and sat primly on an overstuffed chair, overwhelmed by the thick carpets, the divans and sofas, the bookshelves and armoires, the rocker and loungers, the rose-print drapery, the crystal and china, the flowers in heavy glass vases, pink dishes of chocolate almonds. The place reminded her of her grandmother's, she said. We wandered from room to room. We drank glasses of cider and bathed and watched Central Park through the living room windows. My mother roasted a chicken, baked a lemon cake, opened a bottle of wine. Anna fell asleep early, on the sofa, while my mother and I reviewed family news. I carried Anna to the second bedroom and tucked her under a quilt.

When I returned to the living room, my mother pressed her palms against my face. We sat together on the sofa near the front window, watching snow drift over New York, listening to a radio broadcast of Vivaldi, to cabs and late-night bustle, until she dozed off against my shoulder.

It was there, in my mother's lush apartment, that Anna and I collapsed. I spent weeks in bed, rising for meals and occasional cigarettes; I seemed adrift, undersea, the water above me impossibly heavy. The smallest tasks took hours, and I seemed to live in my robe.

Anna rose early and immediately dressed; in daylight she was strong. Not so at night. At 2 A.M. Anna moaned and wept. I lifted my head. I lifted my body, slid over to her. She flinched when I touched her, but she was already shaking. I whispered, *Anna, it's Arthur.* She turned and clung onto me, her nightgown sliding up from her calves, her legs clamping around me, her face buried in my chest. As usual, I pretended I could take care of her.

In a few minutes my mother knocked on the door. "May I?"
"Yes, yes, come in."

She stroked Anna's hair until Anna gazed up, tear streaked and disoriented.

"Here we are," my mother said, her voice heavy silk. "Anna, would you like a bit of cocoa?"

The tears welled. My mother sat patiently at the edge of the bed. Eventually, Anna stopped trembling.

"Oh, there, it's fine now. Bon," my mother said. "Maintenant, nous buvons du chocolat. Is that right?"

She held Anna's hand, and I felt Anna's legs unhinge from mine. Together they stood. Together they shuffled toward the bedroom door. When they'd become silhouettes in the doorway, Anna leaning against my mother, my mother called over her shoulder, "Arthur, darling, get some sleep."

From the living room I heard strains of classical music. "When I was a girl," I heard my mother say. "Quand j'etais une petite fille."

I did not wake until noon. In front of the bureau Anna brushed her short waves, fussed with a barrette. I sat up. "How are you?" I said.

"Fine." Her voice was solid and calm. "This morning I walked outdoors." Then, more confidentially, she said, "And last night? How did I sleep?"

"My mother gave you hot chocolate."

"I thought so. But this morning I was in the bed again. I thought this chocolate was my dream. Your mother, an angel of God."

I pretended that, once he'd met Anna, Manny would immediately comprehend my marriage. Like my mother, he'd accept it as a gesture of kinship rather than an act of passion. I would take an apartment nearby, and he and I would do what we could to rekindle our relationship. But Manny did not come to New York right away. He was by nature a recluse and had escaped neither the closet nor his tangled, suffocating family. His sister Edie clung to him, and I knew he found New York daunting. He admitted none of this: he wrote that he couldn't leave his bookstore and offered to pay my way to Buffalo.

I couldn't bring myself to telephone and answered by letter. *It will take me some time to readjust. To be honest, I am quite exhausted. No need for worry, of course: mother is taking good care of me, and I couldn't be happier to be in New York. But I do need to rest. I'll be there as soon as I'm myself again.*

I wrote and rewrote subsequent letters until they were so hermetic, so relentlessly cheerful he would neither question my state of mind nor believe stray rumors of my marriage. *You sound better,* he wrote back. *Can you get some time away? Please.* But even after several weeks, travel to Buffalo seemed beyond me: my arms were too heavy to pack a suitcase, my legs incapable of climbing onto trains. And he was a grown man; he claimed to love me. I ignored his request and reiterated my own. *Let your family watch the bookstore. Come to New York.* Our letters grew increasingly terse.

Once I was steady enough to leave the apartment, I sought out men. Fidelity to anyone seemed impossible in the face of such wild loneliness. I crossed town to drink in Greenwich Village, at the Salle de Champagne. I attended the opera alone and scanned the audience for men in frippery and mascara. Times Square left me more depressed than anything else, and I went there only on my loneliest, most despairing days. Eventually, the bar at the Astor Hotel—quieter, more discreet—became my regular haunt.

But after these encounters I would still long for Manny. Whether he was real to me then or simply an idea I didn't know. There was a yearning. I called it Manny.

After several months, Anna and I blinked and opened our eyes. Anna's cousin Justine, we learned, was in Palestine. That night, we went for a late supper at the Savoy, drank dry champagne, heard Clemente's marimba band. Suddenly, we were on holiday: for a season we acted like a young New York couple. I took a job in my Uncle Len's import/export firm, and on my days off Anna and I walked Fifth Avenue, spending extravagantly in Bonwit's and Saks. At the Museum of Modern Art we saw Picassos; at the

Metropolitan we heard "La Traviata." I bought tickets for Broadway. We gorged on New York, then hid ourselves away in my mother's huge apartment.

Each morning, light entered the bedroom in pale shafts. Anna's body had filled out: she was curved and sleek. I slept holding her, spooned around her. Asleep, she seemed like water, a sigh floating against me. For hours I gazed at her hair against the pillow, short thick waves the color of walnuts. If I concentrated hard enough, everything else would disappear. But for all our intimacy, Anna and I had never made love. It wasn't a matter of ignorance or simple inhibition: I had slept with women before. I pretended I admired Anna the way I would admire a sister, glad for her that she was attractive. Of course, I knew better. There was between us a precarious balance of caution and desire.

One afternoon, when we were reading on the sofa, I began absently stroking her ankle. She set her book on the coffee table and confronted me. "I am not innocent," she said.

The next week she became more direct. We'd been out to see *Carousel*, which Anna found ridiculous, and which left her happy nonetheless. We'd had drinks. After midnight we tiptoed through the dark apartment, whispering, gleeful, trying not to wake my mother. We lay on the bed, Anna singing bits of *Carousel* songs, purposely mangling the lyrics to make me laugh. Then she placed my hand on her breast. She kissed my face, ran her hand the length of my chest, rubbed up against my cock.

"Anna—"

She opened her legs, pushed against me, kissed me deeply. I fell into her, undressed her, and we rolled and pressed against each other until I entered her fully—fierce, sweet—a lovemaking both strange and certain. After sex we continued to kiss, slowly, stunned by desire.

She watched me. For days I was tender with her, smitten. We made love again and again, every time Anna initiating the sex. I lost myself in the pleasure. It was almost enough, this life with Anna. Almost. And yet, still the craving for men, the undeniable desire to again taste Manny, to roll against him and feel his mouth close over me. Below the rhythm of Anna, the sounds of the men I met in New York, he remained a solitary beat I could not ignore.

Within a month I panicked. Suddenly, almost recklessly, I disappeared to the Astor for an evening.

The following night, Anna touched me and I stopped her. "This is good," she said.

"Anna. I don't expect to change."

There was a moment of almost crystalline stillness. "I want a child," Anna said.

I closed my eyes and she kissed me, little kisses all over my face. "Give me this child," she said.

"And then? Anna?"

She kissed my eyelids and lips, and pulled me to her.

When spring began to take hold, I was still behaving like a husband. A fine mist fell over New York, twilight air a soft gray. I tried to breathe it in. I tried not to think. One Thursday, on my way home from work, I bought pink tulips; I entered the foyer of my building preoccupied, shaking water droplets off the bouquet, while I nodded to Charles, the potbellied doorman, and walked to the elevator. I almost didn't notice Manny sitting on the high-backed marble bench, head in his hands. I couldn't see his face, but the set of his shoulders and the curve of his neck were unmistakable.

"Manny?"

Charles the doorman observed my approach. Manny lifted his head—eyes slightly red, skin paling in the dim light, lower lip pinched between his teeth. My face flushed. Sweat began to slick over my palms. I wanted to burrow my face against his neck. Awkwardly, I patted him on the back, but his shoulders stiffened when I touched him. "How long have you been here?" I said. "If only I had known. Come upstairs."

Manny shook his head.

"We don't have to stay here. I'll take you out."

He made no move toward the elevator, instead giving me a flat stare. "Come on," I said, as if the apartment would be empty for us.

"I've been upstairs."

"Oh."

"Oh is right." He sighed, leaned against the back of the bench, cocked his head to the left. "I met your wife."

I glanced at Charles, who was standing close enough to eavesdrop. I lowered my voice. "Listen, I have a lot to explain. Let's go out. *Please.*"

"I took the train, Arthur. All day on the train."

"Come with me." I spun around to Charles, handed him the tulips, and pulled a five-dollar tip from my wallet. "Deliver these to my mother."

"Let's go," I told Manny. "Now."

The bartender at the Astor nodded when we walked in. A sandy-haired man I'd once gone home with smiled, his gaze lingering as we crossed the room. I ordered two scotches and lighted a cigarette.

"Manny," I said. "I had to get her out of Germany."

"I guess that makes you a hero," he said.

"Of course you're angry."

He pressed his lips together and stared at the ceiling.

"I've missed you," I said.

"You think I'm a fool."

"No. I should have told you right away—I should have cabled you from Europe."

Manny shrugged and sucked his scotch.

"Her family's dead. I thought I could help her. It wasn't love." But my voice wavered ever so slightly, and Manny said nothing.

"Ask my mother," I said.

"I shouldn't have to."

When I told him I loved him, he pushed his drink away. "How would you know?"

He rose to go to the men's room and I followed. He ignored me. I waited until he finished at the urinal, and then I went to him, pressed my chest against his back, kissed him on the neck. He pushed me off with enough force that I stumbled backwards. "Arthur, stop." He glared and ran the tap, bent over the basin, and splashed water on his face.

Small tremors swept through me. My throat hurt. I stepped away, loitered at the men's room door and followed Manny back out into the bar. He continued out to the hotel entrance, speeding up as he moved toward the street. I ran up and grabbed his arm. "Manny, you're exhausted. Let me get us a room. Two rooms."

But he shook me away, flagged a passing cab, hurried into it, and slammed the cab door behind him. I called his name, banged on his door, shouted *please*, and leapt back as the wheels began rolling. Then Manny disappeared, a streak of yellow in the dark.

The apartment: tulips in a crystal vase on the coffee table, and beside them a ribboned package of books, rare first editions— Shaw and Joyce—and a fifth of good scotch.

"A friend of yours was here," Anna said, her face blank. "I asked him to stay, but he left."

Not long after Manny's visit, Anna's pregnancy was confirmed.

My insomnia recurred, and when I slept, my dreams would bury me at the bottom of Lake Erie, weighted by stones from German cathedrals. Boats passed above me. The city of Buffalo was refracted light, visible but elusive, and Manny had vanished. I woke dry-mouthed, puffy-eyed, my heart racing. I called Manny at the bookstore. At first he hung up, but after a few tries he stayed on the line.

"I'm just thinking about you," I said. "How are you?"

"Suspicious."

"I can't say I blame you. But I wish you weren't. I was thinking maybe we should make some plans. Start with a little vacation. I'll be up there soon," I said. "I promise."

First, Anna was morning sick. My mother fed her dry toast and crackers. Once the morning sickness abated, my mother fed her steak dinners. Together they breakfasted. Together they lunched. Shopped. Frequented beauty salons. Together they redecorated the spare room for the baby. My mother cooked up pounds of liver, brought Anna glasses of milk, bowls of fruit and cream. In the evenings they played cards and listened to radio concerts: they seemed happy, and only then did I realize how completely Anna had become my mother's daughter. I trudged off to work. Restless. I chain-smoked and paced and tried not to snap at either one of them.

I called Manny again: the second time, he stayed on the line with me and remained laconic, but said to give my mother his regards. The third time, he made a familiar, heart-stopping sigh. "Arthur," he said, "what a mess."

"We'll get through it," I said. He didn't even know about the baby. I intended to tell him, but that sigh. The drop into intimacy. I'd explain in person, I decided. Soon. And so, as I courted him over the phone, Manny's tone continued to soften.

———————

After Anna's first trimester, I scheduled a week off to go to Buffalo. I neither asked Anna's permission nor warned her in advance: I made the arrangements with Uncle Len, called my cousin Rita, and arrived home from work with my list of travel errands. I found Anna and my mother in the nursery, holding paint samples up against the walls, varieties of yellow.

"Yellow and white," my mother said, "safe colors."

"Good choice," I said. "I'm planning a little trip. A few days, a week."

Anna raised her eyebrows. "For all of us?"

"No. Not this time. Just me."

My mother set down the samples. "A little travel can be a good thing. We'll finish this later."

"A little travel where?" Anna said.

"Buffalo."

Her face closed.

Dinner was unusually silent and strained. Anna stared into her lap. Forks scraped against plates. My mother glanced from me to Anna and back, then poured herself a goblet of wine. I wanted whiskey and cigarettes, wanted to flee to the Astor and flirt with a stranger. Instead, I cleared the table, brewed a pot of tea, set the macaroons out on a plate.

"You save all his letters," Anna said.

"Of course."

"Why 'of course'? It is not 'of course.'" Her voice grew louder, more insistent. "You see me? Your wife. You know? Your *wife*."

"I never lied to you."

Her hands balled into white-knuckled fists. "So that makes it fine. You and your Manny. You and your friends from the Opera."

My throat and eyes stung, and I steadied myself against a chair. "I told you," I said.

"And what is this?" she said, pointing to her belly.

I walked away from the table, summoning a voice not unlike my father's. "I'm going to see Manny. And that's that." I sat on the sofa and lighted a cigarette. I thumbed a magazine.

"Tell me what this is," she shouted.

I couldn't answer and didn't try.

Finally, a sharp, familiar taunt, "Are you a man?"

I looked at her then. It seemed as if my lungs had collapsed, but numbness had instantly set in. "I suppose not," I said.

Then Anna was a blur rushing past, the bedroom door slammed, I heard the stony click of the lock. I leaned over, sick, holding my knees; I closed my eyes and sucked the air.

"Tea, darling?" my mother said, bringing my cup from the table. She kissed me on the crown of my head, stroked my hair. She sat beside me and let me weep. Rocked me against her, shushing me.

After several minutes I calmed. Mother handed me my cup of tea and continued to stroke my forehead. "Why don't you wait until the baby's born?" she said. "Until Anna's got that baby in her arms."

Later, when I walked into the bedroom, Anna's face was blotchy and streaked with tears. She rushed over, imploring, wrapping herself around me.

I stayed. I stopped calling Manny. I stopped meeting men. I never argued. Anna and I remained careful with each other: I honored my obligation and gave her neither cause for complaint nor marital pleasure. Once, late in her pregnancy, I found Anna and my mother standing in the living room, Anna's blouse pushed up to her breasts, my mother's left hand pressed along her belly. They were grinning. When she saw me, Anna's expression dropped into wariness, and she began to tug at the hem of her blouse. But my mother did not move her hand.

"Come here," my mother said, "it's kicking." She held my hand to Anna's belly; through Anna's skin I felt a soft jab into my palm. Only then did the tension ease.

Again, I planned a week off and made hotel reservations at the Statler in Buffalo. Anna knew nothing of this, but two nights before my departure, she woke in terror—the first time in weeks. I rocked her back to sleep and watched her through the night. That week, I stayed in New York, shopping for a bassinet, shopping for a carriage, reading novels with Anna. I was startled to find myself wanting to be near her. Not inside her. Not rolling with her in sex. Next to her. Holding her hand. Hugging her to me. Pressing my ear against her belly, listening. Pressing my lips to her belly, speaking.

On workdays I'd put on my suit, drink my coffee, and linger in the bedroom. But once out of the building, I'd be swept up by the city. Other lives would rise before me, waiting.

Dear Arthur,
Your Aunt Myra's spreading rumors about you. I thought you should know.

Dear Manny,
Myra never liked me. Family matters detaining me — I'll explain when I see you.

The day Anna went into labor, the air smelled of snow. At five A.M. I called a cab: Anna wide-eyed in the back seat, my mother smiling and petting her head. At the hospital I waited and sat with Anna and waited more, as her labor dragged on. Beyond the delivery rooms, other fathers waited and paced; one round-faced Italian man asked Anna's name and announced that we were lucky men.

Natalie emerged purplish white, dark-haired, and startled. Anna and I stared at her, smitten, dopey, touching her tiny fingers, rocking her, amazed at how she slept, amazed at how she woke. The fact of her mouth. The fact of her eyes, milky blue. My mother came in to visit. Uncle Len stopped by with flowers. Then Anna slept. Natalie slept.

I tried calling Manny from the hospital, not knowing what to say. His sister Edie answered the phone; I hung up without speaking. But when Natalie was six weeks old, I bought my ticket to Buffalo. Anna sulked when I left. I knew she might not forgive me. That Manny might not forgive me. I knew I'd have to be steadfast with both of them while they twisted in anger and pushed me away. But I had only the vaguest inkling of the storms that lay ahead—Anna's bitterness, Manny's rage, his frightening depression, my own despair. I did not yet recognize the permanence of leaving my mother's home. But that morning, as my train headed north, I was filled by a strange and certain faith. On the verge of winter, our hearts were expanding. *Natalie.* The rest of us would somehow find our way.

Common Light

I

Marilyn's sister Edie is waxy, the color of mashed bananas, cancer seeping out of her and contaminating plain air. Like carbon monoxide, Marilyn thinks. You can't smell it but you swoon anyway. The perceptible world warps in random jumps and starts, and you have to learn to balance on one foot. To lipread. To remain unalarmed as your myopia transforms a trash bag into a body in the street, a bush into a leaping dog. Still, the postman arrives on time, Bells' Market stocks Jaffa oranges, good cuts of beef, Buffalo elects doltish mayors, and Irv Weinstein reads the news at 6:00, as he has for decades: part of the warp is the semblance of normalcy. Marilyn considers this at night, in her big bathtub, as she appraises her own body, the bulges and loose skin at her belly and hips, the hardness of her calves, the slope and soft tissue of her breasts, the dark mole on her shoulder. Her husband, Sam, walks in, thin and silvery, tilts his head at her, bends down for a kiss. His lips are the same temperature as the water; he slips his tongue into her mouth, slides a hand over her left nipple, and the world seems fluttery, opaque, tinted with larkspur. But only for a moment. There is the matter of Sam's blood pressure pills—whether he remembered, whether she should ask. She breaks from the kiss and strokes the back of his hand. Sam sighs, his face inscrutable. Only after he leaves does she realize she is squinting.

Edie doesn't have a Sam. No bohemian children, no conservative ones. No grandchildren screeching into the phone line. Still, family means shared knowledge, coded into your bones. Cells, genes, ribbons of DNA: how much can you outrun? Count up the separate years, weigh each body's private life; in the end, how Edie is Marilyn?

Imagine you find a lump. Imagine dizzy spells, disorientation, shortness of breath, your veins glassy, small implosions scattering through you like fireworks too close to the ground, your cells forgetting what they are. Interior life gone awry. When do you admit your body is forgetting how to be your body, how long do you wait? Not more than ten seconds, Marilyn thinks, but Edie put off trips to the doctor. Months passed before she revealed her diagnosis to her sisters, and by that time the cancer had leaped organs.

Edie tried to pin it on their brother, who's lived in Manhattan for decades. "He should have stayed here," she said. "This wouldn't have happened."

"Uh huh. So, Manny gave you cancer?"

"Marilyn, don't be simple."

You can't blame cancer on celibacy either, Marilyn thinks, or on eccentricity. But what if you could. Blame it on bad attitudes. Blame it on the souring years, on the small madnesses of the self, suddenly translated to the structure of the body. Blame it on lack of serenity. None of this will happen to Marilyn: if you keep the surface smooth, what's beneath will fall in line. Each week, as she drives Edie to her radiation appointments or waits at the pharmacy for Edie's prescriptions, Marilyn wraps herself in this belief.

Domesticate the thing. Only during brief, rare moments does she still let her own wildnesses loose.

In the bath, Marilyn lays her hand over one nipple, then the other. A National Geographic special hums from the TV in the next room: more sounds of water, a commentator explaining how divers compensate for undersea pressure. It would be better to have Sam back in the bathroom, his hands instead of hers sliding over her breasts, his hands instead of hers slipping down between her legs, finding the tender spots, fingers rolling across her clitoris and easing into her: in that space of time she would wholly let go to him. Touching herself she feels halved, a slice of mind set apart and watching.

The other sisters—Sylvia, Dora—aren't always there when you need them. They kick in for Edie's new television, but after two weeks, when Edie throws the remote at a home health aide, it's Marilyn's answering machine that bleats: *Mrs. Rosen, Joelle Brown calling. Your sister's upset today. I think you should come over.*

By the time Marilyn arrives at Edie's house, Edie's barricaded herself in her bedroom. Joelle has stationed a chair outside the door. The careful order of the living room deteriorates near Edie's shelves of porcelain knickknacks: animal miniatures lie scattered, askew, body parts fallen to the rug below.

Joelle waves at the animals. "I didn't know she could lift her arm that far. She hit the china dogs."

"I can see that," Marilyn says.

"I told her you-all should get her a commode."

"Oh."

Joelle is right, of course; all the aides have been murmuring "commode." Edie's getting harder to handle and should have had one weeks ago. But buying a commode seems another breach of Edie's privacy, yet another raw exposure of her body's secrets. Bad enough that her big body is regularly slung into hospital gowns, part after part lifted onto the x-ray table. Those breasts, enormous and untethered, one now diminished. When the doctors found cancer in Edie's breasts, she barely abided the sequence of humiliating surgeries and lectures by full-breasted nurses about how to wear a prosthesis and what kinds of clothes would suit her new form. No wonder that after the surgery, Edie glared and knocked her hospital Jell-O to the floor. *Whoops.* No wonder she's throwing remotes.

"I'm terribly sorry, Joelle," Marilyn says. "I hope you're still willing to help us out."

"I'm all right." Joelle nudges a china shard with her foot. "Too bad about that poodle."

Edie emerges from the bedroom, haughty, saunters out to the sofa, waving Joelle away and propping herself up with pillows. Her swollen right arm is packed into an ace bandage; her head is wrapped in a scarf, her face puffy and grim.

Joelle raises her eyebrows. "I'll be going now. You've got roast chicken and some casserole for supper."

Edie fixes her gaze on the settee near the window, but the corners of her mouth curl under. It's up to Marilyn to thank Joelle, who nods and disappears.

There is, at least, a sharp gleam to Edie, no painkiller haze. Marilyn picks up the remote from the coffee table and tosses it onto the sofa near Edie's hip. "Funny. I thought you liked her."

"Remember who you're talking to," Edie says. She clicks on the remote and the silence in the living room fills with hospital soap opera voices. No one in the hospital has cancer: these characters have amnesia and car accidents and affairs. One of the doctors, a good-looking blond, is the soul of seduction. You can hear sex in the slimy way he says, *I'll take a look at that chart* and *Let's order a CT scan.* Edie never misses an episode. Today, he's confessing his love for a married woman: as Marilyn crosses into Edie's bedroom and gathers up Edie's wig, cosmetics, and jewelry, she gauges the fake vulnerability in his voice. *Why didn't you tell me,* the woman says. From the bathroom Marilyn collects a facecloth, a towel, hypoallergenic face wash and cream. In the kitchen she fills a white bowl with water, spills nothing as she carries it to Edie.

I was afraid, the doctor says. He checks to see whether the woman believes him. She's a blue-eyed mess of confusion and desire.

"Feel like freshening up?" Marilyn says. She dips the facecloth into the bowl.

For an instant, Edie is a dreamer at the edge of her dream, vulnerable and open: the story has made her compliant. She glances over the tubes and compacts and shapely bottles, the array of clip-on earrings and pastel faux pearls. "Okay."

The truth is, the doctor says, *I've never loved anyone the way I love you.*

Edie holds still as Marilyn smooths the soapy cloth over her face, rinses it, smooths the cloth over her face again, dabs her skin dry. With her fingertips Marilyn rubs face cream into Edie's cheeks and forehead, something she's done for her daughters and grandchildren. A beauty parlor game. There's foundation to apply. Rouge. Lipstick. "Which one Edie? The coral and the red have matching polish."

Edie points at the dark red and tilts her chin forward, letting Marilyn run the lipstick over her mouth.

"Nails too?"

It's what I've always wanted, the woman says. Slow lounge music plays as the camera closes in for the kiss. *But what about James?*

Edie shrugs.

"Let's do them and call Sylvia. Maybe she'll meet us at the Your Host for coffee."

The kiss lingers and the camera pulls back to reveal the doctor's wandering hands. Edie straightens her shoulders, buttons her cardigan sweater. "Why not," she says.

Marilyn massages Edie's hands and slicks red polish over the nails. The red gleam guides her—landing lights, she thinks. And beyond them the flow of TV chatter continues, still distracting Edie from herself: the wig is next, another moment of exposure. Without hesitating, Marilyn unties the silk knot and methodically pulls the scarf away, exposing Edie's bald head.

You have your own happiness to think of, the doctor says.

Edie gums her lips, smudging the lipstick. She looks like a soft cactus, bursting into bloom on one side, remaining prickly over the rest. If Edie were not Edie—if she were Sam or Sylvia or Dora—Marilyn would run her fingers over the stubble, very softly. Instead, she scoops up the wig and tugs it over Edie's scalp.

There's a knock on the door of the doctor's office. *Don't worry about anything*, the doctor tells the woman. In a louder, less intimate voice, he says, *I think we should find you a good specialist*, and opens the door.

Marilyn holds up a mirror. "Which earrings?"

<hr />

Every third weekend Manny flies to Buffalo from New York and stays with Edie. Then Marilyn remembers her life with Sam: she and Sam make love in the late afternoon. She's taken to keeping her eyes closed during sex, even when she's moving above him, until the sensations build to a speeding blur, until she's a body and nothing else. Sam slides his hand along her hips and presses, his signal for her to stop moving. "What is this?" he says. "Why don't you look at me?"

She stares at his puckered navel, his long white arms. Pictures the arms loosening from their sockets and dropping off the side of the bed. "Can't I just feel you?" she says.

They've been making love for thirty years. "I don't think so," he says. "No."

At dinnertime, Manny calls. He nearly shouts that Edie looks wonderful, which means she's wearing her wig and prosthesis, she's smoothed foundation over the radiation burns. "We were thinking about driving to Esmond's for dinner," he says, "but I don't know. I had a long week. If it's all the same to Edie, I'd just as soon relax at her place. Some takeout maybe. Some television."

This year, Manny's face is careworn, his suits hang off him loosely, but otherwise he seems unchanged: a shy, bookish man, a dapper scarecrow, sweet and ineffectual. A mystery knotted up against the mystery of Edie, as in childhood—Edie and Manny off on their own, a tiny, separate family. But now there is New York and Manny's friend, Arthur. Mention Arthur to Edie and she spits.

Marilyn drinks an extra glass of wine after dinner. "I don't want to look at anything," she tells Sam. "I want to be blind."

When Edie's asleep, Manny calls her back. "How is she really?" he says.

Some days upset, disoriented, Marilyn tells him, some days better.

"It's just the chemo," Manny says. "She misses her job."

"I'm sure you're right." Soon enough, Edie will be back in the classroom, herding first graders around. September will be normal, Marilyn says. A totally boring fall.

Pretend, anyway. It helps, doesn't it? Pretend wanting to be blind isn't weird. Pretend Manny's life is not unusual. He shares an apartment with Arthur Blum in Manhattan, and they have shared one apartment or another on and off for thirty years. "The bachelors," Dora calls them, which is true enough, but there is something nasty and unseemly in the way Dora says the word. Sometimes Manny seems less like a bachelor than like an overtired boy; other days he seems ancient, condensed, a Giacometti statue. Marilyn can't quite keep a fix on him, but lately no one's in sharp focus.

II

A Thursday. Marilyn arrives at Edie's an hour after Joelle's shift; the TV trumpets Oprah. Edie is curled under a knitted afghan, the hills of her body surprisingly small. *Drank 16 oz. juice,* Joelle's note reads. *Picked at lunch. Had bath. No trouble.* Marilyn turns down the TV, settles herself in the kitchen with *Recipes for Healthy Living,* and begins a vegetable-and-grain casserole to leave in Edie's freezer. Edie prefers salami sandwiches with chicken fat, which is a problem.

At 5:00 the clock radio in the kitchen goes off: a clip of President Reagan's speech, a woman's voice predicting sleet. Mid-April and *sleet.* Ridiculous.

"Edie? Time for your pills." Marilyn fills a water glass and collects three vials from the counter. "Pills and dinner, Edie. What do you want?" She sets the water glass on the coffee table, touches Edie's shoulder; Edie's still curled under the afghan. "Edie." Nothing. "Time for your pills, Edie."

And then time becomes shimmery, both racing and slow. The blue of the afghan seems immutable, but Edie's skin is the color of cooked turnip, her lips open and chapped, her eyelashes invisibly thin. Marilyn digs through the nightshirt and bandages to find a heartbeat. Edie's stubbornly elsewhere, not dead—still breathing, still keeping a pulse. She shakes Edie once, again: Edie's head bobs against the pillow. Marilyn's own skin is clammy, her gorge rising. She dials 911.

No matter that Edie is still breathing on her own: Marilyn rolls Edie onto her back, tilts Edie's head, seals her mouth around Edie's, and blows in air. She turns her own head to listen for Edie's exhalation, counts, blows again. It's all she knows how to do. Edie exhales light, acrid puffs, and Marilyn wills herself not to gag. When she hears the distant wail of the siren, she checks to make sure Edie's clothes aren't wet from urine, reknots the blue scarf over Edie's scalp, rubs rouge on Edie's cheeks.

In her coma, Edie floats. It's something Marilyn has never witnessed, something unimaginable for a woman as plodding as Edie, but there she is, serene. *Just a body.* The world beyond the hospital drops away. Sylvia arrives. Dora arrives. Manny flies in from New York. Breathable air has a thick, sour scent; the light seems alternately bluer and more ghastly, severing Marilyn from ordinary life. Elements remain: Sylvia, thick waisted in a navy blue dress, thick ankled in orthopedic shoes, white hair pulled into a bun, smelling of Dove soap and cheap mints, murmuring at Edie's bedside; Dora, flapping up and down the corridors like a trapped sparrow, sharp tongued with the nurses, bringing coffee for Marilyn and organizing the watch; Manny, sad-eyed in his tailored suit, patting Edie's face and telling her he loves her. Sam's on the outside with the other husbands—Sylvia's Eli and Dora's Max—who arrive at lunch hour and after work, staying briefly.

He buys Marilyn cafeteria food and tries to convince her to come home. They repeat this scene daily, but her house seems foreign and useless. She sends him ahead and stays as late as the nursing staff will let her, reading books out loud to Edie, leafing through family photo albums, speaking to her as if she might respond.

The fact that Edie can't respond makes conversation with her —Marilyn has to admit—far easier. The thought shames her a little, but no more than her growing attachment to the vigil. She wonders about her own perversity—is this pleasure?—and decides that the vigil offers relief, a comfort in numbers. They are all overlapping, she and her sisters and Manny, merged at the edges, as if an earlier, irretrievable time has been superimposed on this one.

Manny's in the cafeteria, sniffing at his coffee. "She looks pretty good for someone in a coma," he tells Marilyn.

"Really?"

He's sheepish, his big eyes batted down, then opening wide to Marilyn. He always was a beautiful kid.

"What I mean is, thanks for looking after her," he says.

For a few minutes they drink coffee to the sound of the cash register ticking, the cafeteria workers calling back and forth about a bar called Mel's. Not until Marilyn rises to return to Edie's room does she recognize that the boyishness is frailty, his sweetness shot through with the old desperation—flickers of his shambling, paralyzed twenties. Now Manny's shoulders have slipped into a permanent sag, and in this cafeteria he seems relentlessly alone. Dora, two tables over, has not so much as glanced in their direction.

It's a relief when Arthur Blum flies in from New York, braving the talk and rumor from the old neighborhood—talk Manny is often spared out of respect for his sisters. When Arthur walks into Edie's hospital room, Manny is transformed, lighter: his body suddenly relaxes. Arthur in his soft Italian suits and thick gray hair and wire-rimmed glasses, distinguished—yes, relax into that, Marilyn thinks. He stands as close to Manny as men can stand together, as close as an embrace, but they are not embracing, not here. For the others, the effect is the same. Dora rises and leaves the room. Marilyn busies herself with a sheaf of newspapers, relies on her peripheral vision. That day and in the days to follow, Arthur takes his turn at Edie's bedside, reading stories, reading poems, reading, of all things, the Bible. Dora won't come into the room while he's there, but Marilyn sees her listening in the doorway as he reads, sometimes in English, sometimes in Hebrew.

Arthur or no Arthur, Manny frays faster than the rest of them. True, he holds Edie's hand and gives her pep talks. He brushes his fingers over the fine short bristles of hair on the crown of her head. He dabs her lily-of-the-valley perfume on her wrists and behind her ears, as if the scent will enter her dreams, covering the urine smell of the room. But when Sylvia or Dora relieve him from his watch, he's back in the cafeteria again, elbows on the table, palms cupped over his eyes. "It's these headaches," he tells Marilyn. "It's just my head," he says to Arthur.

III

The call comes when Marilyn *is* home, drying off from her shower. It's afternoon, the tenth day of Edie's coma. "She's back," Manny says. "She's right here." He'd been reading the *Buffalo News* out loud to Edie, he says, hockey stories, and Dora was there. The noise that rose from Edie was louder than the other noises they'd heard—a sputter. Then Edie's eyes were open and she asked for her wig.

Marilyn drives to the hospital swimming in gratitude: ordinary highway traffic, ordinary cumulus clouds, common light. She strolls through the hospital corridors like a lover approaching a tryst. But at Edie's door she hesitates. Edie's propped up in bed, flinching while Dora applies lipstick to her mouth. "Don't get it on my chin," Edie says. "Marilyn's the only one who does it right."

"It isn't on your chin. But it will be if you talk while I'm putting it on."

Marilyn clears her throat and approaches Edie's bed. "I'm relieved to see you awake," she says. "I've been worried."

Dora holds the lipstick out to Marilyn.

"I suppose so," Edie says. "I suppose that's how you'd be."

You can't really quantify luck, but Marilyn tries anyway. Edie's return: lucky, sure, but how lucky? From one to ten: plus eight. Yet she's unchanged, her ornery self, made worse by fear and illness and lime Jell-O: minus four. Better when Manny is around: plus two. Marilyn adds up the numbers while she settles Edie into her pink satin bedjacket and faux pearls, finds a straw for Edie's cup of apple juice, while Edie mumbles about inconsiderate health aides and TV static. Plus one. Minus two. Edie's midsentence when Arthur glides through the doorway with a vase of yellow roses; Edie stiffens, her gaze richocheting around the room.

Minus six, maybe minus nine.

"Hello, Edie," Arthur says. "How good you look."

"What are you doing here?" Edie's voice is already clipped and shrill.

"I brought you some flowers."

Edie pulls away from Marilyn and eyes the roses: spectacular long-stems, the sort husbands send their wives for anniversaries. "You've got a lot of nerve."

Arthur licks his lips. "Would you rather I come back?"

"Rather not."

"I see. Did I do something?"

Edie grunts. "You would ask a question like that."

"I don't mean to upset you," he says.

"What a crock," Edie says. "Just look at yourself. Look at Manny."

Minus eighty, Marilyn thinks, minus one hundred. She steps forward, blocking Edie's view of Arthur. "*Edie.* Arthur's here to wish you a speedy recovery. Arthur, I'm sorry. Edie's not really herself right now."

"I think maybe she is." He leans around Marilyn and sets the flowers on the table next to Edie's bed. "We'll talk about that some other time, Edie."

"No we won't," she says.

"Have it your way then."

"Take those flowers out of here."

"I'll be back later."

"I said take the flowers away," Edie shouts, but Arthur is already out the door. With her left arm she flails in the direction of the table, knocking the roses to the floor, water spilling out in a long puddle, the vase rolling under the bed. She mutters the word *faggot*. Marilyn, already kneeling by the roses, pretends not to hear. From the hallway comes Dora's voice, "What did you do to her?"

And Arthur's voice, dry as sand, "She doesn't care for roses."

"She's obviously not in her right mind yet," Sylvia says.

"You never know with Edie," Eli says.

And then, as Marilyn lifts the roses up from the floor, Manny races in, pale and shaken. He sags at the foot of her bed. "You're here," Edie says, her voice tinged with shame.

"I'll just get a towel on this water," Marilyn says, and for a moment there is only the swish of the towel against the floor tile, the soft click of Marilyn's shoes over to the bathroom sink, water dripping against the ceramic basin. When Marilyn emerges from the bathroom, Manny's standing close beside Edie, patting her hand.

Later, from across the cafeteria, Marilyn watches Manny and Arthur taking quick swigs from a whiskey flask, Arthur pocketing the flask in his coat. Then Arthur talks with his hands; Manny cocks his head to one side, shakes it, edges closer to Arthur, and replies. Marilyn can't make out any of it. She orders three cups of coffee, loads up the tray with cinnamon rolls, creamers, packets of sugar, and walks the tray over to their table. Manny's face reddens, but as she approaches, she only hears him say, "You sure upset her." Arthur, as he leans against the back of his chair, replies, "When haven't I."

IV

When Edie leaves the hospital, Manny installs himself in her house, refusing to return to New York with Arthur. He cooks Edie's increasingly small meals. He checks her at midnight. He checks her at three A.M. He keeps track of her medication, confers with her doctors, takes her for drives on the milder days, rents a wheelchair and pushes her along through Delaware Park. He walks Edie to the bathroom, and when the aides are absent, he guides her to the toilet, looks away as he pulls her nightgown up, slips her underwear down, helps her clean herself. In the early evenings he calls Marilyn and tells her how much Edie has eaten and how lively or tired she seems that day. Hope flutters in and out of his voice, as if Edie's awakening will be followed by other dramatic miracles.

"How's Arthur?" Marilyn says.

"Fine."

"Are you seeing him soon?"

"What?"

"Are you seeing him soon?"

Manny pauses, begins again. "Did you meet that new aide—Margaret?"

As if he's sworn off Arthur. As if doing so might absolve him in Edie's eyes. Might rescue Edie, who is beyond rescue.

In bed, when Sam is on top, Marilyn keeps her eyelids half-open, so he is blurry, impressionistic. Orgasms elude her. During ordinary conversations, he often sighs.

In only three weeks, Edie dies—a Tuesday morning, dogwoods still in bloom. Maybe in death she'll revert to floating, Marilyn thinks, but Edie is simply a body in a casket, thinned by illness, powdered and rouged, the skin of her hands translucent. Already she's crossing into another medium. Leaving what to take root in the rest of them? Rawness, panic, paralysis. Cancer? Weeping, of course, weeping and the desire to nap for days. Relief, guilt at the relief. Manny sits in the front row of chairs, head in his hands, and stays there as the funeral director closes the casket and covers it with gladiolas.

After the rest of the family arrives, Rabbi Goldberg prays and speaks of Edie's life as a teacher. He uses the word *everlasting,* and he wears the knowledge of suffering like a second skin. Marilyn's alert enough to notice Manny stumbling through the funeral service, his confusion more apparent than his grief. He ignores Arthur, who's just flown in. Later, at the house, he repeatedly walks into Edie's bedroom, stands there, and walks out again.

"It's like he's surprised that she's dead," Dora says, pocketing a Kleenex. "What else would she be?"

As the house fills with visitors and mourners, Manny slips into the extra bedroom and turns on the portable black-and-white TV, closing the door to everyone.

V

Marilyn sits at Edie's kitchen table, now Manny's kitchen table, repeating herself.

"Why don't you try some of that sandwich? That's good salami. Do you want me to heat up that soup?"

Manny looks at her dolefully and takes a small bite.

"What are we going to do here, Manny? You going to seal yourself up in this house forever?"

It's as if he's found a way into Edie's coffin. For a month he's been living in the house Edie left him, refusing to put it on the market, refusing to fly to New York, where Arthur is waiting, calling and waiting. Doesn't he see? He lets Marilyn clean out one of Edie's closets: old shoes, some of her dresses. One bureau of garments. But the rest stays in place: the porcelain menagerie, the pictures of dogs and kittens, everything down to notes in Edie's hand. Somewhere there are diaries, letters, more clues to Edie. Locked away from everyone but Manny.

His clothes and books lie scattered in the second bedroom, but sometimes when Marilyn comes over, she finds him in Edie's room, on Edie's big bed. Staring at the ceiling, the shades drawn, the room shadowy.

"Come out of there, Manny," she says. "I have cleaning to do."

"Headache," he says, "I've got a headache."

"Here. Two aspirin. Have you been outside today?"

"Outside?"

Get up, Manny. We're going for a walk.

Get up. We're going to Sylvia's.

Get up. I'm taking you to Dr. Jordan's office.

But when Marilyn gazes at that big bed, she herself longs to lie on it, to feel the ruts and crevices Edie's heavy body made, to briefly imagine her own way into Edie.

Manny. Get up. Time to shave and shower.

Sometimes he does. She drives him to her house for dinner, or the Your Host for coffee and bow-tie danish; he reads the newspaper comics and the horse-racing results. She takes him to the psychiatrist Dr. Jordan, who covers pages with Manny's history of "bad spells," his visits to New York doctors, his rest vacations at the shore, and then prescribes expensive pills.

Every few days, Arthur calls her from Manhattan. "No change," she says. "The usual," but the word *usual* has become infected. One weekend, then another, Arthur arrives in Buffalo, and Manny bathes, shaves, goes to movies. He lets Arthur rearrange furniture, pack up the fake cats and dogs. He eats the pasta Arthur cooks. But when Arthur leaves, Manny slumps back into Edie's bed. After four weekends Manny won't even get up for Arthur, pills or no pills. *Inpatient treatment,* Dr. Jordan says. *Think about it.*

Marilyn can only picture the sadistic nurse from *One Flew Over the Cuckoo's Nest.* Wait, she tells him. Can't we wait?

"You can't keep this up," Dora says. "Look at you. You're exhausted."

"What am I supposed to do?"

Dora clears her throat. "When was the last time you had a few days away with Sam?"

Marilyn lies. "The last time Arthur was here."

"Oh yes. I forgot. Arthur. How long do you suppose that will last?"

"It's been years, Dora."

"Don't be a fool. Manny will take everything you've got. If Sylvia had the nerve, she'd say the same thing."

"If you aren't going to help, just keep out of it."

"Did I say I wouldn't help?"

VI

Summer: suddenly the mugginess swells, even in Buffalo.

Marilyn and Sam take a long weekend in New England. Mostly she sleeps on the porch of a Vermont guest house. Mostly he plays golf. They are both, it seems, too tired for sex; for now, Marilyn tells herself, it's enough to sleep in the same bed.

When they return to Buffalo, Manny is missing. Manny's house: one silent room after another, sour walls, the rumpled chenille on Edie's bed, the near-empty medicine cabinet, the dirty forks in the sink. The dim basement. The back garden wild, untrammeled. She calls Sylvia, Eli, Arthur. They haven't spoken with Manny for days. Dead on the street, she thinks. Hanged in a park. Overdosed in a motel.

"Mental Health Center," Dora says. "I arranged it with his doctor." The minute Marilyn left town, apparently. Dora packed his clothes, drove him downtown, checked him in. "That's some attitude he's got," Dora says. "But no wonder." Together Dora and Manny signed papers, insurance forms, permission for drug therapy, psychotherapy, electroshock. Consent in Manny's raggedy scrawl.

Marilyn pictures Manny, forlorn, screws in his temples, rigged up to a Frankenstein machine, his skin the color of stuffed olives. He lifts one hand and drops it, he opens his mouth to speak, all in slow motion. Next he is on a gurney, speechless and drooling, his eyes smoked out.

She finds Sam in his study. "Did you know about this?" she says. "You knew, didn't you?"

"No."

"Don't lie to me, Sam."

"I didn't," he says. "Leave me alone."

When Marilyn walks into the Center's common room, Manny is sitting in a vinyl armchair. His clothes are wrinkled but clean; he needs a shave. Everything is too big: his shirt, his trousers, the chair. Cheers drift over from a TV basketball game, which no one is watching. Stray yells echo in the far corridor. A few men play cards. They sit several feet away from Manny: he's alone, kneading his fingers. He glances up as Marilyn approaches him, runs a hand over his face.

She kisses him on the cheek. "How are you?"

"You know it's these headaches I've had," he says. He holds his head and stares into his lap.

"I've been worried about you."

"I'm all right," he says. "I'll be all right."

"Do you want to see Arthur?"

"I'm kind of tired now," he says. He seems to be talking to the floor tiles.

Marilyn pours Arthur a scotch and slides it across her kitchen table; he runs his finger over the rim of the glass, glares at Dora. "You could have waited," he says, "should have."

Dora frowns. "For what?"

He takes a long sip, sliding his gaze away from her, to the windows. "Nothing was different from the day before," he says. "I've got that right?"

"Right." Dora says. She crosses her arms and leans back, smug.

"And you didn't call Marilyn."

"Marilyn—excuse me, Marilyn—would baby him into her grave. She never knows when to say no."

"I noticed you didn't call me either."

"Why should I?" Dora says.

Arthur taps his finger on the table, waits.

"You think you're his husband," Dora says. "I can't stop your delusions."

"Shut up, Dora," Marilyn says.

And Dora turns to her, curious, shakes her head. "You're blinder than Edie."

"And you're as spiteful. You had no right," Marilyn says.

"But I did." She gives Arthur a cool once-over. "He's the one who doesn't."

"Oh please," Marilyn says.

"You a rescue dog, Marilyn?" Dora says. "Better wise up."

"And you better leave," Marilyn says.

Dora rises, glances at Arthur, her eyebrows arched, lips tight. "I can see I did the right thing."

Marilyn waves at the front hall. "Go on."

The front door slams; beyond it the screen door slams. Arthur pushes his scotch over to Marilyn, lights a cigarette.

VII

Saturday afternoon. Arthur's in Marilyn's laundry room, pouring fabric softener over Manny's clothes.

"I picked him up a few summer things." Arthur holds up a white cotton polo shirt. "What do you think?"

Marilyn fingers the neckline. "Nice," she says. "He won't have to iron."

He opens packages of boxer shorts, drops the shorts into the machine, pushes the start button. "I wanted to bring in some plants," he says. "Little geraniums. The nurse said no." He shrugs. "Can I buy you lunch? You and Sam?"

"Sam's playing golf," she says. She pictures him as a tiny tan-and-white figure on a field of green. "Let's go."

Arthur is smiling. *Tandem,* she thinks. It's as if the two of them are off on a bicycle, pedaling up some hill, steep, steeper. The rest of the landscape drops away. They shuttle back and forth to the Mental Health Center, confer with the doctors, search out the boundaries and gaps in Manny's memory: he remembers Edie's bed, forgets their trips to the park, loses whole years with Arthur. Arthur brushes it off. "We have plenty of time ahead of us," he tells Manny.

Today they bring Manny cheeseburgers and fries, take turns sitting with him in the common room, reading magazines. Arthur is animated and unflappable; he coaxes Manny into drinking a chocolate shake. But Manny only answers yes or no to Marilyn's questions. She excuses herself to walk outside: new layers of clouds have drifted in from the west, lowering the gray-white ceiling. It might stay this way for days, no clearing, no rain. The noise of the street seems distant, as if she's pushed the mute button on a TV remote. Often by midafternoon her torso seems like someone else's, her throat and hands nearly ceramic. When she returns to the common room, she stations herself near the door, a far-off observer. Arthur's gestures are still dramatic and his smile looks genuine; this might mean progress. She can hear the undulations of his voice, waits for the punctuation of Manny's answers, misses them. When Arthur rises to leave, Manny stares at his feet and says nothing.

Marilyn drives Arthur back to his hotel, and he invites her into the bar. "We need a big drink," he says. She orders a gin and tonic, takes a long sip, and feels her muscles loosen. She slides one of his cigarettes out of the package, toys with it, lets him light it for her. In the dim, air-conditioned bar, Arthur is beautiful. But he was beautiful in the laundry room as well. Soon he is talking about his mother, how elegant she was up until the end, how strong. He doesn't mention his own devotion, but Marilyn hears it in his voice, a light hum. "She was quite a woman," he says. "Very fond of Manny." He touches Marilyn's hand, orders her another drink, asks if she's hungry. The bar and the steadiness of his voice are a refuge, and she feels her skin warming; is this what it's like to be loved by Arthur? What Manny has felt and has forgotten. Maybe, to Arthur, she's sitting in Manny's place. And for her? She can't decide whose seat Arthur occupies.

After a week of daily trips to the Center, daily lunches or drinks with Marilyn, Arthur fails to show up for visitors' hours. Manny sinks into his chair and pats Marilyn's hand when she kisses him. He doesn't ask about Arthur, and she searches his face for awareness of the absence—a wrinkling of the brow, stray glances at the door. Nothing. He's wearing the white polo shirt, but what does that mean? Maybe Dora was right to bring him here. Venomous, but right. Marilyn reads the newspaper aloud to him while Manny kneads his hands. After an hour he says he wants to sleep.

Later, she calls Arthur's hotel room and gets no answer, checks her answering machine, questions the nurses at the Center. She stops at a Friendly's for iced coffee, holds the glass against her cheek. She leafs through the paper she's already read to Manny and finally tries the hotel again. The clerk confirms that Arthur is still a guest.

Hushed blue corridor, rows of closed doors, distant elevator bell: you could hide out here for a long time. At room 508, Marilyn knocks. "Arthur? It's Marilyn." Knocks again. "I think you're there. Are you all right?"

The door swings open on a disheveled Arthur: barefoot, his shirt hanging loose, his eyes red, his skin very white. He is holding a cigarette, weeping, crumbling in front of her. The air in the room is sharp and sweet with liquor fumes. He presses his lips together hard and waves her into the room.

"What's happening here, Arthur?"

He closes his eyes. "I'm running low on cigarettes."

"Uh huh."

He leans back onto the bed, sprawls, the cigarette smoke rising above him. "It's just sickening," he says. "It makes me sick."

She perches at the edge of the bed. "What can I get you? What can I do?"

Her offer breaks him: he rolls onto his stomach, hides his face in the bedspread, his shoulders rising and falling in wild heaves. She should lift him up, she thinks, find a way to make him stop. Hold his hand, at least, but now even that seems like too much: her own throat is constricting, her rib cage feels scraped and raw. She ought to slip into another room alone, close the curtains and hide. For a moment she lets herself fall against the far side of the bed, lies there listening to Arthur's clogged breathing. Counts along. Finally, she lifts her hand and pats him on the back—tentatively at first—and his heaves seem to soften. She pushes herself up, sits beside him, rubs his shoulders as if he is her husband, smooths the hair on the back of his head, strokes his right hand.

"Come on Arthur. Sit up." Says it again, until his breathing slows and he rolls onto his side, props himself up on an arm. "That's it."

"I don't know what to do," he says.

"No," she says. Whiskey fumes waft up from Arthur's mouth

and skin, the world beyond the room pitches and leans, too jagged to touch. But there is the room itself, the steadiness of furniture, and after a few minutes, Marilyn tugs at Arthur's hand. "Come on." She helps him to his feet and steers him into the bathroom, turns on the shower and holds her hand in the spray until it's hot. She unbuttons the linen shirt, pulls it away from his chest, patchy with silver hair. He rubs his eyes with his hands, and she doesn't know whether it's for tears or embarrassment, but he doesn't protest, doesn't flinch. She unbuckles his belt, slides his trousers to his ankles, slides his boxers off, trying not to look, looking anyway, noticing the soft skin of his thighs, his penis, the lip of circumcision. "Okay, now," and Arthur is sobbing again. She makes hushing sounds, opens the shower curtain, holds his arm, and guides him into the tub. He's wobbly on his feet, and she can't hold him there. "Sit down Arthur." He listens. She slides him under the shower spray and soaps his skin. For a moment he buries his head in her arm, then closes his eyes and leans back, lets her fill the tub, drinks from the water glass she brings him. She sits on the floor tile next to him, holding his hand, until the water cools.

Her life seems reduced to this moment: her dress damp, the floor cold, Arthur naked and bereft. She towels him dry as if he were one of her children, leads him to the bed, chooses a pair of khaki trousers, a sport shirt, a jacket. Boxers, socks. "You can do this part," she says. She empties the ashtray, rinses the whiskey glass, adjusts the fan while he dresses.

In his clothes, Arthur can almost pass for calm—the fabric shoring him up. He touches her arm and starts to apologize, but she shakes her head. "Let's try the coffee shop," she says. "Get something to eat."

They take a table near the window. Conversation begins as a slow wash of phrases they've used before: opera season, Broadway, Bloomingdale's. Borders of the life Arthur will return to. Arthur asks about her grandchildren, whether she thinks she might travel. They don't mention Manny, Dora, or Edie, and they don't talk about her marriage. Marilyn doesn't say aloud that the past is a shaky foundation. That love is evanescent, that light itself unravels. She believes such things. But here at the center of heartbreak, there is the surprise of Arthur, holding her hand in a

coffee shop. The tables and chairs keep them in place. The waitress brings platters of omelettes, refills their cups, and the world
revolves around their fingers. There is the heat of the coffee to
think of. The texture of bread in their mouths. Passing clouds
shot through with indigo. The ordinary chatter of the women at
the next table. The commonplace greetings of the men.

II. Northeast Corridor

Sharks

When Matt's stepmother calls, he imagines his head ballooning with water, the skin around his face and skull thinning until he's translucent and freakish. It takes hours to recover: in the meantime he's irritable and distracted, he smokes too much, his girlfriend, Alice, finds reasons to go to the movies without him. His father checks in quarterly, but Louise calls twice a week, sometimes more. She calls when his father is off at work, before Matt leaves for his bookstore job. She calls in the evenings when his father ignores her. "Matty," she says, "you're the only one who understands women."

Sometimes Matt screens her calls and locks himself in the bathroom or convinces Alice to pick up. When Alice is in a good mood, she'll wink at Matt and improvise excuses: *He's playing Parcheesi today. He's out pricing Harleys.* Lately, though, Alice can't be persuaded to do much.

Tonight Alice is at her graduate seminar on the psychology of women and girls, and Matt answers the phone, hoping for her raspy hello. But it's Louise, starting right in about Christmas, which Matt always spends with his mother. The edges of Louise's consonants have already begun to blur.

"I don't see why we can't trade this year. Why can't we have Christmas Eve?" Louise says. "The 23rd isn't the same."

"Can't do anything about it," Matt says.

"Your mother could be more flexible."

Not really. Most years, his mother books solo travel plans for Christmas—bird watching in the Galapagos, hiking through Mayan ruins—but when Matt says he wants to see her, she drops the plans and becomes almost maternal. He isn't going to pass that up. "It isn't just Mom," he says.

"Why don't I call her?" Louise says.

Matt shakes his head at the empty kitchen. "If you want. But don't expect much."

"You're probably right," Louise says. "She's got that stubborn streak."

"Louise. She's my mother."

"Of course she is. A fabulous mother. Look how beautifully you turned out."

Matt chain-smokes, opens a beer, pours black beans into a pot of water. He records a cassette of saxophone greats for Alice's car: he's been trying little surprises and gifts, puzzling out what kind of attention she needs. Roses have no effect, the yo-yo and soap bubbles trap dust, and the herbal bliss massage oil has disappeared altogether. She locks him out of the bathroom when she's in the tub. A tape seems harmless enough. He throws some cumin over the beans and tries to read a little Joyce, which quickly gives way to televised basketball.

Matt's on his third beer when Louise's daughter, Tanya, calls. She's already twenty-two, five years younger than Matt, and her good looks astonish him. Sometimes Matt thinks of her as a very smart Rapunzel: she still lives on Long Island with Louise and Dad.

"Just wondering," Tanya says, "about Christmas." Plaintive.

"Sorry," he says, "for you I would, but I'm going to Mom's. The usual thing."

"I thought so."

"Listen, if you're going nuts, call me. I'll drive up Christmas night."

In the background he can hear Louise mutter. He thinks he hears "Joan," his mother's name. He thinks he hears the word "bitch."

"Tell Louise I can hear," he says, and for a moment Tanya muffles the phone. He imagines her skin, which is milky, delicately veined. When she returns, he makes a joke about mothers wanting to invade their children's bodies. Her laugh tweaks a little, as if her throat is partly closed.

He's about to say good-bye, but it occurs to him that his father might have something to do with this phone call, might even have asked to see Matt on Christmas. He stops. "Is Christmas Dad's idea? What did Dad say?"

"Nothing," Tanya says. "Not a thing."

Everyone at the bookstore where Matt works is a lunatic; all day, delirious Christmas shoppers jam the aisles in long lines. The clerks eat bottles of Advil and wash them down with Diet Coke and cold espresso. Matt's on the information desk every third shift: the rest of the time he rings up sales and wraps books in silver paper, fumbling with the ribbons. *Merry Christmas*, he says. *Happy Holidays. Have a Nice Day.* Most days, he has to skip his breaks; after work he ends up napping or drinking more beer than usual.

The thought of his own shopping sends sharp little spasms through his temples. His mother wants ornithology reference books, and Alice requested some novels, but Louise claims that buying books means he isn't putting enough thought into the gifts. So, a week before Christmas, Matt takes the train to Copley

Square and buys Louise a silk scarf and a pair of earrings. The clerk at Saks avoids eye contact. *Merry Christmas,* she says. *Have a Nice Day.* Afterward, he combs the antique stores and galleries for something small and perfect for Tanya. On Newbury Street he finds a cameo brooch and a miniature kaleidoscope. Then he gives up and does the rest of his shopping at the liquor store and by telephone. A gift certificate from L. L. Bean for his impossible brother, Larry, overpriced Broadway tickets and a high-end bottle of scotch for his father.

What he really wants for Christmas is a trip with Alice to a B&B in Maine or Cape Cod, someplace beautiful and deserted, stripped clear of distractions. Dunes. He wants to eat lobsters and pour champagne into Alice's mouth and make love with her there. He's already suggested this for New Year's.

"*Decadent,*" Alice said. "I'll have to think about it." Then she wandered into the living room to meditate. After that the scenes he'd pictured seemed pale and tawdry, and he couldn't bring himself to ask her again. For a few days she said nothing about the holidays; then she announced she'd go to his mother's for Christmas but planned to spend New Year's Eve with her grandmother.

The drive from Boston to Long Island is slow and icy, but for miles Matt feels almost festive. Busy interstates always give him a sense of possibility; in a small, shy way, he feels like Jack Kerouac. He smokes Camel Lights and listens to Dizzy Gillespie. Then he picks up his brother, Larry, in Great Neck. Larry doesn't like cigarettes and he doesn't like jazz. Also, he detests Louise.

"A fake," Larry says. "A real phony."

Larry chews gum with his mouth open, and in between sentences he brays. Matt tries not to wince, but sometimes he can't help it.

"A fake," Larry repeats.

The car in the next lane skids and rights itself. "Who?"

"You know who. Wife number three."

"A fake what?"

Larry brays again. "You name it."

"A fake fake then."

"What?"

"A fake fake."

Larry sticks his fingers in his ears. "I can't hear you," he says.

A flake, Matt thinks.

He hasn't told Larry about the phone calls. Not even the one last spring in which Louise used the words *your father* and *heart episode* and *emergency room* in the same sentence. Larry walks with a small limp, the sort of thing people notice and then stop noticing; the problem is that he thinks the way he walks. He's smart, accomplished, but certain cognitive functions have been shortened a little. Once, in a weird moment of candor, Larry told Matt that the limp has kept him from developing relationships with girls. *Girls.* In high school this was probably true. But Larry's stuck to the notion ever since, instead of developing social skills. Last summer, the weekend Matt and Alice and Larry all stayed at his mother's house, Larry hung about the bathroom door in the morning and stared through Alice's T-shirt at her nipples. Finally, Alice crossed her arms over her chest and returned to the bedroom. "Your brother gawks," she said. "Don't say anything. Just get me a bathrobe."

Around Louise, Larry's beyond containing himself. He snickers. He makes jokes about her cleavage and, of course, her intelligence. No one laughs, even though Larry is often right about Louise; in a cruel sort of way he's got her pegged. It's like beating up on a blind person, only Louise isn't defenseless.

Matt slows to a near crawl as he turns onto his father's street. It's a neighborhood of white Christmas lights and discreet wreaths, tall hedges and wrought-iron lampposts lining the roadsides. But garish blue lights blink in the windows of his father's house. A plastic elf stands by the door. Matt parks on the sanded half of the driveway, kills the engine. He climbs out of his car with a shopping bag of gifts and the bottle of scotch, and locks the driver's-side door, but Larry doesn't move. "*Larry*," Matt says to the windshield. He walks around to the passenger door and raps on the window. "C'mon, Larry," he says. He opens the door and hands over the bag of gifts.

When Matt rings the bell, his stomach clenches. There's Louise, peeking out the front windows, swinging the door open; she's wearing a green silk dress too light for this weather, but it suits her, a V neck with soft draping, her gold chain and earrings gleaming against it. She steps out next to the elf; her mouth is peach tonight, and she's wearing some expensive scent, a lot of it. "You're here!" She kisses Matt's cheeks and pulls him against her suddenly and for slightly too long. Her body is one tall pillow. When she lets go of him, she's brushing snow out of his hair, and he feels as if her fingers are already inside his head.

"Hello, Larry," she says, and kisses the air next to Larry's face. "Presents?" She takes the shopping bags he's carrying. "Did you bring presents?" She ushers them into the overheated house and squeezes Matt's arm. "How sweet of you. Your father will be so pleased."

"Honey? Charles? The boys are here."

"Let's get you warmed up," she says. "Let's get you something to drink. We have eggnog. And of course the usual things. Whatever you boys want. Larry, you can hang your coat in the back closet." She holds her arm out for Matt's coat, then hands it to Larry.

"Honey? Charles?" When no one responds, she stares at her green suede heels. "Your Dad's had a long day."

Then Louise is quiet for a moment, and Matt can hear Christmas carols piped through the speakers in the living room and kitchen. It's familiar and sentimental, the sort of stuff the bookstore plays, that he ought to know instantly but can't seem to place. "Who's singing?" Matt says.

"I love this stuff. So seasonal," Louise says. "Bob Crosby."

"Bing," Larry says. "It's *Bing*."

Louise shoots him a look, then smiles and shrugs. "Bing," she says. "Of course."

———

In his reading chair in the living room, Matt's father scans the *Wall Street Journal* and strokes an obese calico cat. "That's my girl," he says, his fingers tangled in fur.

"Hi, Dad," Matt says. He bends to hug Charles in the chair, but there's no way to get past the newspaper and the cat, and Matt's right arm dangles awkwardly: his movement is like a strange hiccup he has to correct. He straightens. "Merry Christmas."

"Right. Merry Christmas," Charles says. "How are you? Everything good? Larry here?" Matt nods and his father's voice rises, a surprising burst of sound. "Larry? Larry? Did you bring back that software?"

Matt licks his lips. His mouth has gone cottony, and he traces the sensation down his throat to his chest and belly, which also seem stuffed with cotton—static, vague, opaque. This happens once in a while. His arms are still loose, and he swings the bottle of scotch from his left hand to his right until Louise takes it and holds it out to Charles. "Look, honey, look what Matty brought."

"Drinks. Good," Charles says. "Matthew, help yourself."

"Oh, and we have wood," Louise says.

Matt has no idea what she means.

"I got half a cord delivered today," she says. "You boys wouldn't mind stacking it, would you? *Larry?*" she shouts at the kitchen door and pivots back to Matt. "And then you can have a nice drink."

The cottony feeling has traveled up behind Matt's eyes. "No problem," he says.

But Larry refuses, claiming he's fighting off a cold. "I was sneezing the whole way here in the car. Wasn't I, Matt?"

Frozen air clears Matt's head. There's some satisfaction in stacking the wood, even though Louise watches out the window and waves at him. He's wearing his father's heavy boots and parka, and there's something satisfying about that too, about feeling the dips and curves his father's feet have made, catching the slight whiff of aftershave and mild body odor from his father's jacket and wrapping himself in it. In fact, Matt likes his father's clothes much better than anything else about his father, even though they don't fit him properly. The clothes are his father minus his father. The scents and aura and planes of the body without the dense, acidic mass.

Matt's halfway through stacking the wood when he notices

that the falling snow smells like pot. There's no one else outside, not in the neighbors' yards, not on the street. Louise waves from the kitchen window again, and she's holding something besides a drink, some slim cylinder, but no, it's an ordinary cigarette, one of her menthol kings. In the first-floor study, Larry bends over a computer, rapt, his face an odd luminous green. Above them, a second-floor window is open. The room's a dark blank, but he can see an ember, a slight trail of smoke. When Louise turns away, he nods and waves at the dark upper window, and the ember makes a quick waving arc back. Tanya will stay there as long as she can get away with it, which can't be much longer. Louise must have already called her.

Louise is always calling her. When Matt first met Tanya, she was fourteen and already beautiful, trying to hide whenever she could: Louise paraded her around. Within a year she'd cooled and hardened. She was still in high school when he'd caught a glimpse of her sitting at the edge of her bed, poking the skin on her arms with a safety pin until a little row of red dots appeared, like strange freckles, or some creepy high-fashion ornament. It's possible she still does this. Or perhaps something else: binge? Purge? Tanya spends a lot of time in bathrooms, but so do most women Matt knows.

By the time he's done with the wood, Louise has made a small dent in the bottle of scotch. "You're a hero, Matt," she says. "Have some pâté."

Louise has managed to get appetizers arranged on trays, but she's lost interest in whatever else needs to be done. The kitchen is blue with cigarette smoke. But here's Tanya, in a long-sleeved black velvet dress, her arms completely concealed. Her hair falls midway down her back, amber and wavy, the strands magnetically aligned. Tanya's all reserve and sophistication: she's just smoked a joint and her eyes aren't even red. She kisses Matt hello and gets down to business. "Let's finish cooking, Mom,"

Tanya says. "What's happening with the green beans? What about the ham?"

Louise looks around as if she's in someone else's kitchen. She pulls the lid off a pot on the stove, peers in, then snaps on a burner, which Tanya adjusts. "Matt brought presents," she says.

Tanya smiles very sweetly. "Thanks, Matt." Then she yanks the ham out of the oven.

"We're doing a *small* Christmas," Louise says, "you know? Not much money this year. I got some soap for your girlfriend. What's her name? The good stuff. I'm sure she doesn't need soap, but it's the good stuff. Tanya picked it out, right? Didn't you, sweetie?"

"Jasmine," Tanya says. "Alice sounds like someone who'd like sandalwood or jasmine. Exchange it if you don't think it's right."

"Of course it's right, how could it not be? You have wonderful taste. And why would Matt's girlfriend return a present from us?"

Tanya shrugs at Matt. "What have we got for appetizers, Mom? Pâté?"

"Of course. Matty's favorite."

"Actually," Matt says, "Dad's the one who's really crazy about it." He swings a napkin ring around his index finger and pours himself a scotch.

"You don't like pâté?" Louise says.

"Sure I do. So does Dad."

"Good. Tanya, baby, why don't you take some out to Daddy?"

Tanya shoves the ham back in the oven. "Okay." She pushes the oven mitts at Louise. "Here."

Once Tanya's out of the kitchen, Louise shakes her head. "She's touchy around the holidays," Louise says.

"I understand," Matt says.

"Of course you do," Louise says. "You understand everything."

Before dinner has even begun, Matt excuses himself and sneaks up to Tanya's bedroom, where he tries to call Alice. It's a habit he's acquired over the years, making secret phone calls from his father's house. Sometimes he calls high school friends who have stayed on Long Island. He used to call his mother, but one year he fell into whispering his unhappiness over the line, and she listened to him as if he were one of her clients. "I'm sorry you're feeling that way, Matt," his mother said. In the background he heard another woman's voice.

"Who's that?" he said.

"Oh, just a friend from work." She didn't offer anything more. He didn't ask her again but later wondered whether the friend had anything to do with his mother's books about androgyny, or her occasional weekend disappearances. Still, when he'd try to follow that line of thought, he'd drift off and reawaken to find himself calculating the phone bill or biting a thumbnail and staring out at traffic.

Tanya's room is spotless, done up in turquoise and cream. The bedspread matches the curtains, which match the pillows and the carpet. Scandinavian furniture, blond ash. One window is ajar, the air chilly, faintly laced with vanilla. Matt checks the dresser top for safety pins, pokes in the wastepaper basket for bloody Kleenex, and finds nothing but neatly written "to do" lists with all the items crossed off. He picks up Tanya's phone and punches in his calling card and home numbers. No one answers, and then some reggae music comes on the machine, followed by Alice's voice: *Leave us a message.* It's the optimist's voice she uses with outsiders, almost cut short by the mechanical beep. "Just wanted to let you know I'm here, at Dad's," Matt says. "Roads aren't so great, so be careful, okay?" He says "I love you" to the machine. Then he dials back and listens to the messages. Her friend Marci, inviting her to a movie. Louise's voice, saying "I can't wait to see you!" and then his own voice, playing back to him, sounding like someone else, as it always does.

Eventually, Larry abandons his computer starship-battle and asks when they'll get to eat. Matt's father rises from his reading chair and lumbers into the dining room, the cat following at his heels. Eventually, Louise gets there too, with the undercooked green beans and overcooked potatoes and beautifully cooked ham. Louise loads up the plates of the men in the family, serves herself and Tanya half-portions, and sends around a bottle of Cabernet Sauvignon. Before they start to eat, she raises her wineglass. "Merry Christmas!" she says. *Happy Holidays*, Matt thinks. *Have a Nice Day.* "Merry Christmas," he and Charles and Tanya toast back. "Christmas," Larry mumbles.

It's not what Matt would call an ordinary meal, but for a while dinner seems okay. He gets Tanya talking about Bloomingdale's, where she works in the cosmetics department and where romantic scandal has decimated the sales team. Someone had to transfer to another store. There's the matter of Larry's promotion, his new condo. "You're looking good these days," Tanya tells him, and for a few minutes Larry beams at her. Charles doesn't speak when there's food on his plate, but before he reaches for seconds, he says a few words about the stock market fluctuations and a new tennis club opening in Roslyn. He wonders aloud about Matt's game. "You're still playing, son?" he says, but his words run together: *You're still playing son?*

Louise is drinking fast and Tanya keeps refilling her glasses with water—first just the water tumbler, then the wineglass as well. Louise pours the water from the wineglass into the tumbler and refills her wineglass with Cabernet Sauvignon. The third time Tanya pours water, Louise grabs at her wrist.

"Stop that right now, Missy." A sharpness in her voice that even she seems to hear. She softens, pats Tanya's hand. "Or Santa might forget your presents."

For a few minutes they eat in silence. Matt wonders whether it's like this in the eye of a hurricane: loud silence, waiting, a debilitating barometric drop. There's not much food left on his plate—some stray potato bits, some fat sliced off the ham. Then, suddenly, a green bean. He glances up in time to see Louise launch another from her plate to his. Surreptitiously, although everyone at the table has noticed.

"I bet you're still hungry," she says.

He isn't. Really, Tanya's the only one in need of spare green beans: that's all she's eaten. Mostly she's been sipping on her diet Coke and drinking water. You'd think pot would make her hungrier than that. He picks up the hardiest of the beans and tosses it back onto Louise's plate. She sends it back; he returns it again.

She laughs and sends over two green beans and throws a small red potato. It's a game now, he's gone and done it, he's into a food fight with Louise. God. He forks up the potato and eats it.

"Knew you were still hungry," Louise says, and throws another one.

He bends down and waves a string bean at one of the cats, who paws it and attacks it on the carpet.

"No fair," Louise says.

"Louise, contain yourself," Dad says. It's in the voice of Matt's childhood. "Contain yourself," Dad repeats. Louise is spilling out over the edge again, but when isn't she? She doesn't stay within the lines, even the lines of her own body, and she never keeps secrets. The one exception—half-exception—is Tanya's father. About him, Louise won't tell much. Instead, she'll say, "My lips are sealed on that subject," and widen her eyes. "I promised my baby," she'll say. "I promised Tanya. No more talk about all that."

But he knows Tanya's father is a businessman in Chicago. A shark, Louise once let slip. A real shark.

"Some of us are just minnows," she said.

Matthew wonders whether Tanya's father did anything horribly sharklike to Louise, like hit her, or hit Tanya, which would be even worse, if you can say such a thing. And if you could say something else: you can see where the impulse to hit Louise might come from. Tanya is another story though. No one should even think of hitting Tanya.

Louise picks up her last green bean with her hand and bites into it, then winks at Matt.

Patience, he tells himself. She's an abuse survivor, of one kind or another.

Matt knows a few things about abuse survivors. Twice a month, Alice volunteers at a battered women's shelter, and she tells him stories about victims who stop being victims or forget how not to be victims, victims who identify with their abusers, abusers who were themselves victims. "It's a real mess, isn't it?" he says. She nods at him solemnly.

That's the gesture he sees Alice make most often these days, the solemn nod. When he first met her, Alice was more likely to kiss his cheek or stick out her tongue. Back then, he was inching his way out of another relationship. His almost-ex would call him when her car wouldn't start. She'd call him when her family upset her. He spent a lot of time bailing her out, something he was good at. Alice usually bailed herself out: she'd look under the hood, check the battery connections, listen to the car sounds, and call AAA. During family crises, she'd buy herself flowers and meditate or go for long runs. He liked Alice's self-sufficiency, her orderliness, her clean lines. Alice didn't seem to need him, at least not for those small, daily rescues. Now, after two years, she still doesn't seem to need him. Not even for sex, which they haven't had much of lately. She's in therapy, working on "issues." He's wondered if they have to do with the battered women. He's wondered if he's gotten too fat. And he's wondered if he's too clumsy for her, if his tongue or his penis are substandard. Have any of his former girlfriends faked it? Have all of them? Surely not *all* of them. Why would they? He's ordinary looking. He doesn't have money. Maybe they sensed he'd jump-start their cars and take them to dinner when their families exploded. The truth is, they'd get his help no matter what. And how hard is it, really, to find a jump-start?

Occasionally, Alice is still tender with him, and funny. Around her he feels, in some remote way, protected. He tries to think of the tender moments. Their early lovemaking. Alice's kissing his fingers and bringing him strawberries in bed. But mostly he thinks of the funny moments, her deadpan imitations, her acid sense of humor.

At the dinner table he clears his throat and announces he really should call Alice, she's been driving in bad Boston weather, he ought to make sure she's okay.

"Use the phone in the kitchen," Louise says.

"No, my room is more private," Tanya says. "The second door on the right."

Matt nods, as if he needs the reminder.

This time when Matt reaches Tanya's room, he closes the bedroom door and opens the drawers he earlier ignored. Her underthings are neatly folded, and he lifts them in the air and shakes them out: black and white bikini panties, bras that are all lace. He gazes through the lace at the fleshy pads of his fingers pressed against the fabric, then drops the bra and digs through the rest of the garments. There's nothing hidden at the bottom of the drawer, not even a $20 bill or a box of checks. He refolds the panties, replaces them, sets one set of lace cups over another, eases the drawer shut. On top of the desk is a text called *Contemporary Pediatrics*. Inside the file cabinet her folders are labeled, arranged alphabetically and by color. *Chemistry, MCAT prep, Resume, Financial Aid '92, Financial Aid '93, Financial Aid '94*. In the desk drawers there are paper clips and staples, pencils and pens and whiteout, clear tape, Elmer's glue, ordinary paper, resume paper, index cards. No rolling papers. No little stash of pot, no bottle of Prozac. No Dexatrim or Xanax. No razor blades. He knows better than to do this, and he knows if he's caught he'll say he was looking for matches. Although his cigarettes are in the car.

He dials Alice again and gets the machine.

The dining room table is a ruin of dirty plates, stray green beans, glassware streaked with wine. Matt hesitates before reentering, then automatically begins to clear. Louise gives his hand a light slap. "None of that," she says, and ushers Charles into the living room. "We'll have dessert in here."

Tanya's already brewed coffee, and she takes charge of the operation, pulling clean cups from the china cabinet, setting up a tray with the silver coffee pot and sugar and cream, forks and dessert plates. But Louise pulls the dessert plates off the tray and turns to Matt. "You help me with the pie."

Tanya shrugs and lifts the tray with one arm, carries it over her head like a waitress at a nightclub. Maybe she's wearing one of those lace things under her dress.

"Whatever," he says.

In the kitchen, Matt can see where Tanya's made small efforts to clear off counter space. Once Louise sets down the dessert plates, she's back to her kitchen distraction: it's as though she's forgotten what the plates are there for. She pours herself a brandy and lights a cigarette. She smokes menthol, but it smells good, and it's been hours since Matt's smoked. He asks her for a cigarette, and she winks and opens a drawer. There's a pack of Camel Lights.

"I thought you might want some," she says.

She tries to light his cigarette for him, but her fingers slip against the lighter. "It's okay," he says, "I'll do it." But she's still leaning close to him as he flicks the lighter, and he has to turn and cup the flame so he doesn't burn her.

They stand in the kitchen, smoking and gazing out at the falling snow, and then he turns to take the ice cream from the freezer. She's like a cat at his heels, and when he turns again, there she is, in close-up.

"Good brandy," Louise says. She offers him a sip.

He takes it. He's still feeling the warm flush of it when Louise leans right up against him and kisses him on the mouth, a long wet kiss. Her mouth is open and he feels her tongue. She tastes of brandy and menthol smoke, and everything about her has a lovely wet warmth. He kisses her back, thinking only of getting the rest of his body into that warmth. Picturing the pink of her throat. Feeling an impulse to reach up and thumb her nipples through the green silk dress. He presses into her, slides a hand up to her breast, and for a moment everything seems fluid, even his skin.

There's the sudden pleasure of her hand against his groin, and what is it that stops him? The drip of the kitchen faucet. Another slow, thick sound: footsteps? The dizziness he feels. The sudden awareness that all this sensation is also Louise, his father's crazy wife. He steps back, and the expression on her face is not the usual practiced coyness, but something younger and more vulnerable. There's a rustling near the doorway, a fluttery movement, then Tanya in her velvet dress, squinting at them.

"Mom?"

"Hmm?" Louise lets her arms drop.

Tanya steps closer, places her palm on Louise's shoulder. She seems taller than usual. "Mom, let's fix your make-up."

Louise raises a hand to her face.

"It's not bad," Tanya says. "Just a little smudging I'll touch up in a minute."

"Okay." Louise lets herself be led off toward the bathroom.

"I'm sure Matt can manage the pie," Tanya says, her voice flat.

In the half-destroyed kitchen, Matt mechanically slices the pumpkin pie, sets three pieces on frilly dessert plates, scoops vanilla ice cream on top, and carries them out to the living room. Charles is pacing, and a wave of nausea ripples up from Matt's stomach to his throat.

"Here you go, Dad."

Charles eyes the loaded plate as if it's a live hamster. He sets it on top of the stereo but holds onto the dessert fork and fingers the tines as he walks.

A Rangers' hockey game slides over the TV screen, but the sound is off, and Larry's standing directly in front of the TV, taunting the slow, fat calico with a catnip mouse.

"Cut that out," Charles says.

"Larry," Matt says. His voice sounds strangely even, separate from his body. "Pie."

And then Larry's docile: he drops the mouse, he takes a plate, he sits on the sofa and quietly eats. He inadvertently smears pumpkin on his chin, but he doesn't ask about Louise and Tanya, and he lets the calico settle, unmolested, on the armrest.

Matt's hands have begun to sweat. He takes the seat next to Larry and slowly, deliberately forks up his pie—one bite, one swallow, one bite, one swallow—despite the edge of nausea. Charles finally picks his plate off the stereo and eats standing up, swaying from side to side and walking in small circles. No one says a word, and finally Larry turns up the volume on the hockey play-by-play.

At the end of the second period, Louise and Tanya are still absent, and Charles cradles the calico in the chair farthest from the sofa, away from his sons. He's half-asleep, or enraged, Matt thinks, both look the same on Charles. Maybe his heart is acting up. All that scotch, all that ham and bad marriage. That would be enough, wouldn't it? Without standing in the kitchen doorway. Why be in that doorway instead of his chair? *He was pacing*, Matt thinks. *Pacing!* The hockey announcer keeps replaying the only goal of the period, a late tip, the goalie sprawled to the left of the net, clips of a defenseman smashing a winger into the boards, the winger later tripping the defenseman. On the sofa, Matt counts his own breaths, the way Alice taught him to, but it doesn't seem to be working: the room appears jumbled and incoherent, and his heart is beating too fast, as if he's mixed amphetamines with vodka. He wanders over to the tree, kneels, and begins to pick out the packages with his and Larry's and Alice's names on them. This seems to take a very long time.

"We'll open these on Christmas, Dad," Matt says.

"What?" Charles says.

"The presents for Larry and me? We'll take them to Mom's and open them Christmas morning."

Charles gazes at Matt's legs. "Fine."

Then the door is all Matt can think of: he finds his coat and carries the presents out to the car. The snow has not abated; a drift is building around the plastic elf. The lawn glows bluish white, and he wonders whether this is what people see during near-death experiences. It seems safer out here, the way the tundra is safe. He could leave now, without saying good-bye, without even waiting for Larry. It's tempting. He lights a cigarette, then a second one, and waits out the impulse.

"Here we are," Louise says. Matt's brushing snow out of his hair, handing Larry his coat, and Tanya's leading Louise down the stairs. Louise has an entirely new make-up job, rosier cheeks, longer lashes, brighter lips. Tanya looks exactly the same: icy and marvelous.

"You're leaving?" Louise says. Her eyes seem to skip over Matt's face.

"It's still snowing," Matt says. "It'll take us a while to get to Mom's."

"But we have waffles for tomorrow morning," Louise says. "I bought waffles and syrup."

"That's nice," Matt says. He catches Louise's eye for half a second, then breaks away and pulls at the fingers of his gloves. "Thanks. But we have to go."

"I don't like waffles," Larry says.

"They're good waffles," Louise says, "and real maple syrup."

"Mom," Tanya says, "we'll have them. You and me and Dad."

"I thought you were staying," Louise says. "I got waffles."

"I'm sorry," Matt says.

For a moment Louise stops. Tanya guides her over toward Charles, but Louise pushes her away and heads for the tree. Then she's on her knees in that green silk dress, rummaging with the packages, finally looking up at Matt, not taking her eyes off Matt.

"Did you get the presents? Charles, did you give them the presents?"

From a few feet off, Matt can smell Louise's perfume. When she reaches for him, he's on the verge of pushing her away, hard enough that she could fall; he's on the verge of falling himself. Her good-bye hug is a thick clutch, and he holds his breath, then tugs his body back from her, watching the walls, watching his feet. Charles shakes hands—a quick shake, the kind you might give a business associate—but he says nothing, not even "Drive safely" or "Talk to you on Christmas." Tanya watches with the expression of a mannequin. When she hugs Matt good-bye, her touch is so light he barely feels it.

In the car, Larry finds a country station, a woman singing "Big Red Sun Blues." Matt keeps his hand off the dial, even though the song makes him feel absurd. He opens a window and lights a cigarette, and Larry says nothing about it. This is Larry's version of kindness, Matt thinks, this is as close as they've been in years. Light gusts of wind rattle the car doors, the smoke hits Matt's lungs, and he can barely contain the welling urge to confess to Larry, to his only brother, how little he understands, except that he kissed Louise and liked it. That dread and desire blur together, no matter how vigilant he is. That Tanya probably hates him now and might for life, but at least would not tell Dad, though what if Dad knows? What if there was, still, some thin wire connecting Matt to Dad, now cut? What still connects him to anyone? To Alice, who doesn't love him? She says she does, but it isn't the sustaining sort of love; it's more like the love of comic books or a pop song from your adolescence, the kind that catches you fast then leaves you with wry fondness. It's possible, not likely, but possible, that Matt's love for Alice is fake, a substitute for something he can't name. When he tries to imagine her in five years, even three years, he can't see her, he can only hear her on the other end of the phone, with an unfamiliar voice in the background. On the Long Island Expressway, Matt wants to confess that he's going to stay with Alice anyway, until he can figure out what to do next, until they're ready to be honest. Matt blows smoke at the open window. He wants to confess that his craving for that warm slickness obliterates everything else.

"Larry," Matt says. "I'm an okay brother, right?"

"What?" Larry says, a little irritated. "Yeah."

"I mean, I know we're not that close."

Larry doesn't answer this, but he lowers the radio volume. "Did you count how many drinks Louise had?"

"A lot."

"No kidding," Larry says. "A lot a lot. Let's skip this next year."

Maybe in a year their father and Louise will have divorced. Maybe by then Matt will live in some other part of the country. Or maybe Louise will tire of Christmas on Long Island and there will be money: she'll convince Dad to cruise the Caribbean. These are the only escape routes Matt can imagine.

Larry glances at Matt once, twice, as if waiting; he blinks and blinks at the oncoming cars and tucks his fists against his belly.

"Okay," Matt says. He turns the windshield wipers up a notch, adjusts the defogger. Beyond the wash of snow, the string of red taillights extends for miles.

Dreaming
of the
Snail Life

———————

On Angell Street, Lucy shrinks to zero, imagines herself a ball of air. *Old habits die hard*, Charlie says, but he doesn't mean disappearing by fractions. He means nail biting. He means tobacco. Sometimes he and Lucy are lovers, but she doesn't tell him much, not even how hard it is to move through the world. She pays attention to the wrong things: anthills, rain, jet exhaust. Most days, she's choked with shyness, a skittish animal. Panic strikes in the line at the bank, the IGA bread aisle, in Charlie's bed—after he's entered her, just as her excitement mushrooms. She's a helium balloon, she tells Charlie, one more thrust and she might pop.

"But what does that mean?" Charlie says. His brow is furrowed. He's biting his lip. He slips his cock out of her and hugs her to his chest, but against her neck she can feel his frown. When she's calm again, he turns on cable and peels oranges for them to eat.

Of course, that's not the end of it. The next day, in the parking lot of her building, he grumbles. He frowns and clucks, and Lucy pictures him at his sous-chef job, sorting through gritty, wilted spinach. "What is it you said you're doing today?" he asks, even though she's told him laundry. Beyond the sound of his unhappiness, she hears a humming. Almost imperceptible. She watches the delivery men from the Red Cross smoking cigarettes in back of the building next door, the cars streak down Waterman. It's clear that Charlie wants to argue right here, in public, outside the building. He's popping his knuckles the way he does when he warms up to say something risky. He says, "Are you like this with everyone or just me?"

"Like what?"

He hesitates and the humming seems louder. "Frigid."

Lucy flinches.

"You weren't like this when we met," he says. "Did I do something?"

She squints to see the cigarette box on the Red Cross stoop— red and white, like the Red Cross logo—and her old longing for tobacco surges. The rhododendrons in front of the building are blooming, white, magenta; she wants to finger the loud, frilly blossoms and smoke cigarettes. The Red Cross men call to each other: *You'll open up tomorrow, Ron?* One of them whistles; one of them climbs into a pickup truck. Smoke out the pickup window, smoke feathering off into the May air.

"What makes you like this?" Charlie says.

His hair is messed up from his baseball cap, sandy spikes in a sandy field. Lucy's neighbor Kate pulls her Olds Cutlass into the parking lot, and the pickup turns onto Waterman.

"You don't listen to me. Have you noticed that?" Charlie says. "You don't listen. What are you doing now? You know that truck?"

"No."

"What's so interesting about that truck?"

"I don't know. It's a truck."

"I give up," Charlie says. "Uncle."

His face is red, as if he might cry out here in front of everyone, in front of the Red Cross guys, a boy on a bicycle, big-assed Kate with her grocery bags. Lucy imagines the lot's car alarms tripping all at once, Japanese, American, and German sirens all blaring incomprehensibly. Crying here is just the sort of embarassing, out-of-control thing she would do, or at least used to do. Now she thinks a cigarette would be more satisfying than crying, perhaps more satisfying than silence, and she realizes the humming, sweet and a little husky, is somewhere above them, a sound coming from the sky. But not the sky. From the third-story fire escape, from Martine, who is sunning herself and her one-year-old boy. Maybe she's singing, but Lucy can only hear bits of melody. *Frère Jacques, Frère Jacques, dormez-vous?* No. Martine's in a silk wrapper, crooning to round-faced Roland, the sort of boy baby that food companies recruit. Then the humming stops, and Martine lifts Roland, steps to the apartment door.

"I said Uncle," Charlie says.

Sweat beads along his forehead and Lucy wants to kiss him there, to keep him from staring at her failings and counting them up in front of her. She can't bring herself to kiss him on the mouth though, not just yet: he could want sex again, she might still vaporize. This possibility creeps up on her the way the past can, if you aren't careful.

"I say Uncle too," Lucy says.

And then the hysteria starts. Martine's. Yelling down at them in French-accented panic. "The door, she's locked," Martine calls. "Lucy? That is you? Lucy? The door." Roland has begun to wail, his face a red ball.

The rungs of the fire escape wobble. It stops twelve feet above the ground and the second-floor section sways a little when Martine kicks her foot against it. "What do I do?" she yells down.

Lucy pretends she's a fencepost, a parking meter.

"Stay there," Charlie yells. "Stay right there."

And there's Kate, with her groceries, shouting up to Martine, "Do I have your spare key?" and handing the groceries to Lucy.

"No keys," Martine calls, but too late, when Kate is already in the building.

The Red Cross guys are watching now. "Fire department," one of them yells. "You want us to call the fire department?"

The one with a lit cigarette approaches. "What's she doing out there with the baby?" he says.

Charlie shrugs.

"That fire escape. Nowhere near code," he says. "Doesn't anybody inspect around here?"

"She was singing," Lucy says. "That's all I know."

And Kate opens her second-floor window, yells up to Martine "Je n'ai pas des clefs, Martine."

"Yes. No keys," Martine says.

"I guess I'll call the fire department."

"No fire," Martine says.

It's only a few minutes before they hear the sirens, see the red flash on Waterman, before the hook-and-ladder truck pulls into the parking lot, and three men in black slickers and hats begin to scurry around the base of the building. Another two go inside.

Charlie taps Lucy's shoulder, and she realizes she's still clutching Kate's groceries. She's hugging the produce.

"See you," he says. His car is the green of new lettuce, his brake lights obscured by the sun.

A fireman lifts Roland out of Martine's arms and scoops him into the third-floor apartment, then Martine climbs in, the silk wrapper making her backside shimmer. Lucy hauls the groceries past the rhododendrons and into the building, up the wide stairs to Kate's.

More often than not, Kate looks like a horse. Her nostrils habitually flare, her eyes habitually widen and twitch. She's six feet tall and ungainly, a big-boned woman who likes to wear halter tops and shorts, exposing more than anyone cares to see. Maybe if she didn't sort through Lucy's mail, reading return addresses, if she didn't pick at the surface of Lucy's life or jab at the underlayers, Lucy wouldn't think of horses. At least, she wouldn't think of thick-legged work horses. She'd come up with another image of Kate, free instead of desperate, nonconformist instead of ridiculous. Instead, there's the horsiness. And the image of Kate walking down the stairs with a little cottage cheese on her lip, although that only happened once.

"Here," Lucy says. "You forgot these."

"I knew there was something else," Kate says. She heaves the bag into the crook of her arm, digs a black plum out, bites it. She shakes her head, plum juice on her lips. "That poor Martine. You know she's pregnant again."

"What?"

"Yup," Kate says. "Already. That little guy's barely walking. Maybe she's Catholic. That's big in France. Catholicism."

It's involuntary, Lucy's step back. "That's what I've heard," she says, and the unwanted image rises, Martine and George on an unfamiliar sofa, Martine ecstatic in her silk wrapper, George naked, above her, humping away.

"When the baby's born, they're getting an au pair. Swiss," Kate says. She licks her lips. "Your friend in the parking lot—what's his name?"

"Charlie."

"Charlie didn't look too happy."

"Sometimes he isn't," Lucy says, and, just as she's about to turn, Kate leans toward her, the grocery bag almost brushing Lucy's arm. She can smell Kate's plummy breath.

"Men," Kate says. "I could tell you a few stories." She tosses a swatch of hair over her shoulder. "Want a beer?"

"Thanks anyway," Lucy says. "I've got plans."

On weekdays, Lucy's a legal secretary in a firm that handles medical malpractice suits, and it isn't working out. Mostly she transcibes long, involved descriptions of cancers and botched surgeries and deliveries of damaged babies. The other secretaries and paralegals like her, but they act as if she's nineteen instead of twenty-nine, and often after work she can't remember her day, except for lunch. The law firm is right next to the art school, and on her lunch hour she passes students in torn T-shirts and wild hair, students with charcoal smudged into their skin, smoking cigarettes and drinking coffee. She sits on a bench with Agatha Christie novels and eats peanut butter sandwiches. Then she goes back to typing more malpractice stories.

She can't explain why she does this work. She's on the wrong side of things. The wrong side of the art/law divide. The wrong side of half the cases: malpractice defense. Most of the attorneys either ignore her or say inappropriate things about her personal life. Her favorite, though, a man named Joel, does neither. He's Mediterranean looking, handsome, in his late thirties. He tells Lucy how wonderfully smart his wife is, and he schedules afternoons off to take his kids to the circus or the zoo. When Lucy is alone in bed and touches herself, she thinks of walking through the Roger Williams Zoo with Joel, past the cougars, past the gibbons, into the grassy fields; she pictures the hair on his arms, his close-shaven neck.

It isn't that Lucy can't have orgasms. It's just that she can't have them with anyone else around. With Charlie there, except in the beginning, when they were strangers. But for the past several weeks she's either cried or stiffened up and felt nothing. Either way, all their lust evaporates. When she's alone, though, Lucy never cries. She'll take off her clothes and dream up strangers, lie naked on the bed reading personal ads until her mind is full of sex words, swimming with bodies, she'll rub herself with her fingers, make herself come more than once. But Charlie knows nothing about that.

"You need help," he tells her. "Don't be so passive."

"No," she says. She leaves him on the bed, locks herself in the bathroom, touches herself in the shower.

In her secret life, Lucy is never as passive as Charlie accuses her of being. She builds altars out of trash: wood constructions the size of toasters, tiny rooms lined with bright scraps of paper, dotted with broken china, coins, hairpins. Something like Joseph Cornell's dreamscapes, imaginary hotels. Dollhouses gone awry. Sometimes bits of her job emerge in them: a champagne cork that means Joel, scraps of legal notices. Sometimes there are plastic zoo animals or drawings of surly-looking mutts. But most often she uses porcelain beads and shells, stones the size of dog teeth, patterned fabrics, candy wrappers that look like fans.

Some of the altars Lucy keeps in storage boxes that she pushes under the bed before Charlie arrives. But her apartment is too small for all of them. The altars have started to occupy tabletops and bookshelves, and Lucy's taken to wrapping them in towels before company arrives. So far, Charlie hasn't asked what the toweled lumps are. She wishes he would, even though she's afraid. Once or twice she's been close to unveiling them: in the parking lot, after Charlie said Uncle, she thought it might be time. But then there was Martine, and Charlie saying, "see you," and for a week he hasn't answered his phone. Now she's started a new altar, and Charlie keeps appearing to her in it. Green crepe paper. The label from a sack of Maine potatoes. Plastic ducks.

She needs more seaglass. She needs stones. At the end of the week, she bikes to Barrington town beach, picks up what she needs, buys a lemon ice on the way home. This gives her unalloyed pleasure, but when she runs into Martine with Roland, then glimpses Kate in a halter top, Lucy worries that in a decade she'll be a hermit hag. Maybe sooner.

After a few more days of no Charlie, Lucy starts sending him postcards that say "Little Rhody" and have cartoonish maps of the state. On them she writes thumbnail stories of animals stuck in the wrong body. Depressed seagulls. Sandpipers longing to be antelopes. Tired antelopes dreaming of the snail life.

———

When Martine and George entertain, which is always, they leave their door to the hall open. Their apartment occupies the entire third and fourth floors of the building; the first- and second-floor tenants are invisible to them, they shout through the lower halls as if no one else can hear. Fragmented English, loud rapid French, too fast for Lucy to decode. She imagines Martine in white, a pattern of tiny lilies on her dress, George in his Italian suit, their friends in more Italian suits and floral dresses, all drinking martinis out of fogged glasses, slipping the onions over their teeth. It's maddening, all those murmurs and thumps, all that laughter. Sometimes at night, Lucy sticks her head under a pillow to block the sound, then strains to hear the conversation.

Weekends are no better. For example, the second Saturday in June, when the florist rings everyone's doorbells but only really wants Martine. Out there on the front porch, a dozen roses, Lucy answering the door, for an instant wondering whether Charlie has lost his mind in some sweet, expensive way. Then Martine arrives at the door, then Kate, Martine blushing, explaining she is turning thirty, look what George sent.

"Happy Birthday," Lucy says.

"Bon anniversaire," Kate says, and disappears.

And then Roland is calling for his Mama, you can hear it all the way to the building entrance. Lucy returns to her kitchen and plants basil seeds in pots, but in an hour the voices of strangers fill the stairwell: Martine's friends. Lucy scans the hall through her apartment peephole while all the Francophiles in Providence linger on the landing and kiss each other on the cheeks, their torsos and faces swelling large, their legs shrinking away. They place hands on Martine's belly and won't let her carry anything except more roses. Eventually, they climb the stairs to Martine's apartment and coo overhead. Lucy can hear them singing in English, their toddlers yowling, then laughter. She cleans a sinkful of dishes, plays a Coltrane tape a couple of notches too loud, and begins to sketch several demented pigeons. After a while there's a knock on her door and she tiptoes back to the peephole. It's the husband, George, that impatient businessman's face. She tiptoes into the bathroom and runs the shower and waits for him to give up. But in a few minutes she hears a key in her lock. She gets to the door fast enough to shove it closed and secure the chain. Out the peephole she can see Kate rolling her eyes.

After a moment, Kate knocks. "George asked me," she says.

Lucy opens the door an inch. "You can't just come in here. It isn't legal."

"You're pissing them off." Kate jerks her thumb toward the ceiling. "I don't like him either. But he's the kind of guy who calls up landlords. Do yourself a favor," Kate says.

Favor echos in Lucy's head: favorite. Party favor. Sexual favor.

Out of favor. "Stay out of here," Lucy says, and she's surprised by her own voice, now gravelly and low, like a man's or a lunatic dog's.

"Fine. But I'm going to stand here until you turn it down."

Lucy closes the door and stares out the peephole, letting Kate wait it out until a song ends. Finally, she lowers the volume and returns to the peephole. Kate is pressing close to the tiny window, her face distorted and huge. "Go away," Lucy says.

"Lucy," Kate tells the peephole. She pauses. "You'll find another guy." Then she disappears.

On Monday, Lucy gets a postcard from Charlie, a photo of the Breakers in Newport. It says, *I need a few more weeks. Don't panic.*

The next morning, when Lucy sees Kate in the hall, Kate raises her eyebrows. Really, Kate's more of an oversized donkey than a horse, Lucy decides. She hurries out of the house and heads downtown. The temperature's begun to spike, an early heat wave. Pantyhose stick to Lucy's thighs as she walks to work. When she gets to the law firm, sweat coats her legs, pools around her toes. The office air is cooler, but she ducks into the women's room and yanks off the hose and throws them in the trash.

Hours later, at Lucy's lunch break, one of the older secretaries pulls her aside. A partner complained about her legs.

"Joel?" Lucy says.

"Oh no. He doesn't care." The older secretary, Donna, nods toward the corner office. It's the defense attorney on the Shelby case, the one against a surgeon who operated without checking his patient's chart. Donna is not unkind. She hands Lucy an egg-shaped pantyhose package.

"I keep extras around," Donna says. "I think they'll be a little big, but they should get you through the afternoon." Donna shrugs. "It's the firm's rules."

"Thanks," Lucy says.

"You might try those summer hose from Hanes," Donna says. "They aren't so bad."

Lucy nods. "*Hanes,*" she repeats.

Hormones do things to women. They do things to Lucy, make her long for Joel to walk past her desk at work, make her lie on her bed after work and fantasize about Charlie naked. He's been gone long enough that her desire for him has returned. Not all those hormonal surges bring desire, though. There's despair. Listlessness. Even temporary breakdowns of spatial perception: those days when Lucy crashes into her own furniture. She knows she isn't the only woman jerked around by chemistry. She knows that pregnant women usually have it worse, and she feels for those women, the theoretical pregnant ones. *Be nice to Martine,* she tells herself, *she's in a hormonal nightmare.* But every time Lucy runs into her, Martine is a happy madonna, hugging fat-faced Roland. Lucy has the horrifying desire to give Martine a hip check.

Rules for the summer: *Don't be rude to pregnant women. Don't antagonize Kate. Wear your Hanes.* Lucy writes these on scraps of paper and sticks them to the refrigerator, as if they might help suppress the growling that's begun deep in her throat. And they do help, for a while. She waits until after five o'clock to ditch her pantyhose, then rides her bike out to the beach and collects more debris; she's starting a new altar, this one with a lot of dried spaghetti and seaglass in it. She listens to music through headphones, compliments Kate on the snapdragons in front of the house. She stiffens up around Martine but smiles at Roland. Sometimes he grins back, his ridiculous baby grin.

And there's Charlie, inching his way back. He's been writing more notes. He uses the words *sad, undermined, failure* when he describes his own emotional state around her. She doesn't mean to be a virus, she writes back. She knows she keeps too many secrets. She admits to missing him. After another round of notes, she asks about meeting for coffee. He sends a card, a movie-still of trains, saying he's off to visit his mother in Connecticut, at the house she's rented. He'll call when he gets back.

And then, as July is getting even hotter, Roland catches a summer cold and can't sleep, cries through the night, cries through the afternoon, exhausted and cranky. Everyone in the house knows about Roland's cold, and soon enough everyone knows that

Martine tries to raise the humidity level by running hot water into the third-floor tub, in the bathroom next to the nursery. It's a Tuesday evening. The version of the evening George eventually tells the landlord is this: he arrives home before the tub is full and suggests they take Roland out. Roland's fever is down, he's restless. It's a nice night, George says, and maybe a picnic, or at least a drive, will distract the baby. They leave the house, Martine forgetting to turn off the bathwater.

And so at nine, when Lucy rides back from the beach, the house is a lurid red from the flashers on fire trucks. Although the halls are dark, there's no smoke, and no one stops her from entering. But the door to her apartment is open, there's a crowd of bodies inside: Kate, four firemen, a man who turns out to be the landlord's lawyer. Lucy hears the fast plink of falling water, she's hit by a musty smell: it's raining in the center of the room and in the south corner, where Lucy's stereo used to be—now black shadows pushed over to the side, with lighter chunks of plaster heaped on top. The floor is covered with water; the light fixtures brim. Someone has removed the towels from the altars to dry the floor, and the unveiled altars are scattered about, stacked precariously, sitting in puddles. A fireman knocks one over. Kate pushes towels around with her feet.

"It was leaking down to the first floor," Kate says. "The subletters there thought it was coming from here. But it's from upstairs. Martine and George just got home."

The firemen focus their flashlights on the ceiling, and one stray light races around the walls and floor. Kate squints at the altars, touches the one for Charlie. By now she's probably seen every embarassment, and so have the firemen: the wormlike Summer Hanes hung up to dry, the Kama Sutra by the bathtub, the pink vibrator on the bedside table.

That first moment, Lucy's stunned calm feels permanent: *just get to the other side of this.* Everything is oddly quiet, except for the dripping ceiling, the shuffling feet, the low staccato sentences of George and the lawyer. They've got insurance, George says. Plenty.

The sounds and voices lull her. Behind her, Lucy senses Martine entering the room. Turns. "Lucy," Martine says. She's got her hand on her forehead, she's flustered and pale. And she starts to apologize, she looks for the right English words. But then it begins: blood surges into Lucy's face and arms, her hands are shaking, about to fly, and before Lucy can stop herself she's shouting, *spoiled bitch, fat French bitch,* yelling, *get out, get away.* Then George starts toward Lucy, pushing the firemen, raising a fist. But the firemen push back, and Kate's calling George, saying, *hold on there, hold on George;* they all corral him into the hall. Lucy's head is buzzing. She tells the lawyer, *I think you should go, please go.* Just beyond Lucy's door, Martine is in tears, George comforting her, the two of them saying how awful Lucy is, what a monster, and just as Lucy lunges in their direction, a fireman closes the door, saying, *Things will get better, you don't want the police. You shouldn't stay here,* another one says. When her shoulders drop, he reopens the door. The buzz in the hall is thickening, other neighbors from the building are gathering, and through their talk Lucy hears Kate inventing history, outright lying to George. *You probably don't know about Lucy's miscarriage,* Kate says, *being around pregnancy is very hard on her.*

"Horse," Lucy yells.

But the crowd in the hallway seems to think she's yelled "whore" and means Martine. George swears in harsh, unfamiliar French and whips a wet towel at Lucy's door.

———

Finally, they're gone, though she can sense George and Martine upstairs, the uncharacteristic silence punctuated by footsteps. Lucy pulls up the shades: the streetlamps and the outdoor halogens are bright enough that she can see without a flashlight. Three of the altars are ruined, the wood soaked with water, delicate parts hanging loose. The center of the floor is still a pond, the buckets an archipelago across it, the perimeter ringed with towels. There isn't enough room to pace. She can't remember where she left the mop. Small chunks of plaster continue to fall, though the water is now merely dripping. Lucy's face is hot, she wants to smash windows, it's been years since she thought she might smash anything, even a beer bottle, but she could climb the fire escape and smash Martine's windows, the seven-foot ones that face south, the head-sized rounds of stained glass. Lucy's hands itch, they're wet, paint and plaster sticking to her palms. The plaster loses form when she lifts it from the floor, it's grainy and cool, pasty—she could wipe the paste on Martine's door; she pictures the broken glass, wet plaster in Martine's hair, smeared across Martine's face, pushed into her mouth, all around them the water rising and rising, the stink of wet carpet and mildew and cat. Lucy realizes she's standing in the pond of water; the fireman was right, she needs to get out.

———

She's never ridden the bike path in the dark; she knows certain spots along the way are dicey at night, near the Blackstone river, the stretch along the bridge, but in East Providence she sees only some kids drinking beer, a few cars pumping music into the night. Mostly, there's the lap of water, the sound of her breathing, the distant thud of a barge docking. She pushes faster, her calves and thighs burn, and after the long stretch in Riverside, the close, tree-lined sections, the small houses, the paved playground, there's water again, the bay, then Barrington, its lawns and houses even larger than usual, the smells changing to salt and green. She takes Middle Highway out toward the beach, past the golf course, past the graveyard. It's after eleven, and far down the beach she can see figures near a campfire, two more figures closer in, one human, one a dog. She leaves the bike beside a beached catamaran, pulls on a sweatshirt, takes off her shoes.

There's a tiny breeze off the bay. Lights from a few boats and shoreline houses. Lucy wades in seawater to her shins: it's nearly tepid, but black and impenetrable—black all the way down Narragansett Bay, and beyond, to Block Island, the Sound, Connecticut, where Charlie is. Bits of paper float on the surface, flecks of white, and below? More opaque bay, refuse from boats, fish, kelp beds, netting, horseshoe crabs, razor clams, bodies maybe. Women. Girls. Drowning victims of one sort or another. Lucy pictures them as glimmers of orange below the surface, enormous goldfish, the popeyes darting, the mouths opening as if to speak; she sees herself among them, touching their pale faces, searching out one she'll recognize. Someone who was pushed, perhaps, or someone who did herself in. One whose marriage went awry. One who went crazy and could only stare at the scramble of night stars, ignoring the house and everyone in it— the babies shipwrecked, the husband fooling with them. Then gone. Lucy imagines Roland, so pudgy and blond, suddenly laboring to breathe. Sooner or later he'll learn the truth of things, of betrayal, or maybe the little one will, the younger one, not so beautiful perhaps, not the first, not the boy, more vulnerable. Small waves lap above Lucy's knees, ripples of white in the black. There are no fish. The women are only a memory of color: light on the bay before dusk.

Lucy's throwing stones into the ocean, she doesn't know for how long. Trying to see by the moon where they land, trying to make patterns of their splashes, rows and hexagons, her own initials. She throws stones until she feels as empty as sea air, a pocket of salt and lapping sounds and nothing else. Then she notices the slight ache in her upper arms, walks back to the bike and the catamaran. She uses the daypack for a pillow, tries to sleep in the sand.

In the morning, early, there are runners, women and men in athletic shorts, a few dogs. The sky is already a hazy blue, and she can see down the bay to Jamestown bridge, a murky line in the distance. Her eyes are crusty and her ribs hurt, but the bay looks familiar again. She bikes up the hill, past the golf course—a wet, electric green—and back through the neighborhoods, along the dank-smelling river, over the narrow bridge, across the East side. Men in hardhats are filling potholes in the Red Cross lot. Lucy's building is quiet, the parking lot half-empty, George's car already gone. The hallway, more quiet: she can't even hear Roland.

In daylight the apartment looks worse than it did last night. But the gas is still working and she can make tea. The bed is dry. In the back of the bathroom closet, the mop: she hauls it into the main room, pushes it through puddles, squeezes dirty water into a blue bucket. If Charlie were here, she'd explain a few things. How other floods have occurred, the one she witnessed on the Massachusetts shore, the way the ocean rolled up the street, soaking the first floor of her family's rented house, leaving salt marks on the walls and sea objects in the yard—conch shells, milk jugs, a muffler, dead crabs she later buried. It wasn't the last vacation house, but she thinks of it that way because already she knew to wander off, already the air in the house was infected with discord, the shouts that were not yet shouts. Soon enough the family would disintegrate: insults yelled down hallways, slammed doors, cigarette smoke clinging to the bathroom towels. Money on the kitchen counter for pizza. They would be better off as fish, Lucy thinks. She'd rather be an egret.

Through the open window there's the smell of tar, coffee from next door, and Lucy leans out to watch the Red Cross guys smoothing pitch with a mechanical roller. Above them the sky is growing more white, a blue diluted with heat and haze. The sun cuts Lucy's eyes, and she retreats into the apartment. There's the insurance agent to call. The electrician. She dials the law firm, meaning to take a personal day, and, when the receptionist answers, Lucy asks for Joel. He's with a client, the receptionist says.

"Tell him," Lucy says, "I've got a family emergency. Tell him I have to quit."

"You want me to tell him that?"

Lucy pauses. The law firm's other lines are ringing, and she wonders which suit Joel is wearing. Then she remembers money.

"I have to say *that*?" the receptionist says.

She knows the receptionist is a skinny brunette named Daphne, but she pictures a nervous parrot. "Just tell him I'll be out today. Maybe tomorrow. Leave him a note." Lucy hangs up before Daphne can object to anything else.

More calls. After four tries, the landlord's line is still busy. Lucy gives up and sets the damp altars out on the fire escape to dry, then sits against the window frame, head in the shade, bare feet in the sun. Her skin is tingly and warm, the achiness diminishing. Maybe she'll return to the beach, her Wednesday set loose, maybe in time she will quit. Maybe today she'll call Charlie. The Red Cross guys tamp the new tar with shovels, and when they stop work she can hear one of them whistling. She leans forward to listen; it's a tune she knows—bits of it slowed, notes skipped here and there—but familiar. One yellow hardhat bobs across the parking lot. The notes start in the octave's middle, jump high, step down the scale, then leap from high to low and back. A piano lounge song, some kind of strut, a song that conjures men with top hats and gleaming black shoes. In the dizzy morning heat, the Red Cross guy keeps whistling a "Night Train" dense with echos of someplace else, saltier, more sweet, an unseen room, ahead, waiting.

Rubies

When Theo meets Molly, he wants to rub her ankles, to take her feet into his lap, slip off the little suede boots and run his fingers over her arches, around the bend of her heel; he wants to tongue the hollows shadowing her ankle bone, then slowly work his way up her calves. She's in the psych department staff lounge—teal jacket, gold hoop earrings the size of quarters —sitting stiff-backed beside Jeff Morgan, the lab director. Lab staff are still settling into their chairs when Jeff starts in on the new protocols, forgetting to introduce her. The assistant director clears her throat and nods in Molly's direction. Jeff stops himself. Molly shuffles papers around while Jeff slaps himself on the head and ticks off her credentials. The new postdoc. Out of Yale. Etc.

Black curls spring down her forehead as she nods to the group. Jeff waves in the general direction of the staff, lists off everyone's names, then returns to the protocols for the toddler inhibition study. The study is long-term, with follow-up after follow-up, each group of kids named after a different gem. *Sapphires*, Jeff says. *Diamonds. Pearls.* It's crazy, but Theo can't keep his eyes off those camel suede boots. After a while Molly's glancing at her feet too, tucking them closer to her chair. Theo fixes his gaze on a patch of carpet in front of Jeff. He works up some nerve and glances straight into Molly's face. He smiles. He writes the word *protocol* on his notepad. Then he writes the words *suede* and *teal* and *Yale*.

"Theo?" Jeff says. "You have enough videotape for next week?"

"Sure thing," Theo says. He writes the word *video* and draws a box around it.

It doesn't matter to him that she's a postdoc and he's only a lab assistant with a B.A. It doesn't matter to him that she's married. She's milk-colored and green-eyed, and the black curls seem a wild shock, even to her. Black Irish, she says. From her father's side of the family. Jeff Morgan has put her in charge of a group of twenty-one month olds nicknamed the Rubies, and he's assigned Theo to help. Every morning before they start work, Molly smiles at Theo and asks him whether he needs coffee. Then she stops smiling and gets down to business: the data she wants updated, the trials she wants arranged, the video schedule, the articles she needs, the supplies from Toys "R" Us. Her eyelashes flick about as she talks, the black curls spill over her words. Theo takes his cues from the subtle changes in her face, works steadily, tries to please her. After a few weeks she smiles at him more often. By then he's in love with her collarbone, which seems sculpted from balsa, at once solid and light. She likes V necks and scoop necks, and that collarbone floats above breasts as round as tennis balls.

Theo starts buying lunches for her. Innocent enough. Harvard Square is full of lunch. Takeout Chinese food and takeout Indian food. Greek salads. Turkey sandwiches. Specialty coffee. Extra large bottles of soda. At first they eat in the office or the far reaches of the cafeteria. Then they begin to have picnics on the playroom floor, her favorite spot. Most like a house, she says, the rest of the building is so antiseptic. In the playroom she forgets that she's the postdoc and he's the assistant, and why shouldn't she? He's only four years younger, and he's equally good looking. Molly hugs her knees and watches the reflections of the inflatable clowns and the big red tunnel in the double-sided wall mirror. He makes eye contact with her reflection, and sometimes she talks about her life, her lawyer husband with the dying mother, how hard things are for him, the husband, how sad, how empty he's seemed for months. How certain parts of their lives together are on hold. She doesn't actually say the word *sex*, but whenever she alludes to it, his lips become very dry. He wants to lie against her on the bright green carpet; he wants to put his tongue in her mouth. Instead, he sits very still.

Theo's careful when he talks about his own romantic disasters: he doesn't tell the whole story but confesses enough to show he's mulled over his errors, he's earnest about change. For example, what he tells about his last girlfriend. "Commitment," he says. "That was my problem. I should have paid more attention to her. I should have been more mature." He skips over the part about the girlfriend's leaving him after he drunkenly propositioned her sister—a mistake, yes, but not unforgiveable, not cause for hysteria and abandonment. He thinks this is something Molly would understand, but something she'd prefer not to. Maybe, just maybe, she'd shake her head at him and smile, as if he were a boy and she his indulgent parent, like the doting mothers of the more rambunctious toddlers.

He shakes his head. "Twenty-six is old enough to know better."

"Maybe," she says, and wipes her lips with a napkin. "But don't be so hard on yourself."

After work, when Theo runs, he feels like he's in a movie. Orange light reflects off the Charles River, a shade darker than the maples; the grass is still lush, the Harvard stretch of Memorial Drive punctuated with reds and yellows. He likes the way his muscles carry him, his speed, the pace of his breathing—everything simultaneously rapid and smooth. Sometimes he veers off from his route into the neighborhoods or down Mt. Auburn to the parklike cemetery. Sometimes he adjusts his pace to other runners, usually men, fast ones, pushing himself to pass them, but nodding and smiling at them when he does. It's the little games he likes best, the ones he makes up. How long it will take him to pass the guy in the blue shorts. How far beyond the intersection before the white Miata reaches him: the second streetlight, he thinks—and makes it. *Safe*.

In November Molly invites him over for dinner, where he meets the lawyer husband, Richard. On the living room mantle there's a color photograph of Richard and Molly in hiking gear at the top of a mountain, kissing, and a black-and-white of Richard in a zoot suit playing a trumpet. The real, sad Richard stands off to the right, pouring Theo a drink. Richard is doing his best, that much is clear: offering Theo the plate of mushroom tarts, asking him about plans for graduate school, saying Molly has spoken highly of his work. And does he play racquetball? Has he tried the Harvard courts? They should play sometime, Richard could teach him, he's patient, he says, he could really use the practice. Plus he knows a place with a view of the river where they can get a beer.

When Molly's in the kitchen clinking dishes and pans, Richard says, "Molly mentioned you've been through a bad breakup. That's tough."

"Thanks," Theo says. "It's getting easier."

"Time," Richard says. He freshens Theo's drink.

It's single malt scotch, much better than he's used to. Theo sniffs at it while he wavers about whether to mention the sick mother. He doesn't want to depress the guy. But it seems rude not to say anything, and there's no easy alternative: he knows squat about being a lawyer. Finally, he comes out with, "I heard about your mom. That's a real shame."

Richard nods and his face seems to pinken. For a moment he looks as if he might cry. Theo has no idea what to do.

"You okay?" Theo says.

Richard shrugs. "It's a heartbreaker."

They stand in the living room swishing their drinks until Molly returns and Richard kisses her on the cheek. "Here's my luck," Richard says. "Look what I've got here."

Molly hugs his scrawny waist. "I think we're ready," she says.

At dinner Molly keeps the conversation light, asking Theo about his childhood on the South Shore, asking whether he sails much, making mild psychology department jokes. *How many researchers does it take to change a lightbulb? None. Grad students do it.* Richard seems to be holding his own, but halfway through the meal he knocks over the drink he's been nursing all evening. Theo hears a gasp and glances up from his veal to see Richard's fingers in the empty air, dismay on his face. The carpet muffles the sound of shattering, but there's the ricochet of an ice cube off the woodwork and a mess of broken glass and spattered whiskey. Richard tears up and excuses himself.

"Honey," Molly says, and reaches for his hand, but already he's pivoted away from her, he's bolting into the kitchen. Now she's at the edge of her chair, her neck craned toward the kitchen door. She's ready to rise and follow him, Theo can see that's what she wants, and here's his chance to stop her. He moves before she does, bends down, and starts picking up the broken glass. "Oh, don't," Molly says, but he tells her "no problem," and she watches him. Then she turns back toward the kitchen. Theo sets the shards on an empty breadplate, places the breadplate on the buffet, and touches her arm. No, he thinks, stay.

"Have you ever been to Ireland?" he says. "You and Richard?"

Dying can take a long time. This is something Theo's known only in the abstract, but on and on the weeks stretch when Richard's mom is better or worse, eating or not eating, sick from chemo or slightly more functional. Molly smiles less often, and Theo makes it his project to get her to laugh. He boxes with the inflatable clown. He leaves her flowers. Not roses: daisies. Alstroemeria. The less intimidating, more platonic kinds. He puts them in some of the other offices as well, so it won't seem so much like seduction. In the business office the secretaries tell him he's a prince and expedite his purchase orders.

The first time he kisses her, they're in a bar. It's a timid kiss, not at all the kiss he wants to give her, but a kiss anyway. On her forehead. She leans her head back against his shoulder and closes her eyes and sighs. Contentment? Resignation? Rejection? No, not rejection, more like reprieve, or a willed forgetting. A week later, it rains miserably. It's a night when Richard is staying with his mother, and Theo offers Molly a takeout dinner at his apartment. That's when he actually does rub her ankles, when he strokes her hair and kisses her hands and then kisses her throat. Molly smells like citrus and leaves and soy sauce. She's wide-eyed but not resisting, and he feels her yielding to him. She begins touching him back, and he unbuttons her blouse, slides her pants down to her ankles, pulls off his own clothes. As he's about to enter her, he thinks of Richard, which adds a lovely sharp twist to his excitement. They make love on his living room carpet, and the pleasure is almost blinding. This is why people become kleptomaniacs, he decides. Because they like it.

For several days Molly is brighter at the office. He can see it in the way she talks to the kids, in the way she jokes with the lab director. Other staff notice and assume her mother-in-law is in remission. Theo sleeps with her two, then three more times, and each time she opens up more to him, each time he is more convinced that he is what she really wants, that Richard is, in fact, pathetic. While the psychologists are preoccupied with other trials, Theo kisses her in the office. He wants to make love to her there, on the desk, but he's afraid to ask. So he limits himself to these kisses and the gorgeous ache of wanting her all the time.

His fantasy life mushrooms. Daily, Theo pictures the different places he and Molly could make love: the playroom floor, the library stacks, her marital bed. After the fourth time they're together, the places begin to change. He thinks about Olympia, Washington. New Mexico. Spain. Places he's always wanted to visit. Cities far away from Richard. Out of nowhere a strange and reckless hope takes hold of Theo, and he finds himself reading the travel ads, scanning the *Globe* for deals to Europe. He orders brochures. He calls Hyatt Worldwide and asks for weekend prices in Montreal and D.C. He kisses Molly in the office and imagines rain descending on New York.

It's only weeks before she begins to stiffen and pull away when he kisses her, before she begins to cry spontaneously, at odd moments. He rubs her shoulders and strokes her hair. Santa Fe, he tells her, St. Lucia. Baja California. But he can't get her to stop. She's all hung up about the husband, Richard. She cries and cries about Richard's sadness, she says she's horrible, she uses the word *guilt*. Theo tries to hide his annoyance. Forget that, he wants to say. I'm here. Forget all the rest. He wants to kiss her hard. Not to comfort her, but he could pretend that too.

It shouldn't surprise him that Richard's mother actually dies. It shouldn't surprise him that Molly breaks off the affair. She does it when he's restocking the toys in the playroom. She walks in and stands too far away for him to touch. She says his name.

She says, "We have to stop."

There's a thickening in his throat, but the rest of his body feels strangely light, aluminum. This could be someone else's life. A moment filmed from the other side of the mirror.

"Is that from a movie?" he says, and she starts to cry.

"You think I don't have feelings for you," she says. "You think I'm ungrateful."

But in fact he has no thoughts. Except that he wants to push himself into her. Except that he wants her to leave. Except that she deserves to cry. He opens a package of Duplo building blocks and pours them onto the floor.

"Okay," he says.

"That's it? Okay?"

He sits on the carpet and begins to sort the Duplo blocks by color.

"You deserve better," Molly says. "You know?"

He hurls a red Duplo block past her left shoulder, his hand acting independently from the rest of his body. Molly stops crying; her mouth is an O. She leaves.

In fact, she takes a two-week leave of absence. While she's gone, the lab director tells Theo that Molly has been praising his work, he's been great with the Rubies, but they need him to code and compile data on an older group, the Diamonds.

The next weekend, Theo picks up the phone and dials an ex-girlfriend from college. It's an impulse he gets every year or two.

"Did somebody dump you?" she says.

"What?"

"Somebody dumped you, right? I'm not judging," she says, "but that's when you call me."

"I call you when I'm thinking of you."

"Who was she?"

"A woman," he says. "A psychologist."

"Not another one of those work things," she says.

He's silent and a little incensed. Over the line there's a sound like a mewing cat.

"Sorry, Theo," she says. "Really, I am."

"Well," he says. "Thanks. What about you?"

"Me? I'm fine. But I've got to put the baby down for his nap." *Baby? What baby?*

"Good luck, Theo," she says. And then she's gone.

It's May when he realizes that the women at the lab—professors, researchers, postdocs, secretaries—have stopped debating social vs. biological influences in early childhood development and instead trade facts about pregnancy. When to do it. How to do it. What to do if the standard method fails. The women talk about timing and fertility and ultrasounds. They talk about lying in bed, after, to encourage the sperm. They have these conversations in the elevators and cafeteria lines, in the hallways, in front of emeritus professors. Molly smiles and adds her two cents. Richard's been picking her up at the office lately, and sometimes he shows up early to watch the late afternoon lab trials for the Emeralds; he stands in the video room with Theo and watches through the double-sided mirror while the toddlers crawl through the wide plastic tunnel and knock down each other's block castles. Richard seems to have lost his pink rawness, his dreary needs: he grins, he claps Theo on the back and spouts about what miracles the Emeralds are. And Molly, Molly's off to the doctor every other minute, she's taken to wearing loose cotton jumpers, she carries wheat crackers with her everywhere. Often there are crumbs in her hair, crumbs on her shoulders and jacket lapels. He wants to reach over and brush them off, but now he wouldn't dare.

Theo is getting thin. Often he can't get himself to eat lunch, and his body seems flooded by speedy, percolating currents that ease up only when he runs. Molly has taken to eating lunch with the other postdocs and only speaks to him about data. She's not unkind, but she won't be in a room alone with him, and she acts as if they've never seen each other naked. You had your mouth on me, he wants to say, remember?

One day, when he's videotaping a group in the playroom, a fair, doe-eyed boy named Sam is bullied away from the Duplo blocks by an imp named Paul. Sam hurtles himself at his mother, who sits in the far corner with the other mothers, discussing day-care centers. Theo keeps the camera on Sam as he wraps himself around his mother's arm. Through the viewfinder Sam is miniature, but his desire to climb into his mother's lap is still palpable. His mother strokes his light, flyaway hair and continues her conversation with the other women. From the video room the world seems very grainy and small, claustrophobic, and more than once Theo's eyes begin to water. He refocuses the camera on the playgroup, occasionally panning over to Sam, who eventually edges back to the toys but sits alone, facing his mother, rolling a nerf ball back and forth on the carpet. When the taping session ends, the director flips on the video room lights, which are stunningly bright. It is all Theo can do to make his way home to his dark, warm couch.

He works. He runs. Alone at night, he watches movies on video. He tries not to socialize at work, and people start kidding him about being a dull boy. But the lab director compliments him, and another researcher in Boston offers him work on a study of young infants. Teaching them to swim: there's a lot they still remember about moving in fluid environments. Maybe their embryonic resemblance to seahorses is more than superficial. Theo knows the study will require dozens of safety precautions, but he pictures baby after baby slipping from the hands of reseachers, champagne bubbles rising as babies tumble to the bottom of Olympic pools and crack apart like glass as they hit the deep-end tiles. He'd have to dive for the pieces, the gemlike shards, collect them on a platter, and offer them up to one after another accusing, bewildered parent.

As summer begins, there's a new crop of undergrad work-study students at the lab, a couple of new female graduate students. He usually picks one out right away and invites her to dinner, but this time they all seem distant as stars, even when they flirt with him, even when they invite him to parties. Their features blur, and he's oddly indifferent to the way they move. He can't imagine touching any woman but Molly, and even her body is strange to him, the belly expanding farther and farther away from him.

In the late evening when he runs, his breath, too warm, blows back into his face. He thinks he hears rowers on the Charles—it's late for that, the boathouses are locked—or maybe he hears couples on the shoreline, pebbles tossed into the water. Night sounds slide around him like phantoms. Beyond the black river, Boston swells, its skyline a ragged smear, luminous and remote.

III. Jessie Stories

Girl
on a
Couch

Dawna loved the mouths of women—the fleshy and fine lips, the pink, waiting tongues, the hardness of the teeth —the sweet and sharp flavors of the body. She napped through our first weeks of college, and, alone, her desire flared. Already her taste was finely honed: she wasn't drawn to all women, or most women. Not Northern white girls—not me, for example. D.C. women. Baltimore women. Women from home, smart-mouthed black and brown girls, savvy and ambitious. In her opinion, all of Boston had only two: herself and Chantelle Jones, a sophomore poli sci major from D.C. who wore huge hooped earrings and tiny braids in cornrows. Otherwise, Boston was a wasteland, especially our campus—overrun with Irish and WASP and Jewish suburban boys drinking from kegs, white suburban girls laughing too brightly and moussing their hair in the bathrooms. Misery stalked Dawna from the moment she landed at Logan airport.

I was seventeen then, still in love with my high school English teacher, Mr. Levinson, a leather-jacketed poet for whom I'd calligraphied all of Allen Ginsberg's "Howl" in purple ink. Dawna had been watching from the hallway when, after eight hours in the car with my parents, I lugged a suitcase into my freshman dorm room, my mother behind me, repeating, "Jessie honey, just take the steam iron," my father pushing extra twenty-dollar bills into my free hand and reminding me to call his Boston friend, Saul Greenberg. Leather baggage with Dawna's name on it lay across the bed near the door; I took the bed in the corner.

My mother bent over and read the address on the garment bag. "Dawna Brown. Maryland. Hmm." She fixed her lipstick, and then we returned to the dorm's front drive, where our station wagon blinked beside five identical blinking wagons, the string of them uncertain and stunned. We unloaded the pillows, linens, and towels, the new teal comforter, the compact stereo, and the boxes of LPs. My mother smiled broadly at the other freshmen, then scouted the halls for likely Dawnas. But Dawna waited my mother out. She appeared seconds after my parents' teary and dramatic good-bye, a round-cheeked black girl in yellow jeans and a white T-shirt. I dried my face on a Kleenex and offered her a chocolate chip cookie from the tin my parents had left. She bit deeply into the cookie and told me she'd never meant to leave Baltimore. "I'd give anything to be at Hopkins," she said.

I nodded as if I understood and then began to unpack. Dawna propped a hand on her right hip and watched me, assessing my stack of peasant skirts and Laura Ashley dresses, my abalone earrings and my bottle of rose oil. She pursed her lips, dug to the bottom of one of her bags, and propped her high school prom photo on her dresser. A tall espresso-colored man rested his hands on her bare shoulders, a sky blue dress fell over the thick hills of her belly and hips, her skin a creamy brown.

"What's his name?" I said.

"Phillip."

"Are you in love?"

She stuck her finger on the glass frame, blocking out her own head.

"His teeth are nice, aren't they?" she said.

"Sure."

She shrugged and smiled shyly. "I love teeth," she confessed, as if this were the real confession. "I'm going to be a dentist."

My grandfather had been a dentist. I understood the profession as respectable and lucrative, but hardly seductive. "Teeth?"

"Let me see." She motioned for me to open my mouth. "Yours are in pretty good shape."

"Thanks," I said. "I floss and all that."

"Um hmm. I can tell."

———

Mr. Levinson had encouraged me to write poems, and when I left for college I resolved to "delve into the minefield of emotion" and pull words from my inner being. With any luck I'd compose scathing protests like Phil Ochs and sensitive confessions like Joni Mitchell. If they were good, I'd mail them to Mr. Levinson. His first name was Joshua, a name I found so breathy and beautiful I made it my mantra and etched "JL" on bathroom walls. I was determined to dazzle him. The day before classes started, while Dawna went off to Minority Students Day, I smoked a joint and wrote about the alienation of the soul (wild pastures of smoke, the silent landscape barbed and ungiving); later, more stoned, metaphors of the body (hands as scattered birds, bodies like rivers stretching to sea). I compared nipples to hard candies and shocked myself, then hid my writing journal under the mattress and wandered down the hall to the vending machines. After ten minutes of deliberation I bought a root beer and a Hershey bar.

Outside, the sun seemed unusually bright, and the quad filled with Frisbee players listening to the Grateful Dead blare from a dorm window. I strolled across campus sniffing the air, my body as light as styrofoam. On the library's landscaped roof, I wedged my legs into a lotus position and gazed over the city of Boston, pretending to be a Buddhist, pretending not to be a virgin.

When I got back to the dorm, our room smelled of floral Glade.

Dawna had left the blue Glade can on my dresser beside my ear-ring tree, along with a note. *Can't you smoke those drugs some-place else?* With my gold calligraphy pen I wrote back, *Really sorry. It won't happen again.* I bought another Hershey bar from the vending machine and left it on her pillow, wrapped in my apology. After that I smoked in the stairwell or down the hall with our neighbor Roz.

If only Roz were my roommate, I thought. She'd grown up in Ann Arbor during the height of the antiwar movement; she had an older brother who was a draft dodger, and she owned the full Joni Mitchell catalogue. Roz had published half a dozen poems in her high school literary magazine, and I thought she was utterly beautiful: long chestnut hair streaked with amber, Irish-fair skin, plush lips, blue eyes hinting of gray. Immediately after I met her, I wondered what she looked like naked. A couple of weeks into school, I shyly admitted to her that I was a virgin.

"Me too," she said. We shook our heads and stared at her room's beige linoleum. "It's a real burden sometimes."

"Like weights around your ankles," I said.

"Constant." Roz cued up a Janis Joplin LP and started rolling a joint on the album cover. "I came pretty close to losing it last spring," she said. She licked the paper and threw me a knowing glance. "God, did I ever come close."

I didn't know whether Dawna was a virgin, but I certainly wasn't going to ask. Later that night, I stood in front of her prom photo and studied the position of her prom date's hands. Touch-ing her shoulders seemed less proprietary than touching her waist, but he was a head taller than she, and the shoulders might be more comfortable for him.

"You breathing all over my picture?" Dawna said.

"He's good looking," I said.

She spat out a short laugh.

"What did you say his name was?"

"Phillip."

I tried to picture Phillip out of his tux. I'd never seen a black man naked. In fact, I hadn't seen any man naked, except for my brother, and he didn't count. I hadn't seen Dawna naked either: she was always careful not to dress in front of me. I wondered what color her nipples were—plum, maybe. Outside the showers I'd glimpsed Roz's: pale pink against floury white skin. Mine were a kind of medium pink, which seemed okay, but my breasts were too big for the spaghetti strap camisoles that were in style. Most of the time, I wore embroidered smocks and underwire bras and prayed nothing bobbed too much when I ran.

"Do you miss him?" I said.

"Baltimore," she said, "that's what I miss."

"Aren't you going home for Thanksgiving?"

"Yeah." She shrugged.

"But you want to be there now."

"I want to be there yesterday," Dawna said.

She wasn't going to change her mind. I knew by the set of her chin, the daily calls to Maryland. I knew by the way she ignored our room's stark walls and ugly floor, taping photos of women from *Ebony* and mouth shots of celebrities to her closet door and leaving the rest bare. I held up posters I'd bought at the Harvard Coop, cheap Van Gogh reproductions, and asked her what she thought. "I don't care," Dawna said. "Do what you like." Those first weeks of classes I'd return to the dorm in the afternoon to find the shades drawn, the lights out, Dawna in a T-shirt and underwear, her legs tangled in dark orange sheets, a pillow over her head. I'd drop off my books and sit on the quad, visit Roz, read in the stairwell. Eventually, Dawna would wake and play her Gino Vanelli album on my stereo, two sides of cloying, breathy seduction, simple lyrics punctuated with moans and sighs. At 6:00 Dawna and Roz and I would walk over to the dining hall together. Then Dawna would tell me about her classes and her phone calls from home. But once we were through the cafeteria line, she'd peel off and head for the group of black students at the third table, while Roz and I crossed the room to find the other people from our hall, somewhere in the sea of white.

A month into school, Dawna's naps subsided. I saw her across the dining hall at the black students' table, animated, laughing.

She spent most of her time with Chantelle and with a man named Tyrone, who studied with her in our room. Tyrone had beautiful muscles and wore shirts unbuttoned to midchest. His skin was the color of walnuts, his features full and broad. He never smiled at me. While he studied, he repeatedly groomed his hair with a pic and rocked his chair onto its back legs. His slightly acrid musk filled our room and hung in the air for an hour or two after he left: often I fell asleep to Tyrone's peculiar scent.

I don't know how many times I returned from dinner to find Tyrone already at my desk, his books and papers spread, my work pushed to the side in a single, undifferentiated stack. Dawna would be at her own desk, poring over chemistry. Hello, I'd say. Dawna would glance up and nod. Tyrone would nod. Then he'd lean the desk chair onto its back legs, touch his hair, stare intently at his notes. He never offered to move or leave. At first I tried to work on my bed, using *Art through the Ages* as a writing surface. But I couldn't think with Tyrone in the room. I'd steal glances at my desk, at Tyrone chewing gum and reading, Tyrone chewing gum and drawing charts in his notebook. I'd toss my books into my backpack and trudge over to the library. Usually by the time I returned he was gone.

After a few of these nights I began to worry about my things. The glass egg paperweight, the shells I'd collected on Cape Cod, the photos of my family displayed on my desk. Tyrone was probably touching them. I felt a strange shiver when I thought of his fingers on the surface of the egg, pictured him leafing through the unfinished letters to Joshua I'd stashed in my drawer. I'd been careful to hide my writing journal in an underbed storage box, my bag of pot in a sock in my dresser drawer, but if Dawna left the room, wouldn't he look?

Of course, when I returned for the night, my family photos were still intact, the shells were where I'd left them, the paperweight untouched. Sometimes gum wrappers littered the floor near the trash basket. I was mortified by my own suspicions. *Racist.* The next time I'd find Tyrone at my desk, I'd nod, quietly leave, and later wonder where I'd left my mail.

Before midterms student couples began to appear every-where, practically throwing themselves in my path. They were kissing in the student lounge, kissing in front of the library, kiss-ing at the doors of classrooms. Men's hands were sliding around women's waists, down over buttocks and hips, women were throwing their arms around men's shoulders, pushing groins against groins. People hugged in the middle of campus and fell on each other in the pub. I languished on the sidelines with the shy, the awkward, and the closeted girls.

I tried harder to be friends with the men on my floor, concen-trating on the crew of juniors who lived in the apartment at the top of my hall: it hadn't yet occurred to me that if they were as cool as they acted they wouldn't be living on campus. The friend-liest of them was a gangly engineer named Aaron. He liked to wander around in tight jeans and no shirt, crumple up Miller cans and try to make "baskets" in the trash can. A heavy-lidded euphoria overtook him when he sang along to Springsteen, and he developed a habit of touching my shoulder whenever he passed me in the hall. Aaron's roommates were an unlikely mix: Larry, a unicycle fanatic who told fart jokes; Greg, a depressed Russian Studies major; and Paul, a sweet Boston Catholic who spent every waking hour with his girlfriend. Other than the ju-niors, only a couple of sophomore men lived on our hall, and Roz had already snapped up the good one, a dewy-eyed artist named Dan. Dan's roommate, Charles, occasionally grinned at me, but everyone knew he wrote short stories from the point of view of rapists.

The fifth week of school, I met and made out with a small-time drug dealer named Tom King, a cocky blond who'd rigged up black lights in his room and blasted Led Zepplin across the quad. "Let's do it," he said to me in the middle of "Stairway to Heaven." My eyes snapped open: I hadn't even decided to like him yet. His breath smelled of beer and Doritos and his eyes were lizardlike slits. Pot smoke clung to both of us. I sat up carefully and feigned interest in the way the black light illuminated the fake stars he'd stuck to the ceiling. "Don't you think it's premature?" I said.

"That's a good one." Without warning he swept his legs over

the side of the bed, stood, and reached for a bottle of Visine. He winced as the drops seeped into each dull blue eye, then ran his fingers through his hair and surveyed himself in the mirror. "I haven't heard that one before." He opened the door, stuck his hands in his pockets, and smirked.

I returned to my dorm and wrote bad elegies in the stairwell. The next day, I saw him in the student center, palming the ass of a French girl named Monique.

That evening at the bathroom sinks, I told Roz about Tom King. She was combing brown mascara into her lashes, rubbing gel blush into her cheeks.

"Don't worry," she said. "You'll find someone better."

"I will?"

"Jessie, of course you will." She crouched to see whether anyone was in the stalls, then straightened and leaned toward me. I was hit with a wave of patchouli. Her teeth seemed remarkably white. "I have to tell you," she said. "I did it. With Dan."

"Roz, that's great."

"He used the L word."

"Wow."

"Yeah," Roz said, her voice sleepy-sweet. She hugged me, which she had never done before. Afterward, she patted my face.

"He's a great guy," I said. "Really great."

"Isn't he?"

When Roz left to meet Dan, my motivation evaporated. I was struck with an impulse to nap: I wanted to climb into bed and conjure up Joshua. Imagine him pining for me. Imagine him sending his leather jacket to me, a note in the pocket asking me to wait. Imagine him rushing to Boston to find me, passionately kissing me outside my art history lecture, on the library roof, by the vending machines. Imagine him insisting we take a cab into the city, where he'd booked a hotel suite.

I shuffled back to my room, where Tyrone was tapping out a drum solo on my desk.

"I need to sit there now," I told him.

"I thought you'd be at the library," Dawna said.

"It was noisy."

"Did you try the carrels? Always sounds like death in the carrels."

"They were full."

"They're never full."

"Well this time they were. I need to work here. I need my desk." Dawna made a sucking sound. "Shit."

Tyrone shrugged and moved onto Dawna's bed: he lay across it, his legs longer than I'd remembered, the arch of his neck more distinct. Dawna stared at me while I settled in at my desk. I opened my notes to the section on High Renaissance: da Vinci's *Virgin of the Rocks*—figures in a pyramid; Michelangelo's nude *David*—muscular body, tightened sinews. I switched to architecture: Bramante. *Tempietto*, round, domed "little temple," pagan influence. I heard a rustling sound from the bed, Tyrone clearing his throat, sighs punctuating Dawna's breathing. I flipped ahead to Bronzino, pictured Tyrone's hand traveling the span of his chest, downward, resting over his crotch. Listened for Dawna's breathing to intensify. *Venus, Cupid, Folly and Time*—1546. Attention to heads, hands, and feet. Cupid fondles Venus. On purpose I dropped my highlighter. When I glanced around, Tyrone was turning pages in his notebook, scratching notes in with his pen. At her desk, Dawna was nodding off into her lab report. She woke up frowning.

———————

Tyrone was not in love with Dawna, that much was clear. I'd seen him in the dining hall, his hands gliding over a fawnlike girl named Coco. And although Dawna had plenty of longing, it was hard to believe she longed for Tyrone. They didn't exchange dopey looks. They didn't kiss. They didn't so much as touch each other's hands when I was anywhere nearby. Night and day, Phillip gazed out from the prom photo.

One afternoon at the soda machine, Charles, the creepy sophomore, pulled me aside. "Wasn't that Chantelle Jones I saw at your door yesterday?"

"Probably," I said. "She's friends with Dawna."

"She's a dyke," Charles said.

"She seems pretty nice."

"You *do* know what a dyke is," Charles said.

"Yeah." Like Sappho, I thought. I just wasn't sure whether or not you could wear dresses.

"I'd watch out if I were you."

"Why?"

He snorted a laugh and shook his head at me. "Freshman girls," he said, "are really dumb."

"Excuse me." I turned and started back to my room.

"Sure thing," he said. "Just let me know what happens."

As if she'd heard us, Dawna soon began to linger with Tyrone in the hallways. They took more study breaks, and sometimes I'd see them down at the vending machines, pooling their change for candy.

In early November I stopped writing to Joshua. I'd only actually mailed two postcards, one from Faneuil Hall and one a blank, gray-toned card labeled "Cambridge in the Fog." I hadn't heard back. I was working on papers about the silliness of Fragonard and the spiritual divisions in *Wuthering Heights*. What Heathcliff really needed was a little understanding, I thought, but my T.A. kept calling him a puppy killer; admitting sympathy would sink me.

Wednesday night the library was choked with students. In a basement carrel I wrote:

> In Brontë's *Wuthering Heights,* fragments of self reside in each character: wholeness cannot be attained individually, only through union, yet among the living, union is *tragically impossible.*

I made a list of character limitations and tragic impossibilities, beginning with Heathcliff and Cathy, and ending up with Joshua. Then I alternately wrote paragraphs and added to the desk graffiti, scratching in *Ginsberg lives!* and, wherever I found it, changing the word "dick" to "Dickens." I managed to eke out a few pages before 10:00, when I left for the dorm.

Beyond the library doors a few bohemian sophomores huddled

with cigarettes. The first real cold snap had set in and the air smelled of snow. Wind swept the upper campus and the desolate hillside lawns, and my footsteps seemed like tiny earthquakes. But as I crossed the residential quad, I could hear club music, disco, which grew louder as I approached my side of the dorm. Christmas lights flashed on and off in my dorm window. The room was noisy and dim and filled with Dawna's friends. Tyrone again. That morning, Dawna had said, "Tyrone's birthday." Not "birthday *party*." Not "celebration." Definitely not "soiree." She'd said, "You're working at the library later, right?"

I peered in from the hallway. Paper plates with half-eaten slices of cake lay on the dresser, the stereo speakers, the desks. Everyone was drinking cheap champagne, and in the cramped space between Dawna's bed and my desk, Tyrone and Coco danced pressed together, eyes closed. Men I'd never seen before were stretched out on my bed, tossing my stuffed bear back and forth. A song ended and Chantelle cued up another album.

I walked on past Roz's room, which had a hotel "Do Not Disturb" sign hanging on the doorknob. In the stairwell I opened my backpack and pulled out my Fragonard notes. Decadence, I'd written. Rococo = materialistic excess. Goofy fantasy. Woman on a swing = stupidity in love. This was as far as I'd gotten, noting nothing about composition, color, line, technique. *She's a very freaky girl* beat through the fire door. No one, not even the R.A., would interrupt a party before 11:00.

After ten minutes I left the stairwell and began to pace the hall, pivoting at Roz's room and retracing my steps. *One one thousand two one thousand three one thousand.* I pushed the stairwell door open again, ate several breath mints, climbed up two flights, and descended. Then I tried the hall again. Someone had kicked my room door wide open, and the hall was flooded with infectious syncopated rhythms, Cheryl Lynn singing "To Be Real." I caught myself pacing to the music, then ducked into the women's bathroom and covered my ears. My neck pulsed, but my face had gone fish white, and the wind had tangled my hair into dirty blond clumps. I sat on the floor, breathing the way my cousin Sandy did for her Lamaze class. Finally, I reentered the hall and approached my room. The air was hot, redolent of jasmine perfume, sweat, spilled champagne. Tyrone and Coco strutted and shook, Chantelle danced by herself, and everyone else was swaying in place.

"Hey," I said. "Excuse me." I pushed past the dancing couple to my bed, which was still packed with Dawna's friends. I threw my bag between two of the men.

"Hi Dawna," I said.

She gave me a once-over. "Tyrone's birthday," she said.

"Uh huh," I said. "Happy Birthday, Tyrone."

He nodded at me. Coco swiveled to get a look, then turned away.

"Well." My hands were trembling. "You all going out?"

"Jessie—" Chantelle waved in the direction of the cake.

"I don't know," Dawna said.

I faked a yawn. "It's Wednesday."

"Yeah," Dawna said.

"I have an 8:30 tomorrow."

"Mmm hmm," Dawna said, pouring herself more champagne.

Finally, I said, "Why don't you go to Tyrone's room?"

"Don't you see a party here?" Dawna said.

"I see my bed," I told her.

"Do I usually have parties?"

"How would I know? But I've got two papers due. I've got an 8:30."

"Those papers aren't due tomorrow," Dawna said.

"I didn't say they were."

Conversations around us flagged. Dawna shrugged and stepped away from me. "Tyrone," she said, "you running low on champagne?"

By then I was too agitated to think. I reached for the light switch and flicked it on, then pushed down the volume on the stereo. In the sudden hush my voice was distorted and loud. "I'm going to sleep," I said. "Nice to see you all."

"Here?" Coco said.

Then Dawna pinched my upper arm. "Jessie, why don't you take yourself down to see Roz?"

"You mean Roz and Dan?"

"Did you hear me say it's Tyrone's birthday?"

"Happy Birthday," I repeated.

"We're having a party here," Dawna said.

"And now you can have it somewhere else."

"Bitch." Dawna pushed her way to the stereo and upped the volume again. "Somebody hit that light."

But no one else moved. I leaned down and snapped the music off; while my hand was on the dial, Dawna smacked my fingers.

"Hey," Chantelle said. She murmured into Dawna's ear, then announced, "Time for a stroll down the hall. Tyrone, why don't you take Dawna down to those machines? Get some candy."

Tyrone glared at her and tapped his foot, his left arm wrapped around Coco.

"Tyrone, are you deaf?" Chantelle said. "I want some candy." She dug silver out of her pocket. "Would you get me M&Ms? Plain."

Tyrone relinquished Coco and transferred his hand to Dawna's shoulder, guiding her toward the door. As she walked out, her hand swept over the left side of my desk, knocking my shells and photographs to the floor. In the near hallway she yelled, "That bitch," and further away she yelled again. The second shout sounded more like *JAP bitch*.

The lounging men stood up; everyone was hushed, staring at me.

"I'm really tired," I said. I retreated to the corner, where I sat at the end of my bed, pulled my knees up, and tucked my head down, so the crowd was invisible to me, a collection of sounds. "Damn," a man's voice said. I heard murmurs in low and high registers, Chantelle's voice saying, "Let's go now," the shuffling of feet, the door closing.

I picked up my shells, unplugged the blinking Christmas lights, and undressed, leaving my blue peasant skirt and cardigan roped over my chair, my tights in a scrunched pile on the floor. I pulled a flannel nightgown on, turned off the lights, and slipped into bed, where I curled into a fetal tuck and stared at the door. Dawna did not come back that night.

For the next three days we didn't speak. Most of the time, I was out of the room, but when we were there together, we made no eye contact, played no music, spoke on the phone as little as possible, left quickly. In the mornings I dressed and hurried off while she was asleep. Some of the women on the hall commiserated with me, but most people said nothing. I approached my anemic R.A. and requested an immediate room change.

"I've been telling Dawna all semester," she said, "there's nowhere to go until January. Race is not an emergency."

By the weekend my *Wuthering Heights* paper had stalled over Brontë's representation of Cathy-as-ghost. I spent Saturday afternoon in the library brooding and trying to write a sestina using the end words *blue, stop, heart, ghost, dream,* and *abyss.* After an hour I changed *abyss* to *night.*

Late on Saturday, the juniors in the apartment down the hall had a party. Bring some friends, they'd said. Bring Roz. But Roz and Dan had disappeared for a Hyatt Holiday Weekend and didn't much like the juniors anyway. I showed up alone, with a box of Mystic Mints cookies and a couple of joints. Aaron ushered me in but stopped in his tracks to play air guitar to the Cars song on the stereo, squeezing his eyes shut at the solo. When he returned to normal, he yelled to his roommates, "Little Jessie's here." I handed him the box of cookies and decided to keep the joints to myself.

"Hey, Jessie." "Come on in, Jessie." "This is *Jessie,*" the juniors shouted. I couldn't tell whether or not they were making fun of me. I'd worn a pair of jeans and a Mexican embroidered shirt, and most of the other women were in tight sweaters, pearl earrings, and lots of eyeshadow. Almost all of them were upperclassmen.

"Jessie, have some punch," Aaron said.

"I only drink wine," I said. "What's in it?"

"Wine," Larry said.

"Port wine," Aaron said, "and juice and soda."

"Sort of like Sangria?"

"Exactly."

It tasted like orange Hi-C. I drank two glasses in the first twenty minutes, while I eavesdropped and tried to be invisible. Eventually, the punch took hold, and I asked a couple of crew-cut juniors where they were from. They sized me up and smirked. "Mars," one of them said, elbowing his friend.

I narrowed my eyes, then glanced beyond them, the way I'd practiced. "I would have guessed Pluto," I said.

After that they were nicer to me. One of them even asked me to dance, but Aaron cut in. He wanted to do the Bump, which even I knew was passé. I went along with it, but he crashed against me with such force I tripped into other couples. "Sorry," I said. "Whoa. Really sorry."

"I'm worn out," I told Aaron. "I have to catch my breath."

"Fine." He steered me into the kitchen and ladled me another cup of punch.

I'd lost count of my drinks when standing began to feel awkward and difficult, when in fact I began to tip. I shored myself up with the cinder block wall and confessed to one junior after another that I had no major.

A redhead in an Izod golf shirt told me he thought art history was "almost as bad as English." He told me he liked some of the nudes, then winked. "What's the famous one?" he said. "The girl on a couch."

"Ingres?" I said. "Manet? Gauguin?"

"She's naked and she's lying on a couch. You know the one."

"I'd like to sit down," I said. "Do these guys own chairs?"

The living room was beginning to vibrate. Aerosmith's raucous "Walk This Way" poured out of the stereo, and all the drunk junior men were jumping in place, playing air guitar, and spilling punch on themselves. The woman standing next to me was squealing, and someone passed a bottle of Jack Daniels. Patches of sweat formed on my blouse, everything had tilted, and my tongue became sluggish and strange. *Bed*, I thought. I pushed myself up and gazed at the door.

"Come on, Jessie," Aaron tugged at my sleeve. "Dance with me."

"Need to go," I said. I waved in the direction of the bathroom, so he'd stop tugging. Dancers crammed the living room and bystanders choked the entryway. I stumbled into them, ducked between them, finally shoved my way into the dorm hall, the floor of which was slanting badly. Aaron was right behind me.

"Where you going?" he said.

"Taking a break." The edges of Aaron wavered and blurred. My balance disintegrated and I reached for a wall.

"It's early." His left hand gripped my shoulder, and he began to twirl my hair around his right index finger. "I don't want you to go," he said. Then he pushed his face against mine and stuck his tongue in my mouth.

I wriggled, and Aaron locked his arms around me. I tried to lower my chin, but he reached down with his left hand, tilted my face back up toward his. "I don't—" I said. "I feel sick." He kissed me again and shoved a hand against my breast. All this in the middle of the hallway.

I shook my head. I started to cry. People were walking past us, most of them drunk, most of them ignoring us. I don't know how long Aaron pinned me there, but it could only have been a minute or two before Dawna showed up, blurry looking and stern. She poked at Aaron. "What is it you think you're doing?"

He ignored her.

"Hey." She shoved him hard, loosening his grip on me. "You see she's crying? You blind?"

"Fuck off," Aaron said.

"I don't think so," Dawna said. "Jessie, you want him gone?"

"Dizzy," I said. I covered my mouth with my hand.

"Lord," Dawna said. In one move she kicked Aaron in the shins and pulled me away from him, dragging me fast down the hall to the women's bathroom. Then I was kneeling in the bathroom stall, Dawna pulling my hair back from my face and tying it with her watch. I was sick almost immediately.

I stayed in the stall for hours, vomiting and crying, dozing off, waking to be sick again. The light fell in tiny needles, and I envisioned my life in the coming years, a sorry Toulouse-Lautrec painting, lurid orange and mustard and green. I'd end up on stupid dates with men who didn't know who Allen Ginsberg was and would call him a faggot if they did. Joshua would never love me and no one else would either. I'd fail art history, live in hovels, lose my teeth. White people would either avoid me or pat my hand, and black people would disdain me for my foolishness and white-girl blinders, for being inept and for being in the way.

Dawna and Chantelle took turns visiting me in the bathroom, bringing me towels and washcloths. At three in the morning, I sobbed to them that I might as well be dead like Cathy in *Wuthering Heights*.

"Cathy who?" Dawna said.

"It's that novel she's reading," Chantelle said, "some character."

"An imaginary dead girl?" Dawna said to me. "You're going nowhere with that."

"Nowhere," I nodded. "The abyss."

At 5 A.M., I showered and went to bed. At ten, Dawna brought me tea and a bagel.

"What were you thinking?" she said. "Just looking at that Aaron makes my skin crawl."

I felt as if my brain had been sucked out of my head. "Yes," I said.

"Have another sip of that tea." She waited for me to drink. "Listen, I shouldn't have slapped you and all that."

"Thanks for helping me out last night," I said.

She turned away and thumbed her notebook. "Eat some of that bagel. The trash basket's right there, just in case."

I spent the entire day in bed, the room dimmed, Dawna bringing me more tea and toast. Roz made copies of all my reserve readings, which I studied in near darkness. In the evening Dawna and Chantelle talked me into eating the wonton soup and steamed rice they'd ordered with their Chinese takeout. Queen of Sheba, Chantelle called me, and handed me a spoon.

That week, Dawna's prom photo disappeared. So did Tyrone. I started leaving little notes, asking Dawna to tell me if she needed the room to herself. She wrote back saying no, she didn't, but that she'd get epilepsy if I played Dylan's *Blonde on Blonde* one more time. Later, she made me swear to steer clear of "those slimy fool juniors," and I started buying us boxes of Mystic Mints. Such was our truce.

In early December I returned from class at sunset—purplish red seeping through tree limbs, the city capped with indigo. I tried to breathe it in. It was the sleep-deprived time of the semester: during my paper writing, I'd altered the graffiti on half the carrels in the library. Dawna had been rushing between study groups and trying to catch up on labs, and I could see from the quad that our room was dark.

When I walked in, Dawna's sheet covered most of her body and most of Chantelle's, but they were jumbled together, angles and curves and slopes, their clothes strewn about the floor. They peered out from the bed, eyes squinting in the sudden light, their movements frozen. I wanted to disappear. I wanted to stare. I didn't know where to look, and my gaze jumped from point to point around the room: floor, elbow, desk, eyelids, ceiling, knees.

"Leaving now," I said. "Going." I flicked the light switch off and spun around, careening into the door before I finally lurched out into the hallway. After I pulled the door shut, I paused, stuporous, in the empty corridor. My forehead stung. I wondered if Roz had any pot. I wondered if I should buy cigarettes or learn to drink martinis.

The last dregs of orange melted into the horizon as I trudged to the dining hall. From the quad I could see my room window, lightless and blank. What *exactly* were they doing? I knew hands were crucial. Mouths and tongues were heavily involved. I pictured a hand on a breast, fingers traveling over pubic hair, tongues on tongues, tongues on skin, but at that point my head seemed too light and the bruise on my temple had started to throb. A thin moon was rising over the dining hall. I wobbled into the main cafeteria; for a few minutes the buzz and clatter distracted me, but then I was scanning the black students' table for Dawna's friends, wondering what they knew. A strange sadness caught in my ribs and I couldn't eat my dinner. I drank sugary tea and left without saying hello to anyone.

Much later, I returned to the room, to Dawna in her jeans and T-shirt, swearing at her chemistry text. The bed had been made; the floor, cleared. Chantelle sat cross-legged on Dawna's quilt, fully dressed, reading about revolutions. I settled down to work at my desk. At 11:00 we opened a box of Mystic Mints. At 12:00 Chantelle left, wishing me good night, then kissing Dawna on the lips.

I never walked in on Dawna and Chantelle again, nor did they flaunt their romance. But now and then Dawna let information drop. That Chantelle's hands were always warm. That when Chantelle smoked a cigarette, Dawna could taste it for hours. That after sex they would spoon and suck M&Ms. That she found Chantelle's mouth beautiful. Men, she said, had never interested her, but she'd tried them anyway. She'd end up wanting their sisters and ex-girlfriends. Being with men just made her lonely and regretful. Me too, I told her, and admitted to the sadness that seized me almost daily.

Just before Christmas, Dawna and I withdrew our room change requests. Second semester, we fell into ordinary routines. I studied Eliot and Pound, read trashy romance novels, and fantasized about Warren Beatty. On weekend nights when Dawna was out, I opened the windows and smoked pot, then danced alone to reggae. Dawna rarely napped and rarely brooded. Often she would disappear with Chantelle, and often Chantelle would read in our room, lying with Dawna on her bed. They touched each other's faces. They touched each other's fingers. Hands rested on thighs. They gave each other small kisses, then returned to their books. Once in a while I'd leave for the stairwell. Once in a while they'd ask me to dinner.

When the weather improved, Dawna began to peer through our window at the residential quad and point to men.

"What about him?" she said to me. "You want that one?"

"Have you got eyes?" Chantelle said. "That's a man with a boyfriend."

"Him?"

"Um hmm."

"What about the blond in the flannel shirt?" She pointed to a beautiful senior from the Mountain Club.

I shrugged.

"No? Jessie, you just wait. We'll find the perfect one."

That summer, I waitressed on Nantucket and wrote poems about the sea. I dated a hapless film student named Kenneth, learned to drink coffee, and stopped being a virgin. When I returned for sophomore year, Roz and I took an apartment off-campus. Dawna was gone, Chantelle was gone, both of them transferred South. I soon fell in with a crowd of artsy leftists, and I didn't think about Dawna much, barely at all really. In the years that followed, I went through a string of boyfriends, off-beat men from monied families. I finished college, took a job in a bookstore, and talked deconstruction at potluck dinners. During one of those dinners, a smart-mouthed woman named Sarah asked me out for drinks. I'd been watching the low-key slink of her hips, her elegant mouth. The old lightheadedness returned: I knew what she meant. Sure, I said, and gave her my number. For days I pushed my dizziness aside, but an hour before my date with her I panicked first about perfume and sweaters, then about earrings and shoes. The spasm of anxiety lasted twenty minutes, after which I collapsed on my couch and waited for the doorbell. My skin had gone clammy and my ribs ached. It was then, as evening crept in, that I found myself missing Dawna, wondering where on earth she'd gone, wishing she would reappear and explain myself to me.

Strays

Between spring exams her second year of college, Jessie sprawled on the chapel steps and wrote in her journal: *I flail in the vacuum, I stumble in the maze, led astray by false prophets.* It was 1981, a year of minor chaos. All across campus, forsythia blazed and blossoms of dogwood peeled open. There ought to be a metaphor for this, Jessie thought, so much anxiety, so many flowers, but she couldn't get past the maze image. She lighted a cigarette and wrote the word *maladjusted*, a term she'd been using to describe herself ever since last semester's intro to psych. College was overrated, she thought. It meant nothing if you didn't know yourself. Even her better-adjusted roommate said so.

From a pay phone in the union she called her mother in Buffalo collect. "I'm a blank page," she told her mother, Elaine. "An empty shell."

"Honey, is it protein? You haven't given up fish too, have you?"

"No."

"Well what do you mean, blank page?"

"I have no history."

"Oh. You'll feel better after that Russian final. You know, your grandfather was born in Russia. Isn't that history?"

"Mom, I have to find myself."

"Again?"

"I mean it. My roommate, Roz, thinks so too."

"Roz is a lovely girl," Elaine said. "But since when did she become the fountain of truth?"

"Fountain of truth? You mean like the fountain of youth?"

"Whatever," Elaine said.

"I want to find myself," Jessie said. "I want to find America." Just like Simon and Garfunkel in the sixties, she thought. Just like Dylan.

Silence. And then, "Jessie, honey, what is it you're saying?"

"I'm going to San Francisco," Jessie said, surprising herself. To sound as if she had an actual plan, she added, "I'm taking a bus."

"You can't be serious."

"I've always dreamed of going there, always," Jessie said. "I promise I'll write." She mumbled a fast "I love you" and hung up the phone.

The bit about the dream was half-true. For weeks she'd seen flyers for the Rainbow Turtle bus line: Explore America! Boston–California! Eight days $199. She'd called the 800 number and noted the mailing address in San Francisco. Land of cable cars. Jessie pictured a gleaming gold-and-green one, bobbing up over hilltops, the cobalt bay in the distance, women in sandals and men with goatees waving from cafes, swilling cappuccino and jotting frenzied poems on napkins and restaurant checks. Late at night, all the radio stations would play jazz; during the afternoons, the Grateful Dead. The air would smell of ocean, hibiscus, Chinese dumplings, marijuana. She could visit Abby Rosenberg, her best friend from high school, who had moved to Haight Street and become a bohemian.

Unfortunately, Abby was unpopular with Jessie's mother, owing to a lack of discretion with drugs. Junior year, Abby had suffered chronic red-eye, and once, after taking acid, she'd been sick on Jessie's carpet. They'd sampled the bourbon, Jessie told her mother, *Abby's a lightweight*. But Elaine remained skeptical and suggested that Jessie spend time with Naomi Block, a girl more awkward and less popular than Jessie herself, and, worse, impervious to poetry. Still, both Jessie's and Abby's families belonged to the same temple, and the mothers had graduated from high school together—that counted for something.

The evening of Jessie's announcement, her father called and made her promise not to board a bus before they'd talked this thing out, and certainly not before exams ended. In return, he said, he'd call the Rosenbergs.

"I'm not asking permission, Dad," Jessie said. "I'm nineteen now. I'm legal."

He sighed on the other end of the phone and waited until she got nervous and relented.

Two days later, Jessie's mother phoned to say she would mail extra money for traveler's checks and a return airline ticket to Boston, along with a list of their friends in the Midwest and California, just in case. Also, to announce that she and Dad would be visiting San Francisco themselves.

"At the end of July," Elaine said. "We'll meet you there. We'll see the sights."

"This isn't fair," Jessie said.

"We can eat at Fisherman's Wharf. We'll visit Alcatraz."

Jessie spent June announcing her plans to Boston friends and speculating that she might never return. It was nearly July when she belted herself into her backpack and rode the subway to South Station to board the Turtle bus. The train jerked and creaked, a tinny, empty string of pods. A few other people lugged suitcases. Jessie adjusted a shoulder strap and pretended to be from Canada: she tried to project ennui, as if she'd been traveling for months. Before her stop, a man in running shorts pushed past her from behind, tipping the backpack and setting her off-balance.

Outside South Station, the Turtle drivers were already loading the bus, which was painted in rainbow-colored stripes, with an amateurish picture of a turtle sprawled across the side panel. Hippies. Jessie was suddenly conscious of how new her jeans were. She couldn't pass for one of them, even if she wiped off her lip gloss. The skinny, redheaded driver walked around with a clipboard and a cup of coffee: on top of the bus, a dark-haired one roped down luggage. After a few minutes, she announced herself to the redhead. He wore a braid all the way down his back, a beard, and a gold hoop earring. He nodded and smiled and heaved her backpack up on top of the bus. Then he moved on to the next piece of luggage. Jessie paced the sidewalk and stared at the trains until the driver on top of the bus called, "You've got a half-hour. You might as well get coffee."

She waved and started walking toward the station, stopping a few paces down to light a cigarette. She inhaled and exhaled dramatically.

Inside the Turtle all the seats had been replaced with wide platforms, foam mats, India print covers. A loft hung in the rear, a refrigerator nestled up front. Stereo speakers dangled off the walls, and the air smelled of sandalwood incense, diesel, old coffee. There was no bathroom. Next to the driver's seat, in front of the yellow line, sat a beat-up folding chair. Jessie chose a spot on the front right platform, a couple of yards from the door, arranged her coffee and donut, and opened her copy of *The Awakening*. She sat cross-legged and glanced up from the novel's first page as other passengers began to board. Most of them looked like college students. Two women spoke rapid French. There was a bodybuilder in his midtwenties, and a ponytailed woman from a mall boutique: manicured hot pink nails, khaki shorts, a hot pink Izod shirt. A trio of scruffy college boys walked by, and behind them a loud, black-clad Brit, about Jessie's age, who claimed he'd hitched all over the U.S. A couple of women with asymmetrical haircuts held hands and didn't speak to anyone else; a green-haired girl smirked at them. Finally, Jessie noticed a skinny adolescent boy, alone, his hair almost white blond. Twelve, maybe thirteen years old—the same age as her sister. He looked as if he should be drinking Slurpees and riding bikes, but he carried himself like a veteran passenger.

The redheaded driver introduced himself as Kurt. Rules of the Road, he said. Respect other people. Respect other people's things. No cigarettes, cigars, or pipes on the bus. Other burned leaves— he winked—in fourth gear only. Let us know if you need a bathroom stop, and give us fair warning.

Jessie responded with small, measured nods: she wanted to seem interested but not witless or overeager. It was the sort of nod she'd seen bicycle mechanics use when they talked about gears.

The driver Jessie had seen on top of the bus wore a red bandana; his shaggy brown hair fell to his shoulders. He introduced himself as Geronimo.

"What?" the Brit said.

"Geronimo. Geronimo Cappellini."

"Angel hair," the manicured girl whispered to Jessie.

"If you'd rather, I answer to Andy," Geronimo said. He explained the drivers' shifts: one of them sleeping in the loft while the other drove. They planned to hurry across "the boring states," slow down and camp more in the West. He made a brief speech about the need for cooperation and respect, and said that the drivers controlled the tape deck music but would take requests. Then all the passengers had to say their names. The manicured girl was named Cynthia. The boy called himself Joey.

"Let's go," Geronimo said. "Let's get on the road." Jessie glanced over at the Brit, at the drivers, at the punked-out girl on the back platform, the smiling, French-speaking French women, the immaculate Cynthia, then gazed out at the South Station trainyard. She took a deep breath of bus air, funky with experience, she thought, funky from real lives lived here, on this Rainbow bus, this once-upon-a-time city bus that had been liberated. On the road, she thought. *On the road.*

At the first highway stop, the smokers crowded together in the parking lot and lit up. A warm wind shot through the roadside maples and over the asphalt, and from the rest stop railing Jessie watched the highway, wheels spinning at high speeds. The boy named Joey lingered near her and asked her for a cigarette. "Okay," she said, "sure," and gave him one, which he lighted and expertly inhaled. He was scrawny, thin arms like bony tubes, blond hair flopping in his face. When she asked him where he was going, he looked her in the eye but jiggled his left foot. "California," he said. "My brother's there."

"That's nice." Maybe there was no brother, but maybe there was. Of course there was. There must be. She could only think up inappropriate things to say: *What exactly are you doing? Where are your parents? I have a baby sister your age.* So she just stood beside him, facing the highway, hot wind and odor of exhaust mixing with the green summer smells of roadside trees. She finished the cigarette, smiled at him, and turned toward the bus.

"You don't have any candy, do you?" Joey said.

"Just mints."

"Oh." He scuffed at the gravel.

"You want some?"

"Yeah, okay."

She offered up the roll and he took five, pocketing two and putting the other three in his mouth all at once.

At the next highway stop, they repeated the routine, Jessie handing over cigarettes and mints, Joey avoiding eye contact and gazing off at the diesel pumps. They headed into the truckstop diner for lunch, but he complained that he had a stomach ache, and ordered water.

"What about soup?" Jessie said. "Soup and ginger ale?"

He shook his head.

"Toast?"

He refused. But when Jessie finished her grilled cheese, he shoved her leftover french fries into his mouth.

"You want a burger to go?" Jessie said.

"No."

"You sure?"

"Yeah." He shook his hair off his forehead, slid out of the booth and away.

At the cash register, she bought a few chocolate bars, a carton of milk, and a bag of chips, which he inhaled on the bus.

Eventually, Jessie thought, she might have struck up conversation with Geronimo anyway, despite her wallflower tendencies. But that evening, when she moved to the folding chair beside the driver's seat, she was thinking about Joey. She didn't notice Geronimo's beautiful skin. She didn't muse about angel hair. After eating two donated ham sandwiches, Joey had finally fallen asleep on the back platform, under the bodybuilder's extra blanket.

"Listen," she said. "I think Joey's broke."

Geronimo nodded.

She waited. "Shouldn't we do something?"

"He's a tough little guy," Geronimo said.

"Yeah. But he's hungry. I think he's running away."

Geronimo seemed entirely focused on the taillights of a truck. Maybe she'd chosen the wrong words, violated some Turtle code: maybe the respect rule meant not speculating about other people's lives. She wondered whether she should retreat to the platform and pretend she hadn't said anything. But after a couple of minutes Geronimo announced that he himself had been a runaway. He'd been born in eastern New York State and taken to Florida, where the cockroaches were enormous. "Palmetto bugs," he said. "Huge." The foster homes had been cold way stations, the orphanage worse; at about fourteen he'd struck out on his own. He didn't know his real birthday, he told her. He was twenty-six, maybe twenty-five, no one knew for sure. He only knew he was half-Iroquois and half-Italian. After he'd moved to San Francisco, he'd changed his name.

"Wow," Jessie said. Her own breathing seemed unnaturally loud. "God. Wow."

———

The next morning, Geronimo set up a food fund for any passengers short on cash. If Joey was running away, Jessie decided, he was running away for a reason. But at least he'd get cheese-burgers, scrambled eggs, milk. Protein, Jessie thought. He needed protein.

She couldn't picture her sister, Emmy, on this bus, only on the ones to middle school and summer camp. On the camp bus, kids sang in warbly Canadian accents, played cat's cradle, tried on each other's shoes, traded the sweets their mothers had packed for the trip. Emmy better stay on that bus, Jessie thought. She'd *make* Emmy stay on that bus. As the Turtle crossed the flats of Ohio, she composed a letter, asking Emmy if the lake had warmed yet, if the counselors were being nice. *I'm jealous, Em, you lucky thing!* At the entrance of a Union 76 truck stop, Geronimo sidled up to her, almost touched her, smiling enough to show one dimple, and offered to mail the letter.

Just because Jessie wanted, more than anything, to find herself didn't mean she couldn't find someone else too. She told herself this in a women's bathroom in Wisconsin, as she brushed her teeth and washed, then checked her face for signs of change. She told herself this as she watched Geronimo pay a diner cashier for his breakfast and refill his coffee thermos: the burnt olive color of his forearms, the way his hair licked the back of his neck. *Stay centered*, Jessie thought, *no ideas but in things*, as William Carlos Williams said. While she was having a last smoke before reboarding the bus, Geronimo stopped beside her to talk, *a wild pony in the sunlight*, and she offered him a cigarette.

"I can't smoke anything," he said. "I only have one lung."

"One?"

"A semi went out of control on a mountain," he said. "I was coming the other way, on my motorcycle."

"Oh my god," Jessie said.

He ran his hands through his hair, lifting it up off his neck. "You know what they say about the bright light you see at death? I saw it. A tunnel spiraling into a light."

"And then you came back."

He nodded and paused, as if in deference to the power of experience. "Of course, rehab took a long time. Half of my ribs were broken." He lifted his T-shirt to show her his scars. His chest was flat and smooth, but long stripes of white scar tissue variegated his left side. She touched one with her index finger. Lightly, as if it still hurt him.

With her other hand, she waved her cigarette. "Should I put this out?"

"You should quit," he said. "You would if you lost a lung."

She nodded solemnly. "I'll do it soon," she said, and took another drag.

In her travel journal she wrote, *Geronimo has really lived.*

That night, while Kurt drove and Geronimo slept, Jessie imagined Geronimo as a small, copper-skinned boy kicking at the pavement. No mother. And no father either. She pictured her own parents evaporating into ghosts and started to cry. Such a lonely life. Such a lonely boy. Where did he belong? After no boyhood, he'd turned into a driver on the Turtle bus, crossing the country for work, for adventure after adventure—wasn't that what drew her here to begin with, adventure? But it would be better for Geronimo to stay in one place. With a *lover,* she thought. It was a word she'd recently started to use. Geronimo needed a lover, needed stability and care. Geronimo needed a home.

She sighed and watched the dark plains rush past the window, dense wheatfields, the sky huge and heavy with clouds. Most of the other passengers were asleep, head to toe in sleeping bags on the huge padded platforms. Soon heat lightning began, crackling down to the horizon, wild jagged lines and brilliant flashes. The air itself seemed green, and Kurt said they weren't far from Wounded Knee. Even if they had time, they wouldn't be stopping: it was inappropriate and disrespectful to bring a bus full of travelers there.

In the flashes of light, Kurt's face seemed shockingly pale, and Jessie crossed her fingers to keep the bus from breaking down. She'd read about spirits in the land, but she'd never felt them before, and these were palpable. No other cars passed for an hour, and then an ambulance sped by in the opposite direction. It was a hard world, Jessie thought, and this electric storm, this night of green clouds and wild wind, this land of the massacred Sioux could break her in half. Geronimo knew it. Kurt probably did too, though, like Jessie, he was an Anglo outsider. She felt too shy to ask him, but Kurt must have sensed her emotion, because he touched her shoulder, then rested his hand on her leg. This calmed her. Suddenly, there was shelter.

The next morning, when Kurt's driving shift was up, after they'd all had breakfast and he was climbing to the driver's loft at the back of the platform, Kurt asked Jessie to nap there with him. "There's more room up here," he said. "Come on." But something in his face said *sex*.

"No thanks," she said.

Kurt smiled and narrowed his eyes. "You're just a little cock tease, aren't you?"

A few feet away, the Brit raised his eyebrows. The green-haired girl smirked, then shrugged. Jessie made her way over the platforms to the front of the bus, blinking her eyes and pressing her lips together.

She didn't mean to be a cock tease. Maybe she'd somehow been unfair; maybe her flaws were worse than she'd imagined. Maybe Geronimo wouldn't be so friendly, just as the urge to kiss him was taking root. All day she sat on the middle platform reading *The Awakening* and playing magnetic backgammon with Joey. Geronimo concentrated on camping arrangements for Colorado, the locations of state cops, and the bodybuilder's drunken, maudlin attentions to an uninterested Cynthia. *Love is never equal*, Jessie wrote in her journal. *Love is always unrequited.* Art is more important than romance, she told herself, and avoided the folding chair next to the driver's seat.

But that night, after dinner at a campground, Geronimo followed Jessie back onto the bus. He uncorked a bottle of Burgundy and poured it into two plastic cups. "Here," he said. "It's been a long day."

They sat on the middle platform and he told her about his trips to Baja, how he learned Spanish while living on the beach. She'd like Baja, he said. She should take the Turtle there. He rolled his shoulders and neck, as if to loosen them. The wine tasted good, and Jessie's fingers began to tingle. She wanted to touch his skin, to rub up against him, but held back and hugged her knees. After the second cup of wine, she stretched out and offered to give Geronimo a back rub, a common practice on the bus.

He said thanks, lifted off his T-shirt and lay on his belly. She could see those white scars again, she could see where that semi had taken his lung and damaged his body, which was otherwise compact and muscular. She petted his head, then rubbed his back with her fingers and palms—*electricity*, she thought, *the world is electric and so are we*—and he continued to talk and give her wine until Kurt made a campfire and started to play a guitar, and the French girls began to sing with lovely accents, a little off-key.

After that, Jessie's attention strayed to Geronimo so often she thought she might be possessed, and decided to let herself go with the experience. She caught his scent from a few feet away, dropped out of conversations midsentence: was that pull what dogs felt, those tame golden retrievers who suddenly yank at the leash? A dog. Dog metaphors, Jessie thought. Oh god. That's what men always came up with. In sixth grade Artie Eldridge called her a dog, which was the worst thing you could be, worse than a slut, worse than a prude. *Worse than a cock tease?* A dog.

The green-haired, punked-out girl named Amy passed Jessie a joint; after she'd taken a long hit and exhaled, Jessie wondered whether it was time to accept her dog-self. Wasn't that how healing worked? She was a golden retriever. A Great Dane. A Labrador. When Geronimo glanced at her, she grinned.

The important thing was *pleasure*, Jessie thought. She fell asleep on the bus repeating the word. The next morning, as the bus pulled into a truck stop, she awoke grateful and wrote in her journal that 1984—only a few years away—would be a year of renaissance, not doom. *The renaissance has already begun*, she wrote, then wandered off the bus, stepping into a shock of cold air. Coffee from the diner warmed her, steam rising up into her face. She liked the steam. She liked the deep wrinkles in her clothes, the slick softness of her dirty jeans. The bus was deep into the Rockies now. She rolled the word "Rockies" around in her mouth: a little like lemon, a little like salt. Geronimo told her they were heading for another campground, this one with showers, a park full of aspens. He squeezed her shoulder. Everything seemed fluttery and green.

Jessie had had sex exactly ten times in her life, all of them during the previous year. She'd never made love on a mountain though. Without wind, with enough heat and shelter, she would have chosen a mountain peak; she imagined making love in the sky. Instead, she and Geronimo left the others for a clearing off a hiking trail. The evening sky turned indigo, the moon rose above the jagged treeline. Jessie and Geronimo kissed, big open-mouthed kisses. *I'm kissing Geronimo Cappellini*, she thought. The idea of the kiss and the kiss itself melted together, the thrills blurring. Pretty soon they'd peeled off their clothes and lay on top of an unzipped sleeping bag. "You're on the pill, right?" Geronimo said.

"No. That's bad for your body." Plus it makes you gain weight, she thought. She carried a diaphragm in her daypack, but for a moment she forced herself to consider the bad things sex could cause: pregnancy. Syphilis. The previous year, a girl in her dorm had caught herpes; the girl's roommate whispered this to Jessie in the hall, how it hurt, how the girl who contracted it cried all the time and broke up with her boyfriend.

"What about you?" Jessie said, and Geronimo frowned.

The frown convinced her to put in the diaphragm. She opened her pack, turned away from Geronimo and smeared the cool spermicide into the rubber cup, trying to avoid pine needles and dirt, then folded the cup and maneuvered it up inside her vagina. It started to slip out of place, and she had to try again, sticky gel coating her hands. By the time she had the diaphragm positioned right, her excitement had vanished, but she pretended and tried to work up another thrill. Geronimo quickly pushed inside her, moved against her long enough to get a rhythm going, and then stopped, telling her not to move. Behind his head she could see a crescent moon, the silhouettes of aspen leaves, spikes of evergreen. After several seconds she tried to move again but he made a sound as if this hurt, and she didn't want to hurt him, that's the last thing she wanted—this was Geronimo Cappellini—and she pressed her face into his neck and kissed him below the ear. Finally, he moved once, twice, fast, and made a low moan so she knew he was coming, although she couldn't exactly feel it.

"You're really something," he said, and kissed her mouth and rolled off her.

She wanted to put his hands back on her breasts, under her hips, between her legs. But he was pointing at the sky, the crescent moon; he seemed to like staring through the trees. He mentioned the stars in Baja. "You should definitely come along next time," he said. How about this time? she thought, but then he yawned and shut his eyes and slept. She was left with the stars and a cool wetness leaking down her thigh. Eventually, she fell asleep too and woke near dawn, pulling closer to his body for warmth. The air smelled of mountains and Geronimo. She could, she thought, fall in love.

For the two remaining days of the trip, Jessie became Geronimo's bus girlfriend, which meant light kisses of greeting, passionate kisses in more private moments, a night during which Jessie managed to place Geronimo's hand between her legs, his mouth on her breast, and to stay interested most of the time he was inside her. It meant that Cynthia, who had decided to sleep with the bodybuilder after all, talked to Jessie woman-to-woman about men and hidden places to have sex. It meant that Kurt stopped talking to Jessie altogether. The Brit took to slapping Geronimo on the back. The French girls smiled at Jessie more often. And Joey, runaway Joey, stuck to Geronimo and Jessie every minute they weren't off fooling around, asking Jessie whether she and Geronimo would live together now, maybe in San Francisco, and what sort of place she thought they would get. How many bedrooms they'd have. How many extra beds.

The third time Joey asked, Jessie said, "Where's your brother's place?"

"In the city. He's got a huge house."

"And you get along?"

"Oh yeah. He's cool."

"Great," she said.

"Yeah. So you'll live in the city too?"

As the bus approached San Francisco, Geronimo listed off the beaches Jessie should visit. Maybe he'd get some time off, he said. She envisioned herself with him, crossing the Golden Gate Bridge for a picnic in Marin: blue ocean, Geronimo on a beach, shrimp and avocado sandwiches.

Kurt raised his eyebrows and frowned.

When the bus pulled up along Embarcadero, the afternoon was damp with fog, rush hour about to begin. Clumps of people waited on the sidewalk; there were backpacks and boxes to unload, and, suddenly, a scattering of bus passengers, the shift occurring so quickly Jessie forgot to get phone numbers. A guy with a dirty blond ponytail and a beard tapped Joey's shoulder and picked up his duffel. He wore a torn jean jacket and a wrecked pair of sneakers, and didn't seem brotherly at all. "Joey," Jessie called, wondering whether she should take him to Abby's, but Joey waved without glancing up; he stared at the cement walk and followed the ponytailed guy toward the BART station.

When Jessie collected her backpack from Geronimo, he kissed her and she gave him Abby's number, written on the back of a Turtle flyer. "Thanks," he said, and climbed back on the bus roof to retrieve more packs. Then Abby appeared, wearing something like a sari, her walnut hair in dozens of tiny braids. Jessie heaved her pack into Abby's little Toyota and hesitated. Geronimo threw more duffels down to Kurt. "Hey," Jessie called, "I'll talk to you later."

He waved and tugged at a canvas pack.

Jessie didn't cry on the car ride to Abby's place, but she did smoke a couple of cigarettes. The bay was gray green, the city a dizzy sequence of figures and lights. Abby smelled like patchouli, and Jessie wanted simply to lean against her and sleep. On the radio a couple of organizers declared a housing crisis, and Abby popped in a tape of a ska band. The bright jerky beat helped Jessie to sit up. She told Abby her hair looked beautiful. She said, "That guy, the one on top of the bus? When I was traveling, we became lovers. He lives here."

"Good for you, Jess." Abby smiled. She held her hand out for Jessie's cigarette. "I thought there was something about him. You going to see him here?"

"Yeah," Jessie said. "Of course."

For the first two days at Abby's, Jessie slept and ate and heard stories about Abby's whirlwind life. Abby, who had cut whole semesters of high school to hang out, now was almost never home: she took art and philosophy classes at San Francisco State, worked in a cafe called the Funky Monkey, spent an hour a day at yoga and three evenings a week in rehearsal for a play called "Wimmin Spirits." Plus she had a part-time boyfriend named Shane, who counseled disturbed kids and played twelve-string guitar. Sometimes Shane lobbied for a bigger commitment from Abby, but she didn't want anyone "tying her down."

"Why not?" Jessie said.

"What do you think the women's movement is for?" Abby said. "So you can do poetry instead of housework."

Jessie didn't respond. She didn't want to be a retrograde dupe of the patriarchy, but love—domestic bliss—could only help her poetry. Also, it wouldn't hurt Abby to do a little housework: the apartment seemed even worse than all-male college dorms. The other roommates showed up only to sleep, and the bathroom was a pit. Her second day there, Jessie began cleaning. No one mentioned the newly scrubbed, deodorized bathroom, but a day later a note appeared, taped to the mirror. *I pray to the goddess, I thank the women, my soul is clean.*

That week, she smoked pot, read books of poetry, and repeatedly dialed the Rainbow Turtle local number. For a while, no one picked up, but eventually a woman answered. Geronimo was out on an engine repair, the woman said. But he didn't call back that day or the next one. When Jessie called again, the answering voice sounded like Kurt. Smug. "He's on the north route, in Seattle. But I'll give him the message."

Sour grapes, Jessie thought. Kurt's. At least the north route trips were short. That afternoon, at a cafe on Haight Street, she began a poem called "Northern Passage."

While Jessie waited for Geronimo's return, she rode streetcars and buses around the city, stopping off at Golden Gate Park, ethnic restaurants, bookstores. She bought sunglasses and spent hours in the poetry section of City Lights Books, half-reading Baudelaire, half-hoping another browser would take note, a poet, for instance, a male poet, a straight, attractive one—but of course Geronimo would be back soon. Maybe she'd never return to Boston: she could cash in her plane ticket and find her own apartment, a light-filled Victorian in Pacific Heights or near the Marina. She'd figure out the money issues later. On postcards of the bay, she wrote, *What a perfect city. There is art and beauty everywhere and I might be falling in love*, and mailed them to friends back east.

But sometimes on the subway the city's strangeness overwhelmed her, and she felt invisible, the only person for miles without a solid, opaque body. She was as inconsequential as a fish. She worried about Joey and began to search for him in the park, where people seemed to be living, and on the sidewalks downtown. Kids loitered near the seamy strip clubs off Broadway and on Powell in the Tenderloin. Some of them were skinny. Some of them were blond. After she'd reassured herself that he wasn't among them, she'd retreat to another black-and-white-tiled cafe. Every couple of days, she checked a city map for the location of Turtle headquarters: it seemed far away, but finding it on the map comforted her, as if Geronimo were already there, sleeping.

One night the second week, Jessie and Abby killed a bottle of

Chianti and started in on the subject of men, the strange distance one can feel from lovers, what it is that draws you in the first place.

"Shane is like the earth," Abby said. "Like gravity. He's a very solid presence. He might have a young soul, but he's a Taurus."

"I bet Geronimo's an earth sign too," Jessie said. "It's just something I sense." She reached over the table for Abby's Drum tobacco and rolled cigarettes for both of them. "I might just stay here," she said. "I'm thinking about it."

"Fantastic." Abby lighted up and held the match for Jessie's cigarette. "Men aren't for everyone," she said. "You know? Out here a lot of women love women. But I've always really liked men. Some of my lesbian friends don't approve."

Jessie had no answer for this. "To each her own," she said. "Live and let live."

Abby cracked a toothy smile. "God, you sound just like your mother."

———

Almost nightly, while Jessie pretended not to be waiting for Geronimo's call, her parents phoned from Buffalo. They grilled her about her money, her health, Abby's roommates, Shane. There were plane schedules to discuss, theaters to investigate, restaurant reservations to make, and also the matter of Jessie's sister, Emmy, whom her parents had decided to bring along.

"We booked a room for the two of you," Elaine said. "We're staying at the St. Francis."

Jessie had ridden the glass elevators in the St. Francis, just to get a view of the city; afterward she snuck into the posh women's bathroom. The hotel had the kind of velvet-lined glamour she associated with Rita Hayworth.

"I'm not staying at a hotel," she said, without conviction. She wondered whether she could wear a strapless, black velvet dress and still be a bohemian. Whether hotels were inherently antibohemian. That morning, she'd seen a baby cockroach in Abby's kitchen and killed it with a saucepan.

Just before her family arrived, she found a note from one of

Abby's roommates on the kitchen table: *Geronimo (?) called. At Turtle house.* She dialed the house and waited for five minutes, letting the Turtle phone ring and ring. After several more unlucky attempts, she stomped off to the Funky Monkey, where Abby gave her pie and continually refilled her coffee cup. All afternoon, at a back corner table, she read apocalyptic sci-fi stories.

Jessie's mother smelled like washed laundry and perfume, her father's dense man-smell mixed with talcum and lemon drops and menthol from shaving. They kissed her in the hotel lobby and promised her things: a day trip up the coast, a dance performance, dinners, desserts. Fat brown curls sprang off Emmy's head; she was tan from camp, skinny and bold. She gave Jessie a hug and a macrame bracelet she'd made at the crafts center.

"Let's get you squared away," her father said. He smiled and kissed Jessie on the forehead, then flagged down a bellboy to carry her backpack. Murmuring couples crossed the lobby and a pianist played jazz standards. Jessie's father ushered the family into a glass elevator, and they glided up to their rooms.

Clean, Jessie thought. The hotel room was the cleanest place she'd been since the last time she visited her parents' house. Thick bedspreads, thick carpets, gauzy white sheers filtering the window light. Emmy fell on the bed closest to the TV and began to flip the channels; Jessie unpacked her things, carefully hanging her dress and skirt, arranging the jeans and T-shirts in wide dresser drawers. Then she stretched out on the second bed and thumbed a copy of *Bury My Heart at Wounded Knee* she'd picked up at City Lights. She made it through two paragraphs, then set down the book and called the Turtle number. Geronimo would be back later, a man told her.

Emmy turned off the TV sound. "What's that about?"

Emmy wasn't a geeky kid—not nearly as geeky as Jessie had been. She was likeable and smart, but also loudmouthed and indiscreet. "You have to promise not to tell," Jessie said.

"Promise."

"Really, Emmy, I mean it."

"I said I promise."

"I met a guy I like. A man I could love. He lives here, in San Francisco."

"Wow," Emmy said. "Does Mom know?"

"No. And you can't tell her. Emmy? I'm trusting you on this one."

"*Okay*," Emmy said, and confessed she'd French-kissed a boy at camp. Once, he'd stuck a hand under her shirt, but it felt more clammy than good.

"God, Emmy, you're only twelve."

"I hate that," Emmy said. "I'm not a baby. And it's not like I'm a slut."

Slut, Jessie thought. Dog. Prude. She remembered her dog-self and grabbed a notepad off the night table. Meanings of *slut*, she wrote, potential poem: on being a slut. She slipped the "slut" note into her pocketbook and pulled out a package of Drum tobacco. "Sorry," she said. "Can I smoke in here?"

"No problem," Emmy said. "I'll get us some Cokes."

─────

Later, her mother breezed in with a list of art galleries; her father sniffed the air and frowned. Then he picked up *Bury My Heart at Wounded Knee*.

"You're reading this?" he said.

"I just started," Jessie said.

"That's great, Jess," he said. He knew a few things because of being an epidemiologist and also a big reader. He mentioned some of the different clans and tribes that had been lumped together. Jews and Native Americans have a lot in common, he said.

"Cuisine, for example," her mother said.

"Elaine, I'm serious," her father said.

"You mean both being targets of genocide," Jessie said.

"Yes, Jessie, that's exactly what I mean."

"Just don't make everyone Jewish," Elaine said. "It isn't fair."

Jessie measured her words. "I know what you're saying, Mom," she said. "But underneath it all, underneath history, we're really all one. You should read Jung sometime."

"That's fine." Elaine stuck the gallery listing into her bag and opened the door. "I'm going to see art."

When Geronimo at last called Jessie back, he said, "You're at a hotel? Good going. I'll meet you there."

"Here?" Jessie said. Emmy was here. *Her parents* were next door. Even if he showed up while they were off in North Beach, it was like bringing him to her parents' house. She couldn't make love with anyone in her parents' house.

"That doesn't really work," she said. "It's a little complicated." She asked him to meet her at the Palace of Fine Arts, then told her parents she was off to meet a friend of Abby's.

"That Shane friend?" her mother said.

"Somebody else." Jessie said. "A girl. Someone Abby goes to school with."

She brought her diaphragm with her. She took a cab. But as the cab approached the Palace of Fine Arts, her stomach lurched, and she wanted to sink down below the door's window and stay there until the cab drove somewhere else. This had to be fear of rejection, she thought. Sometimes love could make you sick.

Jessie paid the driver and circled the little pond to the temple, violet stone columns shooting up to a dome. Geronimo stood directly below the dome and listened to his own echo. He wore the same red bandana, the same stained jeans, the same blue T-shirt he'd worn through much of the trip west.

She leaned against a column and said his name.

"Hey." He walked over and kissed her on the mouth. "Where are we going?"

The light had a queer fuzziness to it, and Jessie's face flushed. He seemed familiar, he seemed like a stranger, and at that moment she couldn't imagine going anywhere. She didn't answer him but instead kissed him again, hoping the fuzziness would dissolve. It only seemed to worsen.

"Something's wrong," she said. "I'm sick."

"You don't look sick." He pushed her hair away from her eyes, ran his fingers very lightly over her temples and cheeks, kissed them. How lovely the sensations were; how queasy she felt. "I'm sorry," he said. "We'll sit down. Maybe you'll feel better."

And she did sit down, on the grass in the sun, and she let him stroke her hair and her face. She kissed him on the cheek and kissed him on the mouth. He was dusty and salty and warm, and Jessie felt trembly, as if she'd been up all night, or to a funeral. She kissed him until she had to double up and lean against him.

"What's the matter?" he said. "I don't get it."

Then she pulled away. "I'm just shaky today. Not feeling so good."

He held her hand and wrapped an arm around her shoulder, hugged her against him, kissing her ear, her neck. He brushed the hair out of her eyes. "Are you coming down from something? It'll get better."

"No," she said. "It isn't that."

She straightened up and squeezed his hand. "I missed you," she said. She meant it. The missing had been real, almost palpable. Now, at the Palace, it took on a bewildering intensity, which made no sense. She only knew that the longer she stayed, the sicker she would feel.

"You're a sweet one," Geronimo said.

They stood and began to walk toward the street. One step, another step, her body off-balance, the dizziness in her legs.

"I think I should go back to the hotel," she said.

"Then let's go."

"No. Just help me find a taxi."

"A taxi, huh?" But he flagged one down, and, before she climbed in, she hugged him hard and kissed him and squeezed his hand again. "I'm sorry about today," she said. "I'll call you later. We'll make another plan."

"Sure," he said. "Call me."

———————————

It was a relief to ride up and down the St. Francis elevators with Emmy, to order room service, to eat dinner in restaurants with candles and waiters who brought anything you asked for. It was a relief to sit beside her father in the hotel bar while he and Dr. Bloom, his college pal, relived the old days; to wander the art museum with her mother. When she called the airline about cashing her one-way ticket, she pictured Abby's crummy apartment and hung up the phone. On the street, she continued to watch for Joey: she kept extra cash in her wallet in case she found him. She didn't know what else to do. She didn't once call Geronimo. For the remainder of the week, Jessie spent every day with her family.

The day before Jessie's flight back to Boston, Abby met her at the hotel bar.

"What happened?" Abby said.

"I thought about what you said," Jessie said. "About poetry and not making too many compromises. I can't just give up everything to be near him. I just can't see it working for us."

"Sorry," Abby said. "You know you're right, though."

"You think?"

"Oh sure. You need your independence. You need to develop your art."

She wondered whether that was the truth. She wondered what art and independence might have to do with love, or whether they always needed separate worlds. "My mother wanted to know if you're free for dinner," she said.

"Thanks anyway," Abby said. "It's my night with Shane."

At the gate for her flight back to Boston, Jessie hugged her mother for the fourth time.

"Jessie, sweetie," Elaine said. "It was a lovely vacation."

Jessie nodded and pushed her face against her mother's shoulder.

"You have a whole month before classes," Elaine said. She stroked Jessie's hair. "You can see your Boston friends."

Jessie pulled away and bit her lip. Her father stood at the window with Emmy, pointing and talking as the planes took off. They were holding hands. Life would be better as Emmy, Jessie thought, and for a moment she wanted only to order Cokes on the plane and sleep in her parents' house and wake up to bowls of cereal and Mom in the backyard talking out loud to zinnias. To hold Dad's hand without being embarrassed.

When Jessie boarded the plane, it seemed that her insides had been scooped out. She buckled herself into the seat and rubbed her fingers over the shiny cover of *Women Speak! A Poetry Anthology*. A woman in a red linen suit took the next seat and buried herself in the *Times of London*. From the plane, the terminal windows looked opaque: maybe her parents and Emmy were still there. Maybe not. On the ground, luggage carts scooted back and forth like large insects. Men holding orange lights waved their arms and left for distant gates. Other planes crossed the tarmac, and from the small oval window Jessie watched them rush down the runway and hover just above ground before angling up and out of sight.

The Good Life

My mother, Sadie—giddy matriarch, geriatric sweetheart—is not as many women as she used to be. Former selves wink like satellites from the far side of her cerebrum: in Chanel suits and tiny high heels, in pastel housecoats and backless slippers, in flowered aprons, in one-piece swimsuits, in pink negligees. I see her fingering mah jong tiles, flirting with waiters, sneaking butter into the mashed potatoes despite my father's kosher mandate. She applies lipstick without ever checking a mirror. At the piano she coaxes out the hit parade. In the kitchen she'll gossip: *Rhoda Dobkins, sour from the day she was born. You watch, she'll mark cards, crimp the corners.* I'm in my thirties, forties, turning fifty, and she asks, *Elaine, honey, did you get enough for lunch?* She pops a chocolate in her mouth and tells me: *It's a good life if you don't weaken.*

At the nursing home I shore Sadie up to keep her from vanishing. I kiss her white cheeks and feed her low-fat cookies. "Coffee?" she says. A word this winter's stroke has left her with. I wheel her out to the main floor, past the TV lounge where Regis and Kathy Lee shout from the big screen and her postwar nemesis Rhoda Dobkins stacks and restacks playing cards. Today my mother notices Rhoda and narrows her eyes.

"That's right, Mom," I say. "Sour old Rhoda." I kiss her again for remembering the grudge.

You're in the good life a short forever, and then it twists. Last Thanksgiving, my mother could still make the trip to my house; she was still talking in full sentences, playing the piano, flirting with her baby brother, Uncle Irv, a lecher and scam artist I invited for her sake. When my sister Margo and I were growing up, Uncle Irv would pinch our behinds and make low mooing noises: my mother adored him in spite of his obvious sleaziness. She adored him in spite of the loans he never repaid. She gave him her shares of the family house on Lancaster and their father's store downtown. Irving was the spitting image of their father, and he courted Sadie with carnations, steady compliments, lunches at the Howard Johnson's on Delaware. In other words, he made her laugh.

At the piano my mother played her medley of song fragments, and Margo sat beside her singing, *Ma, he's making eyes at me* and "Dark Town Strutter's Ball." Sadie was still managing to hit most of the notes—her fingers curved from arthritis, the nails polished salmon, still wearing her diamond engagement ring, still wearing her wedding ring. Hands of a queen, always, even as those fingers stiffened and rebelled. Queen of Hearts, my mother.

So there we were, Uncle Irv already into the hard liquor, my youngest, Emily, singing along with Margo and my mother about dancing off their shoes, my husband, Daniel, carving the turkey, our London-bound son, Adam, parked in front of the football game, and Jessie, my oldest and most confounding child, Jessie, taking the coats of our cousins the Goldbaums and plying the rest of us with wine. Jessie had arrived from Boston with the look of a sated cat. Twice she'd hugged me for no apparent reason. She'd lifted a gerbera daisy from the centerpiece and stuck it in her hair, and for once she was wearing aqua instead of black. I thought maybe Daniel wrote her a check; I thought she was going too fast with the Merlot. We were on the third bottle by the time we sat down to eat. Jessie bided her time, waited until we were past the appetizers, grinning from the wine, until Daniel was done with his speech making and our mouths were stuffed with food.

"A toast," Jessie said, "to true love." She glanced in the direction of the Goldbaums, a still-young couple.

My younger daughter, Emily, choked.

"That's what it is," my sister Margo said. "Jessie's in love."

Jessie smiled at her father, batted her eyes at Margo, and gazed at me. "I have a girlfriend," she said. She wasn't even blushing.

Silverware clattered. Daniel covered his mouth with his napkin. The light in the dining room grew oddly sharp, and I took a long swallow of water.

Adam elbowed Emily. "Told you," Adam said.

My palms began to sweat and I clutched my napkin. "What do you mean?" I said to Jessie.

"Just what you think I mean," Jessie said.

"Let's talk about this later," Daniel said. He was a little green. He nodded at the turkey carcass. "There's still a lot more food."

"And wine," Margo said. "Let's try the Pinot Noir." She stood and yanked the cork from a new bottle, then circled the table, leaning over our shoulders, her rainy scent wafting counterclockwise as she filled the glasses.

"A girlfriend?" Irv said. "Like the way a man has a girlfriend?"

"Sort of," Jessie said.

His eyes glazed over. "I've seen that," he said.

"What?"

"I've seen that. A little place downtown. Girls Girls Girls."

"Uncle Irv," I said.

"Is she a looker?" Irv said.

"She's beautiful," Jessie said.

"Who's beautiful?" my mother said.

"You are," Irving said. He blew Sadie a kiss across the table. He slurped at his wine, spilling it onto his checked sport jacket. "So long as we're making confessions," he told Jessie, "let me say that I also have a girlfriend."

"Who has a girlfriend?" my mother said.

"Irving," I said.

"Such a flirt," my mother said. "Flirts with all the girls. Never serious."

"Is," Irv said. "Nothing but serious."

"What's her name?" Jessie said.

"Gertrude," he said.

"I don't know a Gertrude," my mother said.

"No," Irv said. "She isn't someone you know."

"You actually date someone named Gertrude?" Emily said.

My mother scanned her plate, a little lost. "Did I have some coffee?" she said.

"I call her Gertie," Irv said. He went misty-eyed at the chandelier, then turned to Jessie. "What about your girl?" he said.

"Emily, would you get your grandmother a cup of coffee?" I said.

"Stephanie," Jessie said. For a moment, she stared off at the beige drapes behind Daniel. I pictured her disappearing into a crowd of women with shaved heads.

"Honey," I told Jessie, "we should talk about this later."

"You don't approve," Jessie said.

"Approve, not approve, they haven't even met her," Irv said.

"Met who?" my mother said.

I sighed. "Emily, make sure it's the decaf."

"Stephanie," Jessie said.

"Didn't you say Gertrude?" my mother said.

"That's Uncle Irv's girlfriend," Adam said.

"Irving," my mother said. "You have a girlfriend?"

"No one who can hold a candle to you," Irv said, blowing another kiss.

Adam wrinkled his nose at Jessie. "It isn't Stephanie Jamison," he said.

"Not that Stephanie," Jessie said.

"Stephanie Jamison? That cheerleader Adam followed around?" Emily said. She set a cup of coffee in front of my mother.

"Shut up," Adam said.

"Who you telling to shut up?" my mother said.

"Emily. Gram, don't you think she has a big mouth?" Adam said.

"A fine mouth. You might try a little lipstick," my mother said. "What a doll. Isn't she?"

"She's a beautiful girl," I said. "Jessie too."

"Oh yes," my mother said. "Real dolls."

"I'm lucky to have daughters like them," I said.

"Oh Mom," Emily said.

"They're your daughters?" my mother said.

"Sure," I said. "And you know what? I'm your daughter. So's Margo."

My mother gazed into her lap. "Imagine that," she said.

Late that night I showered, soaped around and around my navel, little cavern, little whirlpool of tucks and creases. Sadie still knew my name. *Elaine*, she'd say, *don't you look stunning. Elaine, give me a kiss.* But "daughter"? I had already merged with Sadie's sisters and cousins and girlfriends, a cast of familiar women, all drenched in fuzzy-edged love. *I never thought Papa would let us study art*, she'd say. *Did you?*

Such fickle things, our bodies and brains. Such mysteries. How does a woman forget babies? For that matter, how did I make a daughter who wants other girls? All those peptides scrambling up and spelling out *lesbian*.

"A phase?" I said to Daniel. "Could it be a phase?"

He was propped up in bed with a colleague's article entitled "Cancer Risks in California Agricultural Migrant Labor Populations" and a spy novel.

"Maybe," he said.

"Like Birkenstocks," I said. "Like marijuana?"

He shrugged. "No chance of pregnancy," he said. "Low risk for STDs."

"Public health talk," I said. "That's not what you said at dinner."

"She's fine." He turned to his LeCarré. "Jessie's just fine."

The Friday after Thanksgiving, I began to clean a house I'd cleaned the Wednesday before. I vacuumed unsoiled carpets, wiped down counters, dusted yet again. While I was mopping the kitchen floor, Jessie decided it was time for a heart-to-heart. "We need to talk." She landed in the chair closest to me.

"Okay," I said. I dipped my mop in the bucket and ran it in front of the refrigerator.

"About Stephanie," she said. "About my life."

"Sure," I said.

She tapped a pencil on the table, then held it like a cigarette, tilted her head, and talked to the ceiling above me. "I was really nervous at first. You know, when things started."

"Uh huh," I said. I rubbed the mop over a speck of yam.

"*Mom*," Jessie said. "Would you stop?"

"I'm listening," I said.

"No you're not." A sliver of hurt stuck in her voice.

I put down the mop. I sat. "Yes," I said. "I am."

"Forget it," Jessie said. She chewed on the pencil end and closed her eyes. Sitting in Daniel's bathrobe, her hair still sleep-wild, Jessie looked like a kindergartner.

"Don't forget it," I said.

She scrutinized my face, wound a loose strand of hair around a finger. "Stephanie was in my women's group," she said.

Since when are twenty-four year olds women? I thought, and then remembered. "Umm hmm," I said.

"Oh God," Jessie said. "I knew you'd be weird about this."

"Honey, I want you to be happy."

"I am," Jessie said. "Very."

"Well that's good," I said. "That's important."

"You're right," she said, softening. "You'd really like her, Mom."

"Sweetie, I like all your friends," I said.

"Yeah. But you know what I mean."

"I think so," I said. "Did you want to go shopping today?"

The next week, Daniel and I received a five-page letter from Boston in which Jessie discussed the failures of past relationships and raved about Stephanie. In closing, she wrote: *I know you*

didn't expect this, but you should be relieved. Stephanie's Jewish.
She had enclosed two bumper stickers: "I ♥ My Gay Child" and
"Straight But Not Narrow." *P.S.*, she wrote, *Uncle Irv's not so bad.*
He has a big heart.

Irv has a big heart? And I'm the Pope's daughter, I thought. I
refolded the letter and sifted through Irv's catalogue of sins, the
worst of which was disappearing for three months after my father's funeral, while Sadie crumbled. Jessie was too young to remember, and why should I bring it up? She'd only defend Irv as
misunderstood. I left the letter on Daniel's dresser and visited the
nursing home.

After a few days, though, I began to waver about Uncle Irv.
Jessie's love life gave me hives, but maybe, just maybe, she could
see a whole different Irv than I could. Maybe this Irv was better
than the Irvs of my girlhood, the prodigal uncle, the sleazy spend-
thrift my father always had to bail out. True, I was impressed by
the kisses Irv blew across the table at Sadie, the Fanny Farmer
chocolates he'd brought to dinner; I was impressed by his weekly
visits with my mother, all those Howard Johnson's lunches when
she again became a woman men attended to. I relented, and for
the next couple of months my tolerance and gratitude surged.
Then, in January, my mother had her stroke, and Uncle Irv once
again dropped out of sight.

"What did you expect?" Margo said. "He's a leech. Mom can't
write checks anymore."

"He could be sick," I said.

"Just warped," Margo said. "Elaine, don't waste your time."

I tried without luck to reach him by phone. I dropped short
notes in the mail. No response. But eventually, in late March,
Uncle Irv called me at home. "Elaine," he said. "I'm having an
emergency. Come to my store."

"You need an ambulance?" I said. "Police?"

"No, no," he said. "When will you be here?" and hung up before I answered.

Emmy was lying on the family room sofa, knees up, a Walk-
man strapped over her head, bare feet flexed on a pillow: she'd
stuck cotton balls between her toes and painted her toenails crim-
son. Her trig textbook was propped against her thighs, and the
TV, sound off, flashed an ice-dancing competition. "Listen," I told

her. "Something's up with Uncle Irv. I'm going to the jewelry store."

She pulled off the headphones. "Alone?" she said, sitting up to blow on her toes. She hit the TV remote and told me she was coming too. "It's not safe to be around Uncle Irv alone."

"For Pete's sake, he's eighty years old."

"He's a creep. Besides, maybe he's got some little pearl studs."

I wasn't sure whether Irv even sold pearl studs: he sold yellow diamonds, old watches, pawned rings in a dingy storefront in the red-light district, the remains of my grandfather's once-respectable business. The place was poorly lit, heavy metal grates blocking the windows; the cases were cracked and thick with dust. When we arrived, talk show voices buzzed through a black-and-white TV. The store smelled of mildew and old cigars. Uncle Irv stared out the filmy, grated window, fingering watch parts. Sagging.

"Good of you to come," he said. "It's my girlfriend."

"Gertrude?" Emmy said.

Irv sighed and rubbed the casing of a silver pocket watch, his eyes moony and distant.

"Uncle Irv?" I said. I waited. Emmy waited. Across the street, a woman in a tight minidress and stiletto heels rummaged in her purse and pulled out a paperback and a cigarette.

"Uncle Irv, you got any pearls?" Emmy said. "Little earrings?"

He dropped the watch and suddenly returned to us. "I'm heartsick and she wants to talk pearls," Irv said.

"What about your girlfriend?" I said.

"She's dying." His jaw tightened, his pupils darkened, and he brought a hand up over his face.

"I'm sorry," I said.

"She wants to meet you," Irv said. He straightened up and picked a piece of lint off his trousers. "I told her I have a niece, and she wants to meet you."

"That's fine," I said.

"Today," he said. "Now." He gave me the address of his girl-friend's apartment and reached for his coat.

"You come too," he said to Emily. "Only don't mention about having a girlfriend."

"That's not me," Emmy said. "That's Jessie."

"Well don't say anything," Irv said.

"Duh," Emmy said.

"Another thing," he said. "She knows me as Don."

"Don?" Emmy said.

"Yeah," Irv said. "Don Jones."

"Is that your middle name?" Emmy said.

"You ask too many questions," Irv said.

"Well what should I call you?" Emmy said.

"Uncle Irv. I told her yesterday. I said you all call me Uncle Irv."

For months, he said, he'd been living with Gertrude, taking care of her. I asked whether she had any family. "Me," he said. "I'm her family." He shook his head, pressed his lips together, and swallowed hard. "So many years."

"Years?"

"Twenty-four." He pulled a handkerchief out of his pocket. "Elaine, don't mention this to Sadie."

We followed Irv down the long fifth-floor corridor of Gertrude's apartment building, a place full of the elderly. All the sound had been sucked out of it. He opened the door to her apartment and called, "Honey, it's me," his voice tender. We stepped into the dim living room, where Gertrude lay on the sofa, propped up with pillows: a tiny paper kite of a woman, her blue eyes pearled by cataracts. She was wrapped in a pink robe, her fuzzy halo of white hair rising above the bedclothes. She was the exact size and shape and colors of my mother—only here was a smaller nose, a sharper chin. I was dizzy with familiarity, and the dizziness increased as I glanced around her apartment. The coffee table. The reading lamp. The sofa Gertrude was lying on. All from my parents' old house. The quilt I recognized from my parents' bedroom.

I circled the love seat: the royal blue fabric was shiny from wear, threadbare in spots, the frame chipped. New, it had floated among trouser legs and long hemlines, cocktail parties in my parents' living room: my father slapping the other men on the back and threatening to light his pipe, my mother smoothing her black sleeveless dress, her hair done at Louie's that afternoon. She was shy and beautiful in these gatherings, my mother: the shyness surprised all of us. She'd sip at her sherry, smile at the men, compliment the women on their accessories, then fade into the background while the waitress she'd hired passed hors d'oeuvres, smoked salmon and capers and vegetable tarts.

"Good of you to come," Gertrude said. She waved in Irv's direction. "Don worries too much. It isn't my time yet."

Then she started to cough: her rickety body shook and her eyes began to water. Uncle Irv stood paralyzed in the corner. I sat her up and sent Emmy to the kitchen for a glass of water. Gertrude sipped and coughed, sipped and coughed, and finally regained her composure.

"Bless you," she said, and nodded at Emmy, who was hovering behind me. "This is your daughter?"

"This is Emily," I said. "My youngest."

Gertrude extended a bony hand to Emmy and motioned for her to sit at the edge of the sofa. She studied Emmy's face and grinned. "I bet you have a boyfriend," she said.

Emmy blushed. Uncle Irv cleared his throat. "You're right," Emmy said. "I'm in love with Leonardo." Someone I'd never heard of.

"An Italian boy," Gertrude said.

Emmy smiled and smiled. "He's handsome," she said.

"And he treats you nice?" Gertrude said.

"Like a gentleman."

"You make sure," Gertrude said.

Uncle Irv, leerer and pincher, nodded along. Earnestly. But he said almost nothing. I told Gertrude I'd grown up in Buffalo, and he looked at me in alarm. I mentioned my mother, and he began to pace. I said we'd always been a close family, and Irv wrung his hands, then interrupted to ask Gertrude whether she'd had her medicine. When I offered to get Gertrude something to eat, Irv asked me to make him a cup of coffee.

Emmy raised one eyebrow. "You live here, right?"

But I put on the coffee and washed a sinkload of my mother's old dishes, while Emmy and Gertrude played solitaire together, Gertrude pointing and Emmy moving the cards.

"So good of you," Gertrude said.

As we readied to leave, Uncle Irv's hands were trembling. He stroked his beard stubble and stared at the floor.

"You need something, Irv?" I said. "Don."

He nodded. "Oh Elaine," he said. "Such a good woman you are. I've always said—that Elaine, she's got a heart."

"What is it?"

"If you wouldn't mind, if it isn't too much trouble," he said.

"*What?*" Emmy said.

"If you could bring some clothes from my house, my mail." And then he drew me aside and waved at the bottles of pills. "This medicine," he said, "so expensive. Could you lend me a little, until my next check?"

"Of course," I said. "How much?"

"A few hundred," he said. "Maybe four."

I glanced at Gertrude under my mother's quilt, the collection of pills. Four hundred, I wrote.

"Leonardo?" I said. Emmy and I were in the car on the way to Irv's house, Sadie's childhood home, and Emmy was punching buttons on the radio. "Who's Leonardo?"

"Brian," Emmy said, meaning her boyfriend-of-the-month. "Better than Don Jones, isn't it? Better than naming yourself after Wall Street."

I turned up Lancaster and began to watch for Irving's block. What I remembered most about the family house was its wood: the waxed parquet floors, the polished banisters, the sliding parlor door, the heavy-grained piano. But I hadn't been inside for more than fifteen years, not since my mother signed over her share of the house to Irving and he banned the rest of us from visiting. From the street, driving by, I'd witnessed the neglect. Paint peeled in long strips. Dead leaves and stray litter cluttered the lawn, and dead stalks of old shrubs shrank against the house. The roof sagged; the rain gutters hung loose. But to either side spread a neighborhood of renovation and fresh paint.

We parked and made our way up the pitted front walk.

"It's not like this on purpose, is it?" Emmy said.

"Emmy."

"Well how should I know?"

The mailbox was stuffed with envelopes, and the postman had taken to leaving them on the porch floor. Emmy scooped them into a paper bag while I fiddled with the front lock. She followed me into the front hall, which was barely navigable, lined with four-foot stacks of old newspapers, a little city of them that expanded into the living room. There the sizes of the stacks were varied, yellow and mustier yellow paper, the table tops and piano black with soot and dust. The dining room stank of urine and wood rot; brown stains spread across the ceiling. But the heavy oak table was empty, and a package of laundry from Quik-Kleen was propped on one of the chairs. Along the far wall, away from the ceiling stains, Irving had set up an army cot, which was surrounded by rumpled clothes and back issues of *Penthouse*.

Emmy held her nose. "Ew," she said.

It was worse in the kitchen, where plastic bags of garbage were piled into a small pyramid, and a slimy liquid seeped from the upper kitchen cabinets. I opened one. Prehistoric canned goods had corroded through the metal seams. I didn't dare open the refrigerator.

"*Disgusting*," Emmy said. "I'm getting out of here."

I felt like I was in prep for oral surgery: lightheaded, my own voice remote. "Meet you outside," I said. I took the back stairs to the second floor, which was as silty as the living room, but emptier. It was clear the roof had leaked for some time: in room after room the bureaus and bedframes, the mattresses and night tables were water stained and mildewed, the floorboards damaged. But the closets held ordered rows of women's clothes on metal hangers: calico dresses, nylon dresses, moth-eaten sweaters. On the floor: fallen belts, stray gloves. The clothes of middle-aged women, my mother's sisters who lived with Irv until their deaths fourteen and twenty years ago. In what had been my grandfather's room, I opened the drawers of the bureau to find a stack of men's shirts, wrapped in cellophane from a dry cleaner that went out of business in 1963.

I made my way to the end of the hall and the bedroom my mother had shared with her youngest sister. Bare walls, twin beds with cherubs carved into the frames, two small wooden rockers, armless, the caning in need of repair. A heavy bureau, empty, a dressing table with a large oval mirror, its silver marred by ink black spots. Nothing in the closet. Nothing in the dressing table. I checked and rechecked the drawers, bending over, sniffing at them. No scraps of paper. No old lipsticks, no ancient face cream. The smell of nothing, a whiff of mildew and dust. I circled the room and sniffed at more: the walls, the bedframe, a rocker, which I sat in. Hard wood, slow motion, creaking. I closed my eyes and rocked, and for a moment I drifted away from myself, as I do when I'm awake too early in the morning. My face and neck flushed, and when I opened my eyes the room seemed even more foreign. I felt hollow and unmoored. Then I heard Emmy's footsteps on the front stairs, and she was a blob in the doorway.

"Mom," she said. "What are you doing?"

I blinked at her. "This was Gram's room," I said.

She walked over to the dressing table and traced a squiggle in the dust, then pulled her hand back suddenly. "This doesn't feel like her," Emmy said. She wrinkled her nose. "Can we go?"

When I dropped Irv's clothes and mail at Gertrude's apartment, I wrote him another check and gave him the name of a cleaning service.

"I thank you," he said, narrowing his eyes a little. "Elaine, you don't mind my saying, you've put on a little heft."

"Heft?"

"Zaftig," he said. And, after a moment, "A fine thing in a woman."

"I'll call you soon," I said, "to check on Gertrude." When I got back in the car, Emmy, my underage schemer, patted me on the shoulder. "We need a drink," she said.

I turned the key in the ignition. "Good try," I said.

"Okay, then, milkshakes." She squeezed my hand. "Cheer up, Mom," she said. "We'll get mocha."

The following week, I called Uncle Irv and asked him how Gertrude was doing. "A miracle," he said. "I think she's going to recover."

When Sadie moved to the nursing home, Margo and I hung a bulletin board in her room and covered it with family photos. *Sadie in Florida, 1955. Sadie and Bill's wedding, 1927. Sadie at Jessie's 3rd birthday.* We left a stack of photo albums on the closet shelf and covered the dresser with framed pictures. Every few months, I'd update snapshots of the kids. In late April, Jessie sent me three copies of a photo of herself holding hands with Stephanie: one print for Sadie's room, one for Daniel's office, and one for the house. Jessie and Stephanie stood in front of a pier— wind-blown hair, toothy smiles, big eyes—cobalt ocean in the background. Stephanie's head tilted toward Jessie, a walnut brown swath of hair flying into Jessie's shoulder. She was more olive-toned than Jessie and even more petite. They looked like girls at summer camp. I handed Daniel his copy.

"That's her?" he said. "She's cute." But he didn't look at the snapshot for very long.

"So you don't have a problem with this," I said.

"No more bumper stickers, right? She didn't send more bumper stickers, did she?"

"Just earrings for Emmy. Pink triangles."

Daniel took off his glasses and rubbed his eyes. "We don't have to wear triangles too, do we?"

"Maybe armbands," I said. "Maybe funny hats."

"She used to like boys," he said, wistful.

"It isn't you," I said. "You know that."

"Maybe I wasn't around enough," he said.

"Honey, this isn't about you," I said. "Jessie is who she is."

"I suppose."

This was not where I'd expected to end up, switching places with Daniel, something we often do. *Jessie is who she is?* Of course, I believed Daniel had nothing to do with her choice. But I wondered about myself. Too overbearing? I thought. Too gratified by her toddler shyness, her attachment to me. Too affectionate?

At first, I didn't take Jessie's new photo to the nursing home; instead, I took one of her and Emmy from Thanksgiving. I sat with my mother and turned the pages of a photo album, going over and over the family snapshots. She touched the pages, but randomly, distractedly, her expression flat and unchanging. I picked up a larger, framed photo of my father and held it out for her to see. She wrinkled her brow and frowned. Then she wouldn't look at me, or the photos. I kissed her. I praised her blue dress. I started to sing to her, but she frowned for several more minutes and tugged at the fringe on her blanket.

At home, Emmy propped one of the prints of Jessie and Stephanie on the mantle, next to her own photo from the Junior Holiday Dance. I ignored it. That Saturday, I took Emmy out for lunch at the grill by the marina downtown, on the shore of Lake Erie. We sat in the wind at the picnic tables eating french fries and chicken sandwiches. Emmy was wearing her pink triangle earrings and Brian's varsity jacket. She told me lesbianism was in. "You know about Jodie Foster, don't you?" she said.

"Let's not talk about this," I said.

"Wouldn't it be great if Jessie dated Jodie Foster?"

"Okay, Emmy."

"I'd go out with Jodie Foster."

I wanted to slap her. I set down my drink and walked off in the direction of the skyscrapers. "Mom," Emmy called. "I'm kidding. Remember kidding?"

She followed me, and I walked faster. "Mom," she said, starting to worry now, starting to be afraid. I stopped walking. Whitecaps dotted the water and smacked against the promenade's concrete wall. "You know I'm in love with Brian," she said. "We're practically engaged."

"What?"

"Figuratively speaking," she said.

"You're not even eighteen."

"Oh right," Emmy said, "I forgot."

In the distance freighters moved south along the shoreline, and above us jagged bits of blue opened up between cloudbanks. I started to cry. Emmy's remaining bravado collapsed. She put her arm around me, awkwardly hugging me. But I didn't hug her back. My nose was running and I choked when I tried to talk. I gave up. Then Emmy started to cry too, red blotches spreading over her cheeks. "I didn't mean to upset you," she said. "Really, Mom."

I pulled Kleenexes out of my pocketbook for both of us and we sat on a bench. "Sweetie, it isn't you," I said.

"Are you sure?"

I nodded. We dried our faces and blew our noses and stared out at the freighters.

"It's these earrings, isn't it?" she said. "You don't like them."

"They're fine," I said. "Really, Emmy. You look very chic today."

In May, when Jessie called to tell me she wanted to bring Stephanie for a visit, I clammed up. I said I'd have to call her back. I knew Jessie would get off the phone and write poems on injustice and death, but I couldn't help myself.

Daniel gave me a long look and turned off the sound on the baseball game. "She's a grownup," he said. "It isn't our place to interfere."

"Okay," I said, "but visiting? You want Jessie walking around the neighborhood with her girlfriend? Kissing? You know there's going to be kissing."

"That's what people in love do, Elaine." He hesitated. Another Yankees batter struck out. "You really think they'd kiss on the street?"

"I don't know."

Daniel shook the idea away. "Kisses," he said. "What's the big deal?"

"It's an example."

"Well, I'm sure they've already kissed," he said.

"That's a fine thought."

"You know what I mean." He sneaked another glance at the game.

I stepped in front of the TV set. "And," I said. "Where are they going to sleep?"

"I thought so," he said. "Jessie's room?"

"Both of them?"

"Jessie wouldn't put up with the study," he said. Mr. Nonchalance. Mr. Modern Dad.

"Okay, Daniel. Fine. You call Jessie. You make the arrangements."

"What?"

"Call Jessie."

He shook his head. "You're the one she always talks to."

"Time for a change," I said.

"Look, I'm not crazy about this either," Daniel said. "I'm just being practical. You know, live and let live. Isn't that what you say?"

"If my mother knew about this," I said.

"Here we go," Daniel said.

"What do you mean, here we go?"

"This has nothing to do with your mother. And who knows, maybe she'd be fine about it."

"My mother?"

"Maybe not," Daniel admitted.

"She'd have a heart attack," I said.

"She's already had one," Daniel said. "And a stroke."

"And just think what another one would do," I said.

"Enough with your mother," Daniel said.

"She's a wonderful woman, my mother."

"Honey, of course she is."

"I can't talk about this anymore," I said.

"Okay," Daniel said.

"Just tell Jessie it's a bad time for company."

"Uh uh," Daniel said. "If that's what you think, you tell her yourself."

"Fine," I said. "That's just fine." I stormed upstairs and spent the night in the study.

Daniel is braver than he lets on. He called Jessie from work and explained that I was struggling with personal issues. He told her that we'd love for her to visit, but it wasn't a good time to bring guests.

Jessie immediately called me at home. "You don't approve of me," she said. Didn't she used to be shy?

"What do you mean?" I said.

"Dad said you were having a hard time. Personal issues."

"That's right, I am."

"I think you're homophobic," Jessie said.

"Excuse me?"

"You feel threatened."

"So telling me I'm homophobic makes me less threatened?" I said.

"You need to face your feelings," she said.

"That's my business," I said. "Not everything's about you."

"I want to come in for a visit. I want to bring Stephanie."

"It's a bad time to bring Stephanie."

"Why? Because of Gram? I want her to meet Gram."

"Wonderful."

"I can't believe you're being like this," Jessie said.

"Like what?"

"Gram loves me," Jessie said. "If she could still talk, she'd say so."

"That's not the point," I said.

"That *is* the point. Gram wouldn't think I'm a mutant."

"And I do?"

"I am *not* a mutant," Jessie said, "no matter what you think." Her voice broke, and then she hung up the phone.

I started to write her a note. *Of course you're not a mutant.* I took a long bath. I wrote in my datebook, *There isn't enough of me.* Then I made a tuna-fish sandwich with extra celery and onion.

—————

Irony was not lost on me. This Stephanie, this wily lesbian who had seduced my daughter into a strange life, and, God help me, into her bed, couldn't wait to visit my beloved mother, but Uncle Irv wouldn't go near Sadie. He'd called me again to say Gertrude had taken a turn for the worse. "And all those medicines," he said.

"How much?" I said.

"How much medicine?" he said.

"No, Irv. How much do you need? You know I saw Sadie yesterday."

"To be honest, a few hundred. You can mail it to the store."

"What about your sister, Irv? Remember your sister?"

"I think about her every day," Irv said. "I pray for her."

"Maybe you can visit," I said.

"Sure, sure," he said. "You'll send the check?"

"When will you visit?" I said.

"Soon. I would take more time to talk, Elaine. Too bad I have business. Give Sadie my love."

Before my daily visits to the nursing home, I started to take long walks. Spring had progressed without my noticing. The pale green coronas on our maples had deepened and spread. The dogwoods had bloomed; tulips filled the border garden. Every few days I brought bouquets to the nursing home. Sometimes my mother would light up when she saw them, but often she'd ignore them. More and more, she'd act the same way with me. The aides from the home coaxed smiles out of her. But when I said hello, her look became blanker and blanker.

The problem was that we'd all gotten older too fast. The problem was that there weren't enough moms to go around. Jessie left a message on the answering machine saying she'd be coming in with Stephanie and they'd be staying at a motel. I walked a three-mile loop through the neighborhood and pledged to behave like a grownup. Later, I called Jessie back.

"You'd really stay at a motel?" I said.

"Sure," she said, faking bravery.

"But this is your home," I said.

"I don't know," Jessie said.

"I'd like it if you stayed here."

She didn't answer.

"Of course, if you're happier at a motel, I understand," I said.

"It's not a question of happy," Jessie said. "It's a question of Stephanie."

I paused. "Stephanie can stay here too."

"What?"

"Stephanie is welcome to stay here too," I said. "Only please don't neck on the front lawn."

"Mom," Jessie said, "have I ever made out with anyone on the front lawn?"

"Backyard," I said. "You and the boy with the goatee. Kenneth."

"That was five years ago," Jessie said.

"It's precedent," I said.

"But I'm an adult now," Jessie said. "I just want to see Gram. You know?"

When my mother first moved to the nursing home, she met up with Frieda Kaplan, an eighty-five-year-old widow who read the daily paper and could still use a walker. The two of them took breakfast at the same table and spent sleepy afternoons holding hands in the TV lounge. When my mother fell asleep in her wheelchair, Frieda would stroke her forehead and call an aide to bring Sadie's extra blanket or prop her head at a more comfortable angle. Every day when I visited, Frieda would report to me on the situation in Israel and on my mother's sleep patterns. Even after Sadie's stroke, Frieda would watch over her. I'd relax a little. Someone lucid, I thought. An almost-mother. But one afternoon in May, Frieda told me that the previous night she and Sadie had gone barhopping and gotten wildly drunk.

"What?" I said. In spite of myself, I felt sparks of happiness. My mother, cutting her eyes at some bartender. My mother silly on Bristol Cream.

"Oh yes," Frieda said. "We had trouble getting back. We had to call a cab."

Sadie napped on in her wheelchair, her tiny feet poking out from her rose afghan, her skin translucent in the late afternoon light.

"Your mother," Frieda said. "She's a real pistol."

Out the window, a thin streak of red ran along the horizon, bounded by woolly clouds and the pink-tinted field behind the nursing home. Frieda patted my hand, her smile gummy and wide.

"Glad you had a good time," I told her. "Glad you made it back."

In late June, Stephanie arrived in a turquoise sundress, all pleases and thank yous, a gold Star of David around her neck.

There wasn't a single pink triangle on her. She brought us snap-dragons and wine. She made conversation about the house, and I made conversation back. I offered her a glass of iced tea. I offered her fruit salad. I offered to give her a tour of the garden. Jessie and Emmy exchanged looks.

"What?" I said.

"Nothing," Jessie said. "Maybe we'll wash up before we go to the nursing home." She picked up a suitcase and led Stephanie upstairs.

"What?" I said to Emmy.

"Nothing," she said. "But when did you get so polite?"

———————————

At the nursing home we found Sadie spiffed-up and alert: hair washed and set, lipstick on, teeth in, her blue-and-white suit neatly buttoned and zipped. She was having a good day. I wheeled her into her bedroom, away from the TV lounge distractions, and we took turns visiting her there. When Jessie came in, she started paging through a photo album with Sadie. *Here's you*, Jessie said. *Here's Irv.* My mother gave no sign of recognition. *Here, this is Elaine.* Sadie blinked, touched the slick pages, then turned her attention to her polished fingernails. Did that mean anything? Jessie closed the album, then started clowning around: she ran my lipstick over her mouth and left kiss marks on Sadie's hands. Sadie cracked a smile. Jessie sang hit parade songs and swung Sadie's arms, jitterbugging with the wheelchair. Then Sadie laughed, a small laugh, but a real one, and she waved at Jessie as if to say, "Oh you're too much." Jessie kissed her on the cheek and said to me, "Did you see that? That was such a Sadie thing to do."

And then Jessie's smile fell, she began tearing up, because what had happened to the rest of Sadie? And Sadie, my mute, distracted mother, reached up and took Jessie's face in her hands, pressed those arthritic fingers against Jessie's cheeks, and looked Jessie in the eye, steadily, as if they were both very much younger.

I gave them their time together. Emmy and Stephanie were in the common room, pretending to play gin with Rhoda Dobkins. I walked on and said hello to Frieda. I said hello to the other residents, the bald men, the dandelion-haired women, some of them talking thickly, some of them shouting, some of them blinking from their chairs. I returned to the common room just in time to see Rhoda throw a couple of cards down, to hear Stephanie say, "*Look at that!*" as if it were a royal flush.

A few minutes later, Jessie emerged from my mother's room, red-eyed and sniffling. Stephanie set down her cards, pushed a strand of hair out of Jessie's eyes, and let her hand linger against Jessie's cheek. Something in me began to loosen. It was the gesture I would have made. The gesture Sadie made. The one you can't stop craving. The one that catches you on the brink of your deepest despair and carries you back, safe, into the good life.

The Iowa Short
Fiction Award and
John Simmons
Short Fiction Award
Winners

1999
House Fires,
Nancy Reisman
Judge: Marilynne Robinson

1999
Out of the Girls' Room
and into the Night,
Thisbe Nissen
Judge: Marilynne Robinson

1998
Friendly Fire,
Kathryn Chetkovich
Judge: Stuart Dybek

1998
The River of Lost Voices:
Stories from Guatemala,
Mark Brazaitis
Judge: Stuart Dybek

1997
Thank You for Being
Concerned and Sensitive,
Jim Henry
Judge: Ann Beattie

1997
Within the Lighted City,
Lisa Lenzo
Judge: Ann Beattie

1996
Hints of His Mortality,
David Borofka
Judge: Oscar Hijuelos

1996
Western Electric,
Don Zancanella
Judge: Oscar Hijuelos

1995
Listening to Mozart,
Charles Wyatt
Judge: Ethan Canin

1995
May You Live in
Interesting Times,
Tereze Glück
Judge: Ethan Canin

1994
The Good Doctor,
Susan Onthank Mates
Judge: Joy Williams

1994
Igloo among Palms,
Rod Val Moore
Judge: Joy Williams

1993
Happiness,
Ann Harleman
Judge: Francine Prose

1993
Macauley's Thumb,
Lex Williford
Judge: Francine Prose

1993
Where Love Leaves Us,
Renée Manfredi
Judge: Francine Prose

1992
My Body to You,
Elizabeth Searle
Judge: James Salter

1992
Imaginary Men,
Enid Shomer
Judge: James Salter

1991
The Ant Generator,
Elizabeth Harris
Judge: Marilynne Robinson

1991
Traps,
Sondra Spatt Olsen
Judge: Marilynne Robinson

1990
A Hole in the Language,
Marly Swick
Judge: Jayne Anne Phillips

1989
Lent: The Slow Fast,
Starkey Flythe, Jr.
Judge: Gail Godwin

1989
Line of Fall,
Miles Wilson
Judge: Gail Godwin

1988
The Long White,
Sharon Dilworth
Judge: Robert Stone

1988
The Venus Tree,
Michael Pritchett
Judge: Robert Stone

1987
Fruit of the Month,
Abby Frucht
Judge: Alison Lurie

1987
Star Game,
Lucia Nevai
Judge: Alison Lurie

1986
Eminent Domain,
Dan O'Brien
Judge: Iowa Writers' Workshop

1986
Resurrectionists,
Russell Working
Judge: Tobias Wolff

1985
Dancing in the Movies,
Robert Boswell
Judge: Tim O'Brien

1984
Old Wives' Tales,
Susan M. Dodd
Judge: Frederick Busch

1983
Heart Failure,
Ivy Goodman
Judge: Alice Adams

1982
Shiny Objects,
Dianne Benedict
Judge: Raymond Carver

1981
The Phototropic Woman,
Annabel Thomas
Judge: Doris Grumbach

1980
Impossible Appetites,
James Fetler
Judge: Francine du Plessix Gray

1979
Fly Away Home,
Mary Hedin
Judge: John Gardner

1978
A Nest of Hooks,
Lon Otto
Judge: Stanley Elkin

1977
The Women in the Mirror,
Pat Carr
Judge: Leonard Michaels

1976
The Black Velvet Girl,
C. E. Poverman
Judge: Donald Barthelme

1975
*Harry Belten and the
Mendelssohn Violin Concerto,*
Barry Targan
Judge: George P. Garrett

1974
*After the First Death
There Is No Other,*
Natalie L. M. Petesch
Judge: William H. Gass

1973
The Itinerary of Beggars,
H. E. Francis
Judge: John Hawkes

1972
The Burning and Other Stories,
Jack Cady
Judge: Joyce Carol Oates

1971
*Old Morals, Small Continents,
Darker Times,*
Philip F. O'Connor
Judge: George P. Elliott

1970
The Beach Umbrella,
Cyrus Colter
Judges: Vance Bourjaily
and Kurt Vonnegut, Jr.

R. Brandon Kershner

Nancy Reisman earned an MFA from the
University of Massachusetts at Amherst.
She is the recipient of fellowships from
the National Endowment for the Arts, the
Wisconsin Institute for Creative Writing,
the Fine Arts Work Center in Provincetown, and the Rhode Island State Council
on the Arts. Her stories have appeared
in *Lilith, Glimmer Train,* and *American
Fiction.* She was the winner of the 1996
Raymond Carver Award.